Nobody

T. Joseph Browder

Published by T. Joseph Browder, 2023.

NOBODY

First edition. June 5, 2023.

Copyright © 2023 T. Joseph Browder.

ISBN: 979-8223847175

Written by T. Joseph Browder.

Table of Contents

For Marie

My Love, My Soul, My Life

1964

He heard the giggling before the snowball hit. It had been meant for his shoulder, but he'd turned at the sound and she'd thrown a bit high, so it caught him just below the left eye. A brief sting of pain from a shard of ice she couldn't have known was in there rose on his cheek.

She turned, still giggling, and ran away. Black hair trailed out behind her, flashing iridescent hues of deep purple and blue in sunlight from above and reflected from snow that lay like a blanket upon the earth.

He smiled.

She stopped after a few yards and turned. Saw that he was neither pursuing nor packing a snowball of his own to throw in retaliation, but rather was standing still, his hand to his cheek. A look of concern crossed her features, and she walked back to his side.

Closer, he could see her thick black hair better, how the light played among the strands as if gently caressing them. He could see her fine features. Her ivory skin, smooth, fresh, and clean, so pristine that faint tracery veins could be seen just beneath the surface. Her eyes so green that when they fixed upon his, his face flushed, heart fluttering in a way his nine-year-old mind didn't understand. At times, when she was this close to him, it was hard to breathe.

"I'm sorry," she said, noting the red mark rising on his cheek. Her voice, always pleasant to his ears, comforted him. She leaned in and brushed the spot with her lips, the innocent butterfly kiss of a child, offered as apology, meant only to soothe.

Had any other girl save his mother done so he'd have pushed her away, angrily wiped the spot with the heel of his hand, perhaps retching as he did so. Instead, he blushed furiously as heat bloomed in his belly and rose to his face. He felt a dopey grin break out on his face but was powerless to stop it.

"C'mon," she said, her face as scarlet as his own, and took his hand. Though they both wore mittens against the cold, the skin of his palm tingled. The pain in his cheek was forgotten.

They ran. Together. After a few steps the cold air cooled their faces and feelings neither of them were old enough to comprehend receded until they were just children again, laughing and playing, voices rising in the afternoon sunshine that smiled down upon them from a cloudless blue sky, bathing them in pure, clean energy as if it knew something of their future together.

As if it were somehow sentient and understood the meaning of destiny.

The Incident at Boone's

When the three heavily armed men in clown masks came through the front entrance and all the shooting started, Robyn Carr knew she'd been concerned about the wrong man.

Her first thought, when he'd stepped up to the counter at Boone's Family Restaurant and Dairy Mart forty minutes earlier was that he was cute for an older guy. He had blonde hair, going grey at the temples, shorn short on the sides but longer on top and parted in the middle. Robyn immediately thought of the lead actor on *NCIS*, a popular crime show her mother watched. Like that character, his eyes were a dusty shade of blue, earnest and expressive, the kind of eyes a girl could lose herself in. He was tall, six-two or three Robyn guessed, and the brown leather bomber jacket he wore, unzipped despite the late November chill, didn't do much to mask the fact that he was solidly built. *Hunky*, her mother would say, and Robyn agreed. Had he been twenty years younger, closer to her seventeen years instead of forty, she'd have flirted with him heavily. Still, he *was* pretty cute, so she pasted on her best Gallup, New Mexico smile before greeting him.

"Welcome to Boone's," she said. "How can I help you today?"

"I'll have the Chocolate Overdose, please," he said. "Large."

Robyn smiled. The Chocolate Overdose, a chocolate shake with chocolate syrup, chocolate chips and chocolate fudge brownie bits mixed in, was Boone's best-selling shake. The treat was more a sundae than a shake, so thick that it had to be eaten with a spoon. It was also a personal favorite of Robyn's.

"Anything else today, sir?"

3

"That'll be all, thank you."

His voice was soft but clear. Soothing, but with an edge of quiet sadness. A voice, Robyn thought, as she exchanged a receipt and four pennies for his five and two ones, unlike the high and loud voices of boys her age, boisterous and full of false bravado. As she moved away to fill the order, she thought that she wouldn't mind listening to a voice like that at length. She stuck a long plastic spoon in the finished shake and returned to the counter where the man waited patiently. She offered him another award-winning smile and handed the treat over.

"Here you are, sir. Have a great evening."

"Thank you," he said. Then: "You keep your head down."

Robyn thought it an odd thing to say but had heard stranger in the year that she'd worked for Boone's. "Will do," she said, giving those cool blue eyes another study.

He gazed back earnestly, said: "I hope so," then moved into the dining area and took a seat at a small table near the side entrance.

Robyn thought that an even stranger response but brushed the thought aside and moved on to other customers. An elderly woman with her grandson, both of whom wanted double dipped chocolate cones. An attractive cheerleader from her school that she had a nodding acquaintance with, who ordered a double cheeseburger, fries, and a strawberry shake. *That's no good for your figure, sweetie,* Robin thought a bit cattily, but filled the order without a word. Two construction workers. A family of four. And still more customers coming through the automatic doors that fronted the restaurant.

It was nearing six o'clock in the evening. Shortly, Boone's would be brimming with activity. As local merchants and banks closed for the day, dozens of workers would be looking for an easy alternative to cooking dinner. The dining room would rapidly fill with tired parents, loud and cranky children, and groups of teenagers who were more interested in hanging out with their friends than eating at home with their families. The drive-through would fill with those in a hurry to get home, or on their way to the movie theater, or just back to their second shift job after their dinner break.

Robyn was clearing a table in the dining room, a long rectangular area at the front of the business with floor to ceiling windows and comfortable seating for fifty-four—though it was common for there to be more than seventy people jammed into the two rows of booths or the tables meant for two lining the periphery. The open arrangement of the dining area was designed to let in light, promote a happy dining experience, and allow passers-by to see the diners enjoying their meals, hopefully drawing them into the cheerful atmosphere as well.

To the right of the main entrance was the Dairy Mart. Much like a small grocery or convenience store, lowboys, tall freezers, and coolers lined the four aisles of goods. At the back of the restaurant was the kitchen, drive through window, and a small manager's office. These things Robyn knew, but didn't think about as she removed burger wrappers, drink cups, and fry containers from a table where several teens had neglected to clean up after themselves and deposit their trash in one of the large containers conveniently located near each of the restaurants two exits.

She hadn't thought of the man with the cool blue eyes since he'd seated himself at the far end of the dining room more than thirty minutes ago, and was mildly surprised to see that he was still there. He was looking past her, towards the sliding doors at the front entrance. Then he looked to the right, out the windows, scanning the parking lot. His shake was gone, the cup likely thrown in the trash receptacle to his left. So why was he still there? And what was he looking for?

Was he waiting for someone? A girlfriend, perhaps?

Robyn decided that was it. A guy like that *had* to have plenty of interested female friends. Maybe a whole *harem* of them with his easy on the eyes looks and that silky, easy on the ears voice. She knelt down to pick up a ketchup pack before someone stepped on it and she'd have to mop up the mess, looked past the legs of other patrons in the three-quarters full dining room, and froze when she saw the gun.

It was in a holster under his left arm, the retention snap open, the weapon hanging free. The design of his jacket had concealed the bulge that might have been noticeable earlier. Robyn knew little about handguns beyond the fact that they were deadly, but this one was big. Huge, like the ones she'd seen Clint Eastwood carrying in those old cop movies her dad and Grandpa liked to watch. Her eyes seemed to zoom in on the weapon, like a perceptual camera trick she'd seen on TV. She briefly looked up at the man's face. He was again scanning the parking lot and didn't seem to have noticed her looking.

Robyn stood, the ketchup pack forgotten, collected the tray of debris from the table, and crossed to the trash bin at the front entrance. She walked as casually as she could with her heart trip-hammering in her chest and adrenaline surging through her veins. She crossed behind the counter, past Robert and Frank, the twin brother fry-cooks on duty, behind the other two counter girls—Emily, a shy and quiet girl of eighteen with straight brown hair put up in a bun, and Stacia, a twenty-two-year-old single mother with smooth, mocha skin and long hair that she kept in tight single braids that brushed her shoulders as she walked.

Robyn crossed to the manager's office. Eric Franklin, an obese and sweaty man with flame red hair who was a little too touchy feely for Robyn's taste was seated at the lone, cluttered desk wedged into the tight space, talking on the telephone.

"I think we have a problem," Robyn began but was silenced by the single finger her manager held in the air, signaling her to wait. She mentally added *arrogant* to the list of things she didn't particularly like about the man.

She waited impatiently, shifting her balance from foot to foot and casting surreptitious glances back towards the dining area. Finally, Eric re-cradled the phone and looked up at her.

"Yes," he said, as if tolerating a great intrusion.

"I think we have a problem in the dining room. There's a man out there...he's just been sitting out there for a half-hour—"

The manager raised his hand to stop her again. "A lot of people like to relax after a meal, Robyn." He wiped a bit of cookie or cracker from his stained shirt and sighed.

"He didn't order a meal," Robyn continued. "Just a shake. But that's not the point. He's watching the windows and he has—"

The hand went up again. He added an eye roll. "He's probably waiting for someone. Look, I don't have time for this. Our evening rush is minutes away and we're already busy—"

Robyn fumed. The eye roll had done it. Never mind his micro-managing every little thing anyone did. Never mind his overly inflated ego or his tendency to interrupt every time someone spoke to him, as if he knew what they were going to say before they did. Never mind the shoulder touch that tended to linger too long and had turned into light caresses down her side, straying too close to her breast and ending way too close to her rear end over the last few months. Never mind those things and more. *He had rolled his eyes at her.* As if she were a stupid child and he endured her presence only because his job required it.

"*Listen* to me, dammit!" she hissed, startling him to silence. "He has a gun."

Unaccustomed to having voices raised at him, albeit as quietly as Robyn had just done, a flash of anger crossed Franklin's face like a reflection of sunlight over the water's surface. He smoothed his shirt over his protruding belly again, blew out a breath, and said: "I hardly think your tone is appropriate."

"Did you hear me?" Robyn said with some urgency. "*He has a gun.*"

The tension that was rising in the office must have been palpable because Stacia joined her at the door and looked on querulously.

"That's hardly cause for panic, Ms. Carr," Eric said. Robyn noted, without surprise, that his demeanor had gone from shocked to authoritative and arrogant in less than two seconds. "New Mexico is an open carry state. Our patrons have the right to carry firearms."

"What's this about a gun?" Stacia asked.

Robyn ignored her. "He's not *carrying* it," she said to her manager. "It's out in the open, like he's ready to use it."

"Oh, hell no," Stacia said and pushed past Robyn into the office. "Mr. Franklin, you have to call the police! I ain't about to be killed up in here!"

"Killed?" Emily cried from behind Robyn. She too had heard the alarm in Robyn's voice and, abandoning the customers waiting in line to be served, had drifted closer to the office door. Her single utterance was loud enough to be heard by several of the customers and concerned murmuring broke out immediately.

"Ladies, *please*," Eric pleaded. He extricated himself from behind the desk causing the trio to back out of the office. "Go back to work. I'm sure there's nothing to be concerned about."

That's when the automatic doors whooshed open and a customer at the back of the line gasped. Robyn turned towards the sound and saw the clowns.

CLOWN NUMBER ONE, WITH green hair, a maniacal toothy grin, and a red nose that was cracked in places as if the mask had been left out in the sun too long, opened fire before the doors fully opened. His first two rounds shattered glass, then lodged harmlessly in a trigonometry book in the backpack of a high school senior. The third round hit the steel frame and spanged back in the direction it came from, narrowly missing the purple coif of clown number two. Neither clown noticed.

The remaining rounds drilled solidly into the shoulder blades and spine of a meaty woman with two small children in tow. The woman, instantly dead, tottered forward and fell into the patrons ahead of her, effectively shielding the children from the rounds fired by clown number two. Those rounds chewed up more of the woman's back, her neck, and the top of her skull before plowing through the neck and skull of the high school student whose backpack had saved him moments before.

Then the screaming started.

The mass of patrons surged forward, scared sheep blindly fleeing the butcher. There was nowhere to go in that direction. An elderly man at the front was pushed violently against the stainless-steel counter. A grimace of pain blossomed across his face as several of his ribs snapped. His six-year-old grandson was pushed downwards by the weight of the throng, a panicked expression on his face. He disappeared below the edge of the counter like a slowly sinking ship and was trampled underfoot.

More gunfire erupted at the back of the line—long, loud bursts that sent slugs careening through flesh and bone, ricocheting off tile and stainless-steel fixtures. Clown number three, with huge red eyes, a green nose, and a garishly pink tongue lolling between rows of urine-colored teeth, stepped between clowns one and two as they reloaded. He opened up on the crowd with twin automatics. More blood and gore flew.

Robyn watched all this in horror, frozen, like a deer in high beams. Mere seconds had passed but she saw the carnage with pure clarity, as if time itself had slowed or she were outside of it, observing with a keen eye. Marty Whitehorse, a regular she knew from the bank, was pushing and yelling at people to *Get down!* before a slug entered the base of his neck and exited through his right eye. A woman she didn't know, wearing a pea coat and knitted cap, wiped what was left of Marty's eye from her cheek before taking two slugs in the shoulder and another through her throat.

"Get your ass down, girl!" She heard Stacia yell and felt hands pushing on her shoulder. Then Stacia was gone, her perfect braids flying out behind her before she collapsed to the floor.

To her left, Eric Franklin was holding his throat. Blood spurted between his fingers, and he turned a circle making *Gaa...Gaa...Gaa* sounds. The noise stopped when three rounds punched through his chest. He hit the floor with a meaty thud.

Then she was hit from the side as Emily, her face a bloody, sodden hole, fell into her legs. Robyn went down in a heap and time snapped back into place as neatly as a rubber band.

She looked towards the side door of the restaurant, the only ready means of escape. The clowns were still at the front of the restaurant, pouring fire into the patrons crouched and screaming there. None of them had focused on the dining room yet, where diners still sat in stunned silence before their meals or were diving beneath the tables, as if those thin laminate surfaces would offer shelter from a hail of angry, buzzing bullets. She was calculating her chances of making it to the door, wondering how many patrons she could usher out with her, when the door was pulled open from the outside and clown number four entered.

He had red eyes with white spirals, cracked yellow latex skin and a pursed, ruby red mouth. He carried a nasty looking automatic rifle with an extended clip that he pointed at a large family seated at a table directly in front of him. A woman at the table screamed. A man tried to shield three girls and a boy, all under the age of ten, with his body. Robyn couldn't see the clown grin beneath his mask but knew that he did. The tight, gleeful grin of a cartoon villain bent on revenge. Robyn, unable to tear her eyes from a sight her soul demanded she not see, watched his finger tighten on the trigger of his rifle.

The man with the dusty blue eyes appeared at the clown's side, tucked his gun under the clown's jaw, and pulled the trigger twice. The latex mask poofed out at the temple with the first round. The tile wall splattered with blood, brain, and gore with the second. The clown dropped like a brightly colored sack of broken eggs.

Clown number two either saw or sensed that something was amiss in the dining room. He turned towards the diners and sprayed bullets at chest height, above the patrons seated or huddled there. The man in the bomber jacket fired back once, hitting the clown above the bridge of the nose. Purple nylon mixed with blood flew from the clown's mask as he fell, spattering the shoulder and mask of clown number three.

Clown three said: "Hey." He nudged clown one and they both looked down at clown two as blood poured from the back of his mask and mingled with a pool of blood already spreading there.

The man with the blonde going grey hair hadn't stopped with his third shot. Hadn't ducked for cover or run for the door. He strode towards the two clowns, his expression intent, unwavering. He stepped past booths with patrons huddled beneath, past crying women and sobbing children, over the sprawled body of a woman clutching her pocketbook. He appeared to Robyn to be a man with a cause. A soldier on a mission. An avenging angel.

The two clowns looked in his direction simultaneously. Though she couldn't see it, she could imagine their eyes widening at the sight of death coming for them. They raised their weapons but neither got off a shot. Clown three took the first slug in the chest and slid down the wall leaving a trail of blood in his wake. Clown one loosed his hold on his rifle and backed up a step, putting his hands in the air.

"Hey, man—wait."

Anything else he might have had to say was cut off by the second slug as it passed between the latex teeth of his mask and obliterated his lower jaw and tongue before exiting his spine. The body dropped to the floor, an evil marionette whose strings had been cut by an uncaring puppeteer.

The man turned towards the counter, stepping over bodies, the weeping and moaning wounded, and puddles of gore. He approached Robyn.

"No!" she cried, crossing her arms over her head. He slipped his gun back into the shoulder holster and crouched beside her, taking her wrists gently in his hands.

"Are you alright?" he asked in that soothing, sadness-tinged voice she remembered from before. "Were you hit?"

Robyn lowered her arms slowly, considering those dusty, cool blue eyes. The man had just killed four people. Quickly, efficiently, and without missing a shot. She should see a stone-cold killer in those eyes, but instead saw only concern. For her.

"I...I'm fine," she managed. Then ran a hand over herself to make sure.

He stood her up and she turned, looking for her own blood mixed with the blood of others on her uniform, using her senses to search for pain. There was none.

The man offered her a quiet, small smile, and despite the carnage around her, she returned it. "I told you to keep your head down," he said, and she seized on those eyes again with her own.

Why did you come here? Why did you save us? Why this concern for me?

"These people need help." She looked around, startled to see that many of the patrons she assumed dead were moving. Sobbing, clutching at injuries. The twins, sensing the slaughter was over, had come out from the kitchen and were moving among the wounded, helping them.

In the distance, she heard sirens.

The man moved away in the direction of the side door.

"Wait," Robyn said. She was uncertain what to say. *Thank you* seemed insufficient. Instead, she asked: "Who are you?"

"I'm nobody," he responded. Then disappeared into the night.

Arianna

C hristmas had come early to downtown Gallup.
Or so one would've thought given all the flashing red, blue, and yellow lights from the thirty-four and counting emergency response vehicles pulled up around Boone's Family Restaurant and Dairy Mart.

Ambulances arrived empty and departed with as many victims as they could safely carry, waved past police cruisers blocking the usually busy street. Cruisers belonging to New Mexico state troopers, McKinley County Sheriff's deputies, and the Gallup Police Department, were parked helter-skelter across sidewalks and entrances, doors hanging open, engines still running. In a town known to have the highest crime rate in the state, typically exceeding that of every other town of similar size in the nation, this was an unusually vicious crime that drew every available law enforcement unit within earshot of a radio.

Thirty-eight-year-old Arianna Price, known as Ari to her friends and closest co-workers, but as Special Agent Price of the FBI to everyone else, wound a black SUV she'd drawn from the Albuquerque motor pool three hours earlier between news vans and other media outlet vehicles. She halted at the upraised hand of one of three officers manning the barricades a half block from Boone's. As one of them approached her vehicle, Price rolled down her window and flipped open her wallet displaying her credentials.

"Go ahead, Ma'am," the officer said and waved at another officer near the blue and white painted sawhorses blocking the road.

"We can all go home now," the second officer muttered to the third, not bothering to hide the scorn in his voice as the SUV passed and he replaced the barricade. "The Feebs have arrived."

Price wound the SUV past cruisers and ambulances, more police, and a coroner's van laden with three zippered black vinyl bags. Finding nowhere to park along the curb near the restaurant she stopped the vehicle mid-street and shut it off. She exited and strode towards the entrance, dodging two coroner's assistants guiding a gurney with a fourth body bag, this one much smaller than the rest, towards the van.

"Christ," the larger of the two men handling the gurney muttered. "What a fucking mess."

"Wasting little kids," The second shook his head. "What the hell is wrong with the world?"

"Oh, the world would be a wonderful place all right," the first replied. "If it wasn't for all the people in it."

Price ignored the exchange, stepped over a depleted med kit on the sidewalk, and entered the restaurant through the side door. She spotted a body on its side near the door, an assault rifle near one outstretched hand. White latex and gaudy hair covered a head resting in a pool of blood. A uniformed officer stood watch to the right of the body. Price flashed her ID and he nodded. She surveyed the rest of the scene, taking in the dining area. Chairs knocked over, a side table overturned, booths and the floor littered with half eaten burgers, chicken strips, melted milk shakes of every flavor, uneaten fries turning greasy and cold under the glare of fluorescent lighting.

Halfway up the aisle on her left the blood began. While the flooring in this part of the building was relatively clear, the area near the registers was spattered in crimson. Puddles and pools of red, mixed with dropped food, ketchup packets, and straws. Coats, hats, bookbags, wallets, cash, and handbags, all resting in slicks of blood, stamped with bloody footprints.

Near the front counter, sitting upright as if casually removed and dropped on the floor, was a child's tennis shoe. Arianna could make out the Keds logo on the side. A once white sock, now solid red, peeked from the top of the shoe. The sight of that tiny shoe sent a shudder down her spine.

It appeared the civilian casualties had already been removed from the scene, the dead to the medical examiner's office, the wounded to hospitals. All that was left now were the bodies of the perpetrators and the investigators on the scene.

Two uniformed officers stood near the registers in quiet conversation, heads bent, their hands resting on the butts of their weapons. They looked up in unison as she walked down the aisle towards them, careful not to step on any debris or blood in her path. She again flashed her ID and they returned to their half-whispered discussion.

Technicians with CSU emblazoned on the back of their vests were bent over the counters or kneeling on the floor, swabbing and collecting evidence, measuring impact marks and calculating trajectories. One looked up from a baseball cap she was carefully holding in one nitrile gloved hand. The left side of the cap was torn away, and the tech was having a difficult time getting it into an evidence bag. The twenty-something with blonde hair peeking out from under her cap nodded when she saw Price's ID, then tilted her head towards the front entrance.

A quartet of detectives in black and grey suits stood there, voices low as they conferred with a native American woman. A fifth man in a dark blue jumpsuit examined three clown masked corpses. The temporal lobe of whomever had been wearing the baseball cap the CSU tech was handling slipped out of the cap and onto the floor with a splat. The tech muttered "*Shit*" under her breath as Arianna headed for the front entrance.

Diedre Goldenfeather, a full-blooded member of the Navajo Nation, was fifty-seven years old and nearing retirement on the night of what the media would later dub the Boone's Family Massacre. She looked up, taking in the approaching African American woman, the dark pantsuit and matching Burberry trench coat she wore, and immediately marked her as a federal agent.

"Arianna Price," the woman said, holding forth an open credentials' wallet. "FBI," she added needlessly.

"Agent Price," Captain Goldenfeather extricated herself from her detectives and the coroner, a Native American man in his late thirties.

"Captain Diedre Goldenfeather." She shook Price's hand, then dropped it and moved in closer. "I wasn't aware that anyone had called the Bureau in on this."

"No one has," Price responded. Her legal authority here was tenuous at best, as the captain would obviously know.

State and local cases could not be investigated by the FBI unless formally requested by that jurisdiction, or unless extraordinary circumstances existed. While an argument could possibly be made for the latter, the former had yet to occur. If it ever would. She was in danger of crossing a line here. One that could impede her own investigation. Offending this woman, who had no doubt faced tougher circumstances and discrimination to attain her position than Ari herself had, would do little to help her cause.

Sensing that Captain Goldenfeather was as intuitive as she was proud, and would value blunt honesty over prevarication, she came directly to the point.

"I'm not here in any official capacity." Arianna said. "I was passing through Albuquerque from D.C. on another case when I heard radio chatter about an unidentified gunman who fled the scene after the shooting. I believe my case and yours might be related and would like to be read in on what you have so far to determine if I'm right. I have no intention of assuming control of your investigation, or disputing jurisdiction in the name of the FBI."

Goldenfeather frowned and backed away from Price, her eyes narrowing. She tilted her head to one side. After a moment's hesitation, she nodded, then smiled.

"You're a Profiler, aren't you?" Goldenfeather asked. "One of the FBI's mind readers?"

"I'm with the Behavioral Analysis Unit, yes," Price answered. "But we don't read minds. We're trained to analyze the facts and statistics of violent offenses to link offenders to crimes through their behavior. Intuition plays a big role in that. How did you know?"

"You read me the second I introduced myself. Knew that trying to bullshit me wasn't going to work and got right to your point. You knew I'd respect and respond to that rather than any of those manipulation techniques they teach you at Quantico. The same techniques all these white assholes around here try, instead of just being open and honest. As if an old Navajo woman is too stupid to tell the difference.

"What you call intuition," Goldenfeather continued, "my grandmother called a sixth sense. I have a fair amount of it myself. It's telling me there's something off here, but that you're on the level about not interfering with my case. So, I'm going to help you out even though I have no legal requirement to do so."

"Thank you," Arianna said, relieved.

Goldenfeather waved the younger woman over to the entrance and Price followed.

"Gentlemen," Goldenfeather interrupted an exchange between the coroner and the homicide detectives. "This is Agent Price of the FBI's Behavioral Analysis Unit. In the spirit of inter-agency cooperation, she's going to *observe* our crime scene,"—she eyed Price meaningfully at this— "and maybe ask a few questions to determine if this case falls under the FBI's definition of domestic terrorism."

After the obligatory round of hand shaking and "Good evening, ma'am's," the coroner bent back to the masked corpses.

"As I said before," the coroner, crouching on the balls of his feet to avoid both the gore and the plethora of expended shell casing littering the floor, said, "the shots that killed our perpetrators were extremely well placed. Each round was instantly fatal, though fired from a distance, as evidenced by the lack of stippling or gunpowder on any of the deceased."

"Witness statements place him on the far side of the dining room when the shooting started," one of the detectives said with something like admiration. "Said he took all four of them in under ten seconds, one shot apiece, except for laughing boy over there at the other door. He popped him twice at point blank range."

"Yes, well," the coroner responded, "I haven't examined that one yet so I can't confirm those statements. As for these three, the witnesses seem to have it right."

"Have you attempted to identify the bodies?" Price asked.

"I was just getting to that," the coroner said. He inserted a finger under the neckline of clown number three's mask, simultaneously pulling up and away on the protruding pink tongue. Long, straight black hair concealed under the mask fell away revealing youthful, Native American features.

The tallest of the three detectives said, "Fuck me. It's Nathan Winter." His face reddened and he looked at Price. "Excuse me, ma'am," he said. She waved his concern away.

Diedre Goldenfeather sighed. "Which means the other three are likely his brothers; Paul, Jacob, and Went."

"Went?" Arianna asked.

"Short for Wentworth," Diedre explained. "They live on the rez. They've been arrested several times for narcotics, possession of illegal weapons, and various and sundry other charges. Paul, the oldest, was questioned in the rape and murder of his girlfriend last year, but there wasn't enough evidence to arrest him. Nathan there," she said, pointing at the youth slumped against the doorframe with a sizable hole in his chest, "was the youngest. Just fifteen. I'd hoped he wouldn't fall in with his brothers. But blood is blood, and to the Navajo Nation that means everything."

The coroner shifted his position and removed the mask of clown number two. Despite the wreckage of the lower jaw, the face could be recognized by the detectives and Captain Goldenfeather as Went Winter. His eyes were wide open, conveying shock and surprise.

"There goes the domestic terrorism angle, ma'am," the shortest detective said. Price noticed he had a bit of mustard on his tie. "Unless you count petty thieves and junkies as terrorists. These four have been assholes all their lives. Drunk one day, high on pot or meth the next. They probably got good and ripped and decided to light up the town old west style. I doubt they counted on Charles Bronson showing up at their little party and fucking up their plans, though."

"You said there were witnesses?" Price asked.

Diedre Goldenfeather replied: "We have several, but most of the people here were too busy trying to get out of the line of fire or too panicked to give us much detail about what happened. We have a seventeen-year-old cashier who interacted with the unknown gunman before all the shooting started, but I'm not sure she'll be much help. I have her outside in a cruiser if you'd like to speak with her."

"I would," Price said.

"I thought you might." Goldenfeather led her back towards the side entrance while the coroner spoke with two of his assistants back from loading the last civilian body into the van.

"These three are ready to go," Price heard him say. "Zip them in and have them ready for the return of the second van." Then he and the detectives moved off to examine the fourth shooter.

"You're not interested in this scene at all, are you?" Goldenfeather asked Price as they pushed through the door and into the carnival lit night beyond. "You're interested in the unknown shooter. The *unsub*, as you'd call him."

"He may be a factor in my case," Arianna said, walking towards a McKinley County Sheriff's cruiser parked nearby. The rear door was open. The young woman in the back seat looked unkept and frightened. A uniformed officer stood nearby.

Diedre Goldenfeather placed her hand on Price's shoulder, halting her. She looked around, making certain no one was within earshot, then spoke quietly but firmly. "Cut the shit, Agent. I may be the small-town Captain of a podunk southwest police force, but like I said, I have a good sense of intuition myself.

"I've had dealings with the BAU. This is the most violent city in all of America. FBI, NSA, Homeland—you're all the same. You travel in packs, like hungry coyotes. Never alone. You're off book here. Rogue. So, tell me what your interest in this unsub is or our *spirit of cooperation* ends with me making a phone call to Washington."

Price eyed the older woman with respect bordering on fondness. She'd seen how she handled her detectives, casually explaining the presence of an outsider in a way her subordinates would accept while allaying any concerns of FBI interference. All without lying—though the absolute truth may have been tarnished a bit. She'd also guessed Price's real purpose here was to investigate their vigilante and see if he was the man she was searching for. And that she was, indeed, part of no official investigation.

Perhaps her grandmother was right, Price thought, wondering. *Maybe she does have a sixth sense of sorts.*

"Have you ever considered applying with the FBI?" Price asked her. "The BAU could use more people with your skillset."

"Child." Goldenfeather smiled a weary and knowing smile. "You're a black woman in a position of authority in white man's world, so you have some concept of what it took for me to get where I am today. I'm too old and too tired to go through that all over again. Washington, D.C. may serve you well, but my people are here, within a hundred miles of where we're standing, and this is where I'm needed. Not only to serve them, but to keep them from getting their foolish asses shot off by some drunken *bilagáana* with race issues."

Arianna smiled at the Navajo word for white man.

"Now," Goldenfeather continued, "tell me what you're after here or get back in your vehicle and away from my crime scene."

"We—" Arianna began, then corrected herself. "*I*—don't have a name for him. No identity, no address, no social, no work or military history. There's no evidence whatsoever that he exists other than eyewitness testimony. He appears during acts of violence, kills the perpetrators, then vanishes before authorities can get to the scene and detain him. What I do have is a description. It's always the same. White male. Medium build. Late thirties to early forties, with greying blonde hair cut short on the sides and grey-blue eyes that are commonly described as *piercing*. He's soft-spoken and well-mannered. At least until the violence begins. I've heard the word *charming* more than once."

Diedre Goldenfeather's eyes widened almost imperceptibly. "That's the very description I got from the witnesses I've interviewed. One lied. Said it was a Navajo man in his twenties. But I knew she was lying and ferreted out the truth. Another used the word sensual, but I think she meant sexy. Told me she lied to protect the man who'd saved her life, and the lives of so many others."

"I've heard both words used to describe him," Arianna replied. "But he's also extremely violent, well-armed, and very skilled with a wide variety of weapons. He once killed an escaped sex offender who'd evaded law enforcement for months with a coffee table book.

Arizona Landscapes, if I remember correctly. Crushed the man's throat with the spine after beating him senseless with it, then vanished from a Phoenix hotel crawling with SWAT teams who'd been closing in on the fugitive."

"You're searching for a vigilante," Goldenfeather said. "The same vigilante, it seems, that ended the violence here. Okay, I understand that. But why go off book and risk your career? Why not call in the resources of your team? Make it official?"

"I've tried that. We searched for hard evidence of his existence for three years. We came up with nothing but anecdotal descriptions time and time again. No fingerprints. No DNA. Nothing. After forty months of investigation the Deputy Director ordered the investigation closed. I've been running it myself, on the side, for almost ten years."

"Thirteen years?" Goldenfeather said, astonished. "Then your vigilante was in his mid-twenties when you began."

"No, he wasn't," Arianna said. "His description was the same then as it is now. I've traced similar acts, by a man with the same description, back over twenty years. I'm not even sure if he's a man at all anymore. He seems to be more of a phantom."

Diedre Goldenfeather stared thoughtfully into Arianna's eyes for a moment, seeking deceit or madness, Arianna wasn't sure which. She then motioned towards the McKinley County Sheriff's cruiser.

The girl was seated in the rear passenger seat, a blanket loosely wrapped around her shoulders. Her hair, tidy and pulled back earlier, now hung loose in clumps around her ears. Dark circles brooded under her eyes and hectic patches of red had appeared on her cheeks as if she'd overdone her makeup.

Chief Goldenfeather sent the young patrolman watching over the girl away before making introductions:

"Robyn, this is Special Agent Price of the FBI. If you're up to it, she'd like to ask you some questions."

Robyn stared vacantly at the seatback in front of her, then gestured to the empty half of the seat. Arianna climbed in beside her while Chief Goldenfeather remained outside the vehicle, but not out of earshot.

"Can you tell me about it, Robyn?" Arianna asked softly, thinking the girl—just a child, really—had to be in shock. Her mind would be a tidal pool of emotion for weeks and months to come. Surges of horror followed by crests of sorrow, undercut with eddies and currents of anger and fear. And guilt, for having survived.

Robyn looked at Arianna for the first time, her eyes alight with fever shine, before looking away. "He warned me," she said. "Told me to keep my head down."

Her hands worked unconsciously at each other, fingers rubbing her thumb, her pinky, her palm. A vain attempt to remove dried blood that had worked its way deep into the lines and whorls.

"I thought it was just an expression." She laughed, a humorless and desperate sound.

"Did he speak to anyone else?" Arianna asked. "Another employee? A customer? Any of the shooters?"

"He waited." Robyn again met Arianna's gaze before her eyes slid away nervously, as if harboring a shameful secret and not knowing who to trust it with.

"He was there before the shooting started," Arianna said. Chief Goldenfeather had told her as much, had indicated the girl had interacted with the vigilante. "How long was he there? How long did he wait?"

"A while," Robyn answered. "Thirty, maybe forty minutes. But that's not what I mean." Her voice dropped to a whisper. "He *waited*."

"I'm not sure what you mean."

"When the first clowns came in," Robyn said, casting Arianna a haunted look that spoke of many counseling sessions to come, "he waited. They were shooting everyone in sight, but he didn't do anything. Not until the last guy came through the side door. The one that would have shot me too. *Then* he stopped them. But not before."

"He warned me," Robyn repeated, now furiously scrubbing at her hands and a red stain on the hem of her uniform. "Told me to keep my head down."

Sensing she'd get no more answers from Robyn Carr this night, Arianna levered herself from the backseat. "I see now why you kept her here and let the other witnesses go."

"Most were sent to the hospital or the station." Captain Goldenfeather gently closed the vehicle door and motioned for the sentinel officer to return. "The others were allowed to go home. We'll follow up with them later. Ms. Carr, however, will require special treatment. Our staff psychologist will be here soon. I'll let him decide what's needed in her case."

Arianna headed towards the street where her vehicle waited. Captain Goldenfeather accompanied her.

"You have all that you need?" she asked.

"Yes," Arianna replied. "Thank you for your assistance." She stopped, retrieved her ID wallet from her pocket, and removed her contact card from it. "If you're ever in need, call me. I'd be happy to return the favor."

"Are you convinced my offender and your unsub are one and the same?" Goldenfeather asked, the card vanishing into one of her pockets as if by magic.

"Absolutely," Arianna answered. They stepped from the sidewalk to the street together. The depleted med kit was gone, returned to whichever ambulance it had come from to be refilled. "His interaction with Ms. Carr—," she motioned in the general direction of the cruiser, "—the fact that he protected her before the others, confirms it."

"Will you continue to pursue him?"

"I will."

"Agent Price," Captain Goldenfeather said as they approached Arianna's commandeered vehicle. She laid her hand on Arianna's arm, stilling her in the act of opening the door of the SUV. "You must stop searching for this man. Go back to D.C. and rejoin your team. Forget all about him. Pursuing him, trying to divine his function in this world, will only lead to your destruction."

"What?" Arianna said, taken aback. She turned to meet the woman's gaze.

"You seek *Biitei*," Captain Goldenfeather said, her voice grave. "A ghost. The spirit of *Bha'a*, the Thunderbird. The Great Protector who is always at odds with *Hinncebiit*, a monster with metal horns and glittering eyes who seeks to destroy mankind. For your own sake, you must let it go."

Arianna stared. Gone was the captain who had seemed so rational, so logical. The woman of fact and truth, the officer of the law who viewed her cases solely with reason and reality. In her place stood an aging Native American woman who now spoke of Navaho folklore, myth, and legend.

"I can't," Arianna said, her voice soft but determined.

"Child," Goldenfeather said, not as a police captain nor as a colleague, but rather as a friend or a mother. "Why?"

"Twenty-five years ago," Arianna explained, "*I* was the girl sitting in the back of a police cruiser. Confused, frightened, angry. Relieved that I'd survived and torn with guilt because of it.

That man who saved Robyn Carr's life tonight? He saved me during a home invasion when I was fourteen years old. Only back then, it was my father and brother he let die before doing anything to stop it.

"And I want to know why."

Black Sunshine

C arl Linsner muttered "*Shit*" under his breath and pushed the accelerator of the grey Ford Econoline to the floorboard. The headlights had reappeared in the rearview mirror, set to high beam, filling the cab of the van with a harsh white fluorescence.

"Thought I lost you, you bastard," Carl said, then turned the vehicle sharply onto a side road, this one dirt with only trace of gravel.

He'd picked up the tail just outside of Lima, Ohio, at a few minutes past three a.m. as he headed for the lake. His first thought had been that it was a cop. A state trooper most likely, cruising state Highway 81 between Lima and Ada, looking for speeders and drunks to fill his ticket quota for the month.

The vehicle had pulled up on his rear bumper at a steady sixty miles an hour, remaining there long enough to run the tag—*Registered, insured, and perfectly legitimate, thank you very much*, Carl had thought—before pulling into the left lane and passing the van at a high rate of speed.

It hadn't been a cop, though. Unless, Carl mused, they'd taken to driving around in solid black '69 Mustang Mach Ones. The ram air-scoop on the hood marked it as the 428 Cobra Jet, though the vehicle lacked the customary racing stripe up the side or any other markings save the familiar pony emblem on the grille. As it blew by him, engine growling like a pack of angry wolves, Carl caught a glimpse of color in all that blackness.

Someone had applied a legend to the side of the vehicle in photoreactive paint. The kind that's only visible when hit with a light source.

It read *'Black Sunshine.'*

Definitely not a cop, Carl grinned and relaxed. *Cops don't dig Rob Zombie.*

The Mustang roared away, taillights fading to miniscule red eyes in the distance before vanishing altogether in the pre-dawn Ohio morning.

As he'd crossed over the Ottawa river, high beams lit up the interior of the van a second time and the Mustang pulled in behind him again. A glance in the side-view showed nothing but the car's rear fender, the rearview offered nothing but the glare of light.

He was waiting for me, Carl thought. *Backed up onto the thin strip between the guardrail and the drop-off and waited for me.*

The Mustang was mere inches from Carl's bumper, the engine screaming loud enough that Carl could feel it through the frame of the van.

What the hell is this? he wondered. *Someone I know who thinks he's funny? Some dumbass kid playing cat-and mouse? Someone I pissed off? A road rage junkie?*

Whichever it was, Carl wasn't sticking around to find out. He floored the gas pedal, accelerating rapidly past sixty-five to seventy. Then eighty. Then ninety. The Mustang remained on his tail as if held there by Velcro, matching Carl's speed mile for mile.

Carl gripped the wheel with both hands, trying to keep the van in the center of the road and to hell with designated lanes. He squinted at the speedometer as it crept past one hundred, thankful he'd sprung for the V-12 engine when he'd purchased the vehicle seven years before. Still, the Mustang remained on his tail, mere inches from his bumper.

Carl weighed his options. V-12 or not, he obviously wasn't going to outrun the Mustang, despite having the larger, more powerful engine. The van was too heavy and about as aerodynamic as a brick on wheels, whereas the Mustang could maneuver like a shark through open water. Furthermore, its driver, Carl grudgingly admitted, had far superior skills than he. The ability to stay so close to the van at these speeds without hitting it or even kissing the bumper spoke to that. As the tandem vehicles roared past a faded and nearly unreadable sign that announced to passersby that Jade Springs Lake and Campgrounds were a mere five miles ahead, Carl decided on a different course of action.

He slammed on his brakes.

There was an immediate sound of squealing rubber, breaking glass, and rending metal. It felt as if a giant hand punched the rear of the van, then pushed it forward and to the left. He heard a muffled cry from the sole passenger in the back of the van but ignored it as he let off the brake, turning into the skid caused by the collision. He applied the gas, not quite gunning the big engine, but coaxing it slowly back up to sixty-five as he straightened the vehicle.

A glance in the rearview revealed the Mustang nose down in a ditch and facing the wrong direction. It must have spun out after the collision and sailed off the road. It didn't look like it would be going anywhere anytime soon.

Too bad you didn't roll, you sonofabitch, Carl had thought, and continued on towards his private compound.

The Linsner Compound had once been known publicly as Jade Springs Lake. A sprawling, summer destination on fifteen heavily wooded acres that boasted four-hundred campsites, two tennis courts, a large playground complete with swings, slides, and a maypole. A large clubhouse overlooked the lake like a sentry. In its 1980's heyday, four diving platforms—one a thirty-meter board that could easily dislocate the shoulders of an unpracticed diver—two water slides, a zipline, and several pontoons and rafts of various uses including one with a large trampoline were installed. The campground was the brainchild of Art Linsner, Carl's grandfather, who'd bought the land on the cheap from the Beckford Stone Company when the quarry they'd operated on that spot for twenty years had flooded in 1956, forming the lake.

When Art died in 1976 the property boasted fifty campsites, largely for fishing enthusiasts, and passed to his son Christopher. It was Christopher who foresaw the camping boom of the late seventies and had the clubhouse built, the lake outfitted with water slides, and installed the remaining campsites and water attractions.

In 1998 Christopher died, passing the property to *his* son, Carl, then a mere twenty years of age. To the dismay of the hundreds of families who called the lake home during Ohio's long, hot summers, Carl closed down the lake and the campgrounds, had a twelve-foot chain link fence erected around the entire property, and declared it off-limits to the public. He lived there, alone, in the once immaculate clubhouse, while the playgrounds rusted, the concrete pads denoting campsites cracked and were overrun by weeds, and the water attractions fell into disrepair.

It was the old access road past the clubhouse and the neglected campgrounds that Carl turned on to as the Mustang's headlights bloomed in his rear-view mirror once again.

Carl cursed. The Mustang should have been disabled. At the very least those hateful headlights should have shattered on impact. Who the hell was this guy anyway? And why was he playing this game?

He knows. The voice came from deep within his subconscious and sounded very much like his father.

Bullshit, he thought. *No one knows. No one* could *know.*

Carl pressed harder on the accelerator, the van shuddering over potholes and ruts in the neglected road. At least he'd left the gate open. It flashed by as the van jolted over the concrete pad that had once marked the location of the welcome booth.

The Mustang didn't slow as it took the turn. Didn't slew to the left as the van had, and didn't seem to bounce and jounce over the potholes and ruts in the road. It accelerated, it's 428-liter V8 screaming like a banshee out for revenge.

It wasn't going to settle for riding his tail this time, Carl intuited as the road forked ahead of him, a long loop that would take him around the periphery of the property. He took the right-hand fork, the accelerator bottomed out against the floorboard. His passenger was crying out in fear and pain at every bump and dip the van rolled through, some considerable enough that his own head bounced against the headliner.

Bright white light filled the world and the Mustang slammed into the van just behind the left tire. Carl could feel it pushing against the heavier vehicle, could feel the rear end slipping out of control, and knew there was nothing he could do to prevent what was about to happen.

The van hit a pothole the size of an Easter basket and rolled.

Carl screamed and uselessly pumped the brakes as the van flipped, airborne for the first revolution, the roof crushing in on the second. The windshield exploded in Carl's face, safety glass harmlessly buffeting his cheeks, forehead, and tightly closed eyelids. The cries from the back of the van stopped, cut off mid-scream. The third and final revolution brought the van to a jarring stop on its right side against a large oak. The remainder of the windows coughed their glass out on impact, the sliding door on the passenger side buckled inwards like a sprung seam on an old tin can. The van looked as if it had been sent to the scrapyard crusher, the job abandoned halfway through.

The Mustang had fallen back after the final impact with the van's bumper. It idled a few yards back, engine purring, the sound of a contented animal after a big meal. The driver side door opened, and a man got out. He was carrying a large set of bolt cutters.

Carl's seat had been wrenched free of three of its four bolts when the van fetched up against the tree. He was unhurt but now facing the passenger side of the vehicle, pinned to the seat by the lap and shoulder belts still attached to the mechanism above and behind him. He was suspended in mid-air with his arms and legs hanging over empty space, a rapid *ticka-ticka-ticka* sound filling his ears. He dismissed the sound, repeatedly pushing the button to release the seatbelt catch jammed shut by the weight of his body.

He craned his neck to the right, peering past the twin mattress now leaning at an angle from the bedframe bolted into the back of the van. He'd bolted that frame into place himself after ripping out all the van's other seats, save the driver's, along with much of the interior. He'd replaced the carpeting, headliner, and sidewall coverings with red and charcoal soundproofing foam, giving the interior the look of a giant checkerboard.

This was the third such van he'd converted in this fashion. The first two sat at the bottom of the quarry, beneath one-hundred and fifty feet of cold, still water.

The right-hand rear door of the van wrenched open. Gravity pulled it to the ground with a squeal of bent hinges. Carl watched helplessly as hands found the release for the left-hand door and it was pushed upwards. A long stick, likely a tree branch that had been severed when the van rolled off the road, was pushed into place under the door to prop it open.

"Who are you?" Carl screamed, renewing his efforts to free himself. He pushed, pulled, and twisted the belt release in his hands to no avail. "Why are you doing this?"

The mattress was pulled from the van and tossed aside. It landed with a *flumph* in the overgrowth beside the road.

The Mustangs high beams revealed the man who'd harassed him in silhouette. The man who'd chased him and driven him off the road, destroying his van and possibly killing his passenger. He wasn't at all what Carl had expected. He was tall, of medium build, and dressed in blue jeans and a brown bomber jacket. His face bore no malice, nor triumph. He didn't grin maniacally. Didn't laugh with pleasure at what he'd done. Instead, he looked determined. Resolute. As if he were doing a job that had to be done, regardless of his personal feelings about the matter.

He didn't look like the sort of man who would pursue a complete stranger with the intent of committing violence.

He eyed Carl sadly, pityingly. Then reached inside and gently placed his fingers under the chin of Carl's passenger. He then nodded, a look of relief briefly crossing his features, and used the bolt cutters to free the unconscious girl from the handcuffs attached to the eyebolts that Carl had bolted into the van.

She was ten. They had *all* been ten. Each of the twenty girls Carl had taken, one a year, over the last two decades.

No one knew. No one suspected. He stalked them and researched them thoroughly. Their habits. They and their families' time schedules. He took them from their beds in the early morning hours, never from the same community twice. He'd taken girls from Van Wert, Celina, Upper Sandusky, Mansfield, and Mt. Vernon. Once as far away as Canton. Drugged them unconscious before they could awaken and alert their mothers or fathers, or the older or younger sibling sleeping in the same room.

Then he spirited them away to his compound to do as he wished for as long as he wished. He'd once kept one, an exceptionally beautiful blonde, for an entire year. He'd forced her to interact with the new girl for a few weeks before he finally grew tired of dealing with two charges and left her naked, gagged, and tied to a tree for the wild animals to finish off.

Most were wrapped in multiple trash bags that he weighted and tossed in the dark waters of the old quarry. Some remained where they'd been when he grew tired of them.

"No!" Carl screamed. "You can't have her. She's mine!"

The man said nothing. He cut her ankles free first. Then her right hand, using the bolt cutters between one hand and his chest as he supported her body with the other to free the left. He hoisted the child in his arms, turned, and walked away without a word.

"Wait!" Carl cried, bucking against his restraints as the man laid the girl on the back seat of the Mustang. "We can share her! We can take others! As many as you like! There are hundreds of them out there! Waiting to be had!"

The man got in the Mustang, backed up a few feet, then turned the vehicle and drove back out the way he had come. Alone in the darkness, the sound of the Mustang fading in the distance, tears rolled from Carl's eyes, down his nose and dripped on the checkerboard-colored foam lining the passenger door, mixing with the liquid already pooling there.

"She was mine," he wept pathetically. "You had no right."

Then he noticed the smell.

He opened his eyes in alarm, craned his head around the interior, and could not see but could smell the gasoline pouring into the cargo area from the ruptured fuel tank. The angle of the vehicle and the ridges of the foam soundproofing were channeling it directly into the cab beneath him. Then he recognized the source of the rapid ticking sound. The vehicle's way of telling him a turn signal bulb had burnt out or was broken, and the electrical impulse that was meant to light it was discharging randomly into the atmosphere.

He railed and screamed, raged and tore at the belt pinning him in place.

Three minutes later the van went up with an unimpressive *woomph* that nonetheless ended Carl Linsner's twenty-year reign of terror.

1972

"I bought this today," she said, and slid the 45 RPM album down the spindle adapter before setting the needle in place. A rhythmic scratching sound came through the quadraphonic speakers as the needle worked its way around the platter before finding the first groove of the track. Distorted guitar chords replaced the usual hiss and pop, then fell off as the mellow baritone of the lead singer took over.

"It's a new song by the Raspberries."

From the couch, hunched over the Algebra and Trigonometry textbooks open on the coffee table in front of him, he barely heard the music. His mind was awash with coefficients, polynomials, and radicals, as he tried to solve for the nonzero in a quartic function.

"Um hmm," he muttered, trying to focus past a mild headache forming behind his eyes.

Math, any form of it, was his nemesis. Numbers were supposed to be logical and absolute, simple to deduce and rationally explained. She had no difficulty grasping the concept of integers and exponentiation. No trouble at all finding the four variables x, y, z, and T, over the rational numbers. She easily plucked the answers from the ether and set them on paper as if they came to her by way of magic. To him, every mathematical formula seemed chaotic, every concept vague and ill-defined, as if someone had thrown a bowl of Campbell's newest soup—call it Chunky Algebra Integers—into his brain and stirred vigorously.

"Uggh," he groaned, and ran a hand across his head, twisting it into a fist and pulling at the hair near his temples. "I'll never understand this stuff. We graduate in two weeks, and I'm sure to flunk this test."

"Hey," she said softly. She returned to the couch and sat beside him; one leg tucked under the other. She pulled his hand from his hair.

"You won't fail the test," she said, and laid her head on his shoulder. "When have you ever failed a test?"

He thought about it and realized he never had. He'd come close once. He'd gotten a D on a science test in the fourth grade, a result that had caused his parents such upset that he'd doubled down on his study sessions, with her, in her parent's basement. They'd both passed that semester with an A.

"It'll come," she said. "And if it doesn't, who cares? You're getting A's in all your other classes. That'll more than make up for a failing grade in Advanced Algebra. Besides, when are we ever going to use this stuff anyway?"

Her closeness: her hand on his brow, her head on his shoulder, the warmth of her thigh pressed against his and her soothing voice in his ear, had a cathartic effect. Numbers and ratios, degrees and functions fled his mind, taking the building pressure behind his eyes with it. He was at peace. Comforted. Cleansed.

"Now," she said and stood. "I'll start the song again. Pay attention this time."

She crossed to the stereo console to reset the record and he leaned back, watching.

So much more beautiful at eighteen than at nine. Her black, flowing hair loose and shining, catching every glint of light from the tension lamps in the corners of the room, throwing back rainbows of deep blue and purple. The snug white sweater she wore accentuated her fine ivory skin where it showed through between her shoulder blades. Her blue jeans, likewise snug, emphasized every curve; her buttocks, the flare of her hips, the taper from her thighs to her knees to her calves. Her feet were clad in a pair of silly rainbow toe socks, an affectation that rarely failed to make him grin.

He seldom thought of her in this way. They'd been best friends since the age of seven and his one attempt to kiss her at her fourteenth birthday party had resulted in her pulling away, shocked and blushing furiously. She'd kept her distance for the remainder of the afternoon, barely waving goodbye to him when it was time to leave. He'd been confused and a bit heartbroken, but their friendship was more important to him than any pubescent imaginings of romance and had remained, their bond eventually strengthening further.

He straightened, swallowed a lump that had taken up residence in his throat, and turned his thoughts back to his studies.

She reset the needle on the album and the discordant guitar melody began anew. She turned and he missed the small frown that crossed her features as he bent back to the algebra texts on the coffee table.

"Hey," she said. "You're supposed to be listening."

"I am," he responded absently, his mind awash with numbers, equations, and functions once again. He looked up and smiled. "I think I've got it this time."

"Uh-huh," she said. He also missed the small pout on her lips.

He bent back to the texts and picked up a pencil.

"Yes!" He said, excited as the numbers and variables slid into place in his mind like a puzzle being assembled. He picked up his notepad and began scribbling furiously, his brow furrowed in concentration.

"If f multiplied by x equals ax cubed..."

"My parents won't be home for hours," she said, her hands on her hips, tapping her rainbow clad toes against the shag carpeting.

"—plus bx to the third power, plus cx squared—"

"The name of the song is Go All the Way."

"—plus dx plus e; where a is a nonzero—"

"I love you. I've always loved you. And I want you. Now."

"—which is defined by a polynomial of degree four—"

"Oh, My God!" she yelled, startling him. He looked up and was taken aback by the look of anger he saw on her face.

"Men are so stupid," she said. Then her face softened, and she hooked her fingers under the waist of her sweater, pulling it off over her head. She was bare underneath.

Her breasts were high and proud, the firm alabaster flesh coming to fine pink points within small areolas. They heaved with youth, vitality, and the nervousness of a young woman baring herself to a man for the first time. Her stomach was taut above the waistline of her jeans. Small tremors passed through the flesh around her bellybutton, a small, flawlessly shaped indentation. She dropped the sweater to the floor and unfastened her jeans, revealing white panties beneath, a tiny pink bow at the waist, just above the pubic arch. She shrugged out of the jeans and stood before him.

She was beautiful. She was perfection.

He swallowed the lump that had retaken position in his throat, certain his heart had stopped. The pencil and notepad fell to the floor at his feet, forgotten. He began to speak but his breath fled his lungs and all that came out was, "Wh?"

"You are my heart," she told him, crossing to where he sat in stunned silence on the couch. Her bare flesh both excited and astonished him at the same time. The creamy skin of her thighs where it rose to meet the pudenda, concealed from sight beneath the sheer panties but not without the intoxicating scent of a woman, sent shivers from his toes to his spine. She placed her hands on either side of his head and lifted his face to meet hers.

"I love you," she said. "My life and my soul are entwined with yours. I give myself to you now and forever. And if you'll have me, if you feel the same, and we're ever apart, no matter the reason, I won't feel whole again, alive again, until you're back in my arms. Not even death will keep me from your side."

Moments later, as he entered her for the first time and two became one—there was resistance and pain for her at first as he gently pushed through her hymen, but her eyes, the deepest green of the purest jade, *held his as she gripped his buttocks, pulling, encouraging him to continue—he realized that a hole in his being, an empty place in his soul he'd never realized was there, had now been filled and that she had completed him.*

Then bliss.

The couple reveled in their love for one another while Eric Carmen, forgotten on the turntable, repeatedly sang of holding close and never letting go. Evening rolled into night and a wise moon rose in the sky casting a shining, silvery brilliance on the Earth below.

Something, somewhere, took notice.

Lonnie

The elevator doors parted before Lonnie Schultz without so much as a courtesy *ding*. He looked out into the stark white and stainless-steel lined hallway, adjusted his hold on the object in his pocket, and smoothed his crisp white lab coat before exiting. Like the car behind him, the hallway, more of an intersection with a set of tightly sealed steel doors at either end, was plain and unmarked. No colored arrows with printed legends marked his path. No friendly numbered signs indicated the floor on which he'd arrived. The elevator button pad had been similarly plain, with no lights or numerals.

In the Mount Nasak facility, one was expected to know where they were or where they were going. If they didn't, they didn't belong, and would likely be arrested or shot for their ignorance.

The sole point of color other than silver or white for the eye to fix upon in the eight-foot by eight-foot sally port was the guard's station. Directly facing the elevator doors, it was comprised of a desk (green) with a high-end computer upon it (black), a chair (brown), and the guard himself (blue uniform and mottled, pasty pink skin) who currently eyed the computer monitor with confusion, as if not believing what he was, or was not, seeing there. He peered owlishly up from the screen at Lonnie as if to confirm his existence, then back to the screen again. Then back up at Lonnie.

"Problem, Fred?" Lonnie asked the forty-five-year-old Air Force sergeant who'd been stationed at this post for the last three years.

"No." Fred answered, obviously puzzled. He made rapid keystrokes on his keyboard. "Yes. I don't know. The computer didn't tell me the elevator was on its way down, and the cameras didn't record anything." He made more keystrokes then looked up at Lonnie yet again. "Now the system isn't responding at all."

Lonnie grinned broadly. "That's because I disabled it and put all the cameras on a loop before I shot everyone up top and came down here."

"Yeah, right." Fred laughed at the joke. "An unauthorized firearm in the elevator would've set off every alarm in the facility."

"Not this one," Lonnie said and pulled a ceramic pistol from his pocket. He shot Sergeant Fred McAfee, formerly of the United States Air Force, between the eyes before the laughter died on his lips. Now there was a new color (red) in a large swath behind the desk for one to see upon exiting the elevator.

Lonnie hummed quietly to himself and rounded the desk.

"Excuse me," he said and dumped the sergeant's body out of the chair before taking a seat. He made keystrokes of his own, entering the personal access code he'd inserted through a back door into the system months before.

In seconds he overrode the safety locks on the eight-inch-thick steel doors accessible from the sally port that prevented more than one of them from being opened at a time. With barely a hum the two sets of doors simultaneously slid open.

"*Ta da!*" He said, then stepped over Fred's body and, ignoring the East corridor for now, headed down the West corridor towards the labs.

Three Level-5 biocontainment labs lie along the North wall of the corridor.

As far as most of the world is concerned, the highest bio-safety level in use is Level-4, wherein the most virulent strains of known diseases, both bacterial and viral, are safely researched and housed. Those few outside of the staff here with knowledge of this facility's unique agenda, the *creation* of genetically modified bacteria, viruses, and toxins of such virulence that their very existence threatened the entire planet, would not dare argue with that misconception, nor admit anything to the contrary.

The first lab was dark, as Lonnie knew it would be. This was the lab he'd spent seven years working in as second tech to Dr. Elizabeth Marshall. For the last four of those years, Dr. Marshall had been working on a promising strain of *Rhabdoviridae*, commonly known as the rabies virus, but referred to in the lab as HRP, for Human Rhabdoviridae Pathogen. The last iteration she'd tested, number one-thousand and twenty-two, had a one-hundred percent mortality rate amongst their rodent and primate test subjects.

HRP-1022 was Lonnie's first choice for annihilating the human race.

He'd been suspicious that HRP-1022 wouldn't fully eradicate the species, regardless of the perfect mortality rate indicated by Dr. Marshall's test results. For one thing, a primate *is* a hominid, but by no means a human being. And humans have a pesky habit of developing immunities to viruses, old or new. One only had to look at smallpox, one of the deadliest viruses in history, which nevertheless claimed only five-hundred million lives during the twentieth century. For another, Lonnie had only been present at forty-eight out of ninety tests and couldn't confirm that Dr. Marshall wasn't padding her numbers to impress the big boys upstairs and in Washington.

Still, to his knowledge, HRP-1022 had been the most promising agent for his designs and he'd decided to move forward with his plans—until Dr. Peter McMillan's half drunken lab tech had, against all policy and procedure, told him about GT-16.

The tech, a thin, blonde woman with the unfortunate mouthful of a name Margeaux Quagliarella, had been celebrating notification of her husband's healthy return from a tour with the Marine Corps in Afghanistan and a pending three-week vacation home, when Lonnie had sidled up to her at the topside lounge with no more intent than to promote himself as a good sport and all-around great guy. An activity he'd become so adept at over the last twenty-seven years that it had become instinct. After a few banal comments, she'd glibly begun discussing the work going on in Lab Three.

"It's a genotoxin," she'd told him, either too drunk or too stupid to realize she was breaking an oath of secrecy and potentially subjecting herself to charges of treason. "And a really nasty one, at that."

"How so?" Lonnie asked. He was familiar with genotoxins, chemical agents that both caused and were used to fight certain forms of cancers. He was also aware that some were responsible for damage to DNA that caused birth defects and other mutations. He'd never considered using one to fulfill his goal, however, as genotoxins were too slow and too unpredictable. A good blast of radiation, say Gamma rays, would be far more effective. But generating Gamma waves with enough energy to irradiate every man, woman, and child on the planet would be impossible. You might as well try to lasso the Sun and drag the Earth into a closer orbit.

"We spiced it up a bit," Margeaux said, pushing her empty glass towards the site bartender, a sad looking man in his forties that made Lonnie think of Droopy the dog, Droopy slowly moved to refill the drink. Margeaux rolled glassy eyes back towards Lonnie and continued: "We wrapped it in liposomes for delivery, added a few DNA and RNA strands to the mix, and *BAM!*" She slammed her hand down on the bar, spilling a bit of her newly freshened beverage. The bartender wiped the spill away without a word.

"It replicates independently and directly attacks the DNA, producing apoptosis in cells," Margeaux revealed. "*All* cells. In seconds."

Lonnie's eyes didn't bug out or even shift to the side. He didn't gasp in surprise or demand more information. He didn't allow the slightest trace of newly piqued interest to show on his face. Rather, he took a slow sip of whiskey, one of the few things that was good in this godforsaken place, and set his glass back down on the bar.

"Apoptosis, huh? Cell death."

"Yes," Margeaux said seriously. "Nearly immediate and absolute throughout every subject Dr. McMillan's exposed to it. Every living cell in the organism just...stops."

Had Lonnie Schultz not been so adept at hiding his true nature from those around him, Margeaux Quagliarella might have seen an odd light shining behind his eyes. The light of madness, now capering and gibbering with glee.

"Virulence?" Lonnie asked.

"Up here?" Margeaux said with a shake of her head. "Zip. Zero. Nada. Too cold. GT-16 likes it warm. It requires a temperature above one-hundred and two degrees to get going and has a narrow initial range of survivability. Anything lower than one-oh-two or higher than one-oh-five and she craps out. Permanently inert."

Lonnie was equally successful at hiding disappointment. This time of year, depending on its rate of replication, the toxin would only take out a few hundred ragheads throughout the Middle East, innumerable jungle-bunnies in South America, a lot of old farts in Florida and maybe the American Midwest. It was nothing like the complete annihilation he desired. Even if it were twice as virulent as the Black Death and reduced the world population by two-thirds, the species would carry on, reproducing like vermin. In another fifty years or so they'd again cover the Earth, depleting what resources it had managed to recoup, threatening to spill out into the solar system as Branson and Musk were near achieving, infecting other worlds with their pestilence. Then Margeaux continued and that insane, yet unseen light began cavorting behind his eyes yet again. "But once she gets going, nothing on Earth can stop her."

"Meaning?" Lonnie prompted, pretending to have another sip of whiskey.

"The toxin replicates at an extremely high rate. *And* it mutates inside dead cells. If it were released in sufficient quantity in a hospitable clime, say a single milliliter in a feverish person in Pensacola, Florida, or Austin, Texas, on a really hot day, it would replicate and mutate inside each of those cells—there's something like a hundred trillion in every human being—and every mutation would increase its survivability factor until it adapted to any temperature variation, any hostile environment, any biological permutation. It would easily cross the human/animal barrier, and, theoretically, could mutate to infect the RNA of plant life. Give GT-16 a dozen or more hot human hosts and there'd be no stopping it. Dr. McMillan calls it a planet killer."

Margeaux took a sip of her own drink—*a fucking Mai Tai for God's sake*, Lonnie thought, *in Nutsack, Alaska*—before continuing: "It's possible it could even survive the vacuum of space and spread beyond Earth."

"Wow," Lonnie said, assuming an air of sober respect. "Guess we're lucky we do all these studies way up here where it never gets above fifty degrees in the summer."

The conversation then turned back to more banal subjects, her husband's return, her upcoming vacation. Lonnie continued to exchange meaningless banter until his internal voice told him he'd behaved within social norms for an appropriate amount of time. He'd then returned to his quarters, the current, ongoing plan taking shape in his mind.

Now, he continued past Dr. Marshall's lab. *That* fine specimen of humanity was currently decaying at a slow rate in her office topside, a bullet lodged in her aorta. Her number one tech, an overweight, pimply faced man of forty-two, was slumped against the wall outside her office, equally dead. The look of surprise that had taken residence on his face as Lonnie raised his pistol and fired it into his chest was still there.

Lab Two was also dark and deserted. This was also to be expected. The Mount Nasak facility, not its real name as it had none and didn't officially exist, had three labs with three, three-person teams. They ran on a rotating basis, with no more than two labs in operation at any one time, the third rotating out every three weeks.

A numerologist might find meaning in all those threes. Lonnie did not. He knew that numerology, just like ethology, astrology, psychology and every other fucking *ology* were no more than constructs of the human mind. Each and every one of them devised as tools with which to mask the corruption and control of other human minds in the name of science. *There's even a* Scientology, *for chrissakes*, Lonnie mused. *And what a load of self-aggrandizing, self-propagandizing assholes that bunch is.*

The three-person staff of Lab Two was currently in Fairbanks. Five-hundred and forty miles away by air. It mattered not. They'd be just as dead as everyone else on the planet in ten days. Less, if Lonnie could make Point Hope by nightfall.

Lab Three, where Lonnie had quite accidentally learned the real action was going on, was bright and tenanted. Lonnie keyed his personal access code into the keypad next to the outer door and it whooshed open. The small control room beyond was held at negative air pressure. If he were to don one of the bulky industrial Positive Pressure Personnel Suits and pass through the airlock and into the lab itself, the negative air pressure would increase, thus keeping any particulates inside the lab where they belonged.

Lonnie had no intention of entering the inner lab and stood at the eighteen-inch-thick reinforced plexiglass window watching the movements of Doctor McMillan, Margeaux Quagliarella, and the third member of the team, a nervous and squirrely little guy named Bobby Maze.

After a few moments, Quagliarella noticed his presence at the window and motioned to Dr. McMillan. The good doctor set down a petri dish and removed his arms from the latex gloves of the fume hood where he was working, crossed to the window, and thumbed the intercom button set into the wall beside it.

"Mr. Schultz." His usually baritone voice, heard through both the speaker of his suit and the small intercom speaker, was distorted and tinny. "You're not authorized to be here. May I ask what this is about?"

"This is about the end." Lonnie replied, thumbing the button on his side of the glass. "For you, now. Later, for everyone else."

"What?" The doctor demanded. "What does that mean? Are you drunk?"

"Not at all, sir. I just wanted to thank Mrs. Quagliarella." As always, he pronounced her name correctly.

"Thank her?" the doctor demanded. "Thank her for what? Mr. Schultz, you are not a member of this team and are therefore violating security and safety protocols. If you don't exit the control room immediately, I'll be forced to call topside and have you arrested."

"I'll rest later," Lonnie said quietly, then clicked off the intercom.

The doctor continued to talk on his side of the glass, his mouth moving but Lonnie not hearing the words. He moved to the control board adjacent to the window and flipped up a clear cover housing a large red button.

The doctor saw what he was doing and began beating furiously against the glass. The two other members of the team began moving clumsily, but rapidly, towards the airlock.

"Ta ta!" Lonnie said with a little wave to the frantic trio inside the lab and slammed his hand down on the button.

Forty-eight jets of Dicyanoacetylene burning at over nine-thousand degrees Fahrenheit filled the room. Those inside didn't have time to scream.

Briefing

The Gulfstream G550 cleared the runway at Quantico, landing gear retracting into wheel wells with a soft thump. Arianna Price, who'd barely made it on board before the lone flight attendant sealed the door behind her and the aircraft began to roll, steadied herself against the back of a seat as the government owned jet punched its way through the electrical discharges and heavy rain of a storm lashing the eastern seaboard, the heavy sky outside the cabin lit with strobes of lightning and answering thunder. The sleek white aircraft clawed for altitude amid downdrafts and turbulence, gaining a thousand feet here, losing a hundred there, until it broke through the thunderheads at twenty-four thousand feet and the cabin was flooded with sunlight. The craft leveled out and continued on to its cruising altitude of thirty-five thousand as the storm raged on below.

Arianna realized she was dripping all over the floor.

"Hey, Ari," Melinda Tran said from a seat directly opposite the one Arianna was clinging to. "How was the *vaca*? Didya catch your ghost?"

Melinda Tran, of Vietnamese descent, was dressed in garish neon green performance pants, a clashing black and hot pink top, and spiked heels. Her straight black hair was cut short in a bob, framing a face that was largely invisible behind an oversized pair of thick-lensed glasses that magnified her brown eyes to owlish proportions. Despite her outward appearance—a look that all but screamed *There's nothing going on up here but wind whistling in a vacuum!* —Melinda Tran was a first-rate agent with an IQ of one-hundred and sixty-five. She was also a better than average shot with a side-arm or rifle, and an 8th rank Dan in Akido. She'd mopped the floor with many a foolish opponent who'd underestimated her size, speed, and agility during hand-to-hand combat training.

She was also the only person at the FBI's Behavioral Analysis Unit that Arianna trusted with the details of her rogue investigation.

"No such luck, Mel," Arianna answered with a sigh, dropping her duffel and a briefcase sized portable office into an adjacent seat. She removed her sodden overcoat and took the same seat she'd clung to moments before. "What's with the get-up?" she asked, gesturing at Tran's wardrobe. "You moonlighting as a prostitute when the call came in?"

The call Arianna referred to had been a text alert from the BAU. Subject *911*. The body of the message read *Runway 02R. Bring go bag. Wheels up in 28 minutes.*

Arianna had returned to her two-bedroom apartment on Wisteria Avenue a mere twenty minutes before receiving the text, strung out from the long drive home from New Mexico, exhausted from two nights without sleep, and frustrated that she'd once again come within a hairsbreadth of her unsub, and he'd once again faded away like mist on a sunny morning. She'd been greeted at the door by her cat, a female Japanese Crested sporting the requisite stumpy tail, onyx over white coloring, and the disdainful attitude the breed was known for.

"Hey, Fred," she'd greeted the animal.

Fred glared at Arianna for a moment, conveying her displeasure at receiving only dry food and having to use a soiled litter box for the past four days, turned, and strutted away without so much as a meow. Her insignificant tail wiggled back and forth as she walked, like an index finger raised and waved in a *tsk-tsk-tsk* gesture.

"Ingrate," Arianna muttered.

She'd dropped her go bag and her laptop off in the bedroom before tending to Her Highness. Fred supervised the cleaning of her litter box and accepted fresh food and water with a single, short, unimpressed *mow* for the effort. Arianna was looking forward to a long, hot shower before collapsing into bed for the next twelve hours when the phone twitted its familiar, beckoning chirp.

The *911* heading of the text wasn't unusual. The BAU was frequently called in with little warning. What *was* unusual was the message to bypass VICAP and the BAU offices and meet at the airport. Once there she'd been signaled to drive directly onto the tarmac and board the Gulfstream the FBI kept on hand for cases that were hundreds, even thousands, of miles away.

There had also been the subtext of the message. An unwritten but *felt* urgency that said: *Be there on time or be left behind.*

"Hooking?" Tran replied, shoving a piece of gum in her mouth and chewing like a horse who'd found a particularly tasty bit of hay among the chaff. "Nah. My mother set me up with another date. *A good Vietnamese boy with good parents!*" She imitated her mother's thick accent precisely. "*Better than all those* mi chang *you go with.*"

"Were you trying to blind him?" Ari laughed.

"No," Tran smiled, removing the false glasses and revealing her soft features. "Just convince him he'd be better off with a nice traditional girl rather than the batshit crazy Americanized model."

Arianna smiled, then looked around the cabin for the rest of the team.

James Austin, a sandy haired, boyish twenty-something whose computer skills were the envy of the numerous hackers he'd helped take down, was seated behind Melinda in deep conversation with Angelica Aguilar. The raven-haired beauty of thirty-two was a former DEA agent whose undercover work had brought down a major cartel player and stopped sixty million dollars' worth of high-grade cocaine from landing on American soil. The op had been a huge success, but the resulting trial had necessarily blown her cover, making any further undercover work with the DEA impossible.

David Remarr, whose sleepy eyes and slow manner of speaking belied an acute intelligence and nearly eidetic memory, was sprawled across a couch at the rear of the cabin, one foot on the floor, one arm raised over his head. He looked for all the world as if he were fast asleep, but Arianna wouldn't have taken any bets on it.

The blonde, blue eyed, six-foot-four and broad-shouldered Arthur Brant stepped over Remarr's outstretched leg as he moved forward from the small kitchen at the back of the cabin towards the cockpit. As usual, he wore a tailored three-piece suit in dark blue, with a perfectly knotted red tie. The aroma of Axe bodywash preceded him. He reminded Arianna of a young Clint Eastwood with better manners, a better wardrobe, and superior hygiene habits. Despite his all-business attitude and a barely discernable sense of humor, he was as beloved to Arianna as every other member of the team.

Team, hell, she thought. *This is my family.*

"Ladies," Brant said, nodding as he approached. He stopped short and did a brief double take as he took in Tran's attire.

"Did the power go off in your building, Ms. Tran?" he asked, not bothering to hide his dismay at her outfit. "Were you, perhaps, hoping to light your way with your clothing?"

"Nah," she said, popping her gum and replacing the glasses on her face. "I was earning a bit of folding green down on Third and Brighton." Third and Brighton had a reputation as an area heavily trafficked by prostitutes in Quantico.

Brant gaped, his blue eyes bulging from their sockets. His head swiveled from Tran to Price and back again.

"She's joking, Brant," Arianna said, struggling not to laugh.

Tran removed the glasses, her levity vanished like a wisp of steam in the cold.

"So, what's going on?" she asked Brant. "Where's Decker?"

Supervisory Special Agent Matt Decker, a twenty-four-year veteran of the FBI, the last seventeen of those with the BAU, was their team leader. At fifty-three he was older than most team leaders, but unrivaled in the number of cases closed under his supervision. He'd passed up promotions to Section Chief for six years running and, just a few months prior, had passed up the bureau's Assistant Deputy Director slot.

"I'd just get fat up on the Hill," he'd explained to Howard Sutherland, the current Director of the FBI. "Old, I already got. Fat, I don't need."

The truth was that Decker abhorred politics in any form or fashion. He felt certain he'd step on the wrong toes at the wrong time in very short order, thus ending a brief tenure as ADD and losing his pension.

"Besides," he'd added to Sutherland, "I'm retiring next year. I wouldn't have time to learn the basics before it was time to pack my bags and head for Florida, much less be an effective leader."

"He's on the flight deck," Brant said in answer to Tran's question. "With Sutherland and Mike Conlon."

Arianna was taken aback. By the look on Tran's face, she was just as surprised by the news. "Head of Homeland Security, Mike Conlon?" she asked.

"The very same," Brant replied. "He'll be briefing us on this case."

"That's—" Arianna groped for the right words.

"—very irregular," Tran finished for her as she and Price exchanged a glance.

Inter-Agency cooperation between the DHS and the FBI wasn't unheard of, not in the digital age where attacks on American infrastructure were launched on an almost daily basis. State and local entities suffered incidents against oil and electrical companies, water purification facilities, and even federal agencies like the Social Security Administration, the NSA, CIA, and FBI were targets. With but a few simple keystrokes, American citizens, most of whom weren't yet old enough to vote, could launch assaults from the comfort of their bedrooms and living rooms. Arianna recalled an attack the previous year that left a small town in Kansas with a population of just over twenty-five hundred people without potable water for three weeks. A logic bomb planted in the town's water control computers shut down the pumps supplying fresh water from the reclamation facility to its twin water towers, diverting sewage and wastewater there instead. The decontamination of the towers alone took two weeks. The hack was perpetrated by a ten-year old girl with a school provided laptop who hadn't wanted her father to work on her birthday.

What was *very irregular* as Tran had put it—and, in Arianna's mind, spoke to the seriousness of the matter—was that the Director of DHS himself would be briefing them and not their team leader. The fact that the briefing would be taking place at thirty-five thousand feet and not in the conference room at BAU headquarters spoke to its urgency.

The door to the cockpit opened behind her. Arianna craned her head around to see Decker step through, followed by Howard Sutherland and Mike Conlon, the sixty-two-year-old Director of Homeland Security.

Decker took a corner position beneath a large screen TV just inside the cabin, his body posture telegraphing that he would be deferring to Sutherland and Conlon.

"Can I have your attention?" Sutherland called out unnecessarily. All eyes were already on him. David Remarr, all pretense of sleeping vanished, sat upright on the couch and pushed a hand through his unruly hair. Brant took a seat across the aisle from Arianna and Tran, while Conlon moved further into the cabin to better address everyone from a central location.

"You all know Mike Conlon, Director of Homeland Security," Sutherland said.

Heads nodded. Conlon didn't waste a second. He began speaking in rapid, clipped tones.

"There's no time for the usual pleasantries. We have a situation in Boston right now that potentially makes the Marathon Bombing look like the work of amateurs."

Mention of the attack in 2013, the five lives lost and the ensuing manhunt that resulted in a firefight that crippled several of Boston's finest and the entire city itself for nearly a week, assured that he had their undivided attention.

"At approximately 5:30 this morning," Conlon continued, "law enforcement conducted a raid on the *Freiheit Fur Immer* group at their compound in the New Jersey."

Freiheit Fur Immer, from the German language meaning *Freedom Forever,* better known to the BAU as the FFI, was founded in the late nineteen eighties by a group of libertarians whose sole political belief was that one should be able to do as one wished without government interference, so long as it didn't hurt others. That included the use of narcotics, bigamy, interracial and homosexual relationships (both social taboos at the time) and the unregulated ownership of firearms. The well-funded founders of the group had purchased fifty-acres of land deep within the Jersey Pine Barrens, far away from the prying eyes of local law enforcement. In less than a year they'd erected a large, self-sustaining, multi-building compound in the middle of that wilderness, where they had maintained a quiet and peaceful existence.

Over the decades, however, their leadership and their ideology had changed. The FBI believed, but so far had been unable to prove, that the FFI, under the leadership of a neo-Nazi extremist named Timothy Coleman, was a front for various criminal enterprises ranging from the manufacture and distribution of drugs, largely methamphetamines, the import, export and sale of illegal weapons, including military hardware, and, most recently, human trafficking.

"The members of this morning's raid were met with heavy resistance," Conlon said, " Six sheriff's deputies were killed, another nine severely wounded. At that point, the state police joined the fray and what was supposed to be a simple raid turned into one of the largest gun battles in that state's history."

"Our intel says there's over a hundred and forty people in there," David Remarr interrupted. "About half of them women and children."

"That's correct," Conlon said. "But, as of nine-thirty this morning, those who were involved in the attempt to repel the assault have either been killed or surrendered, and the remaining members are in custody. That situation, as ugly and violent as it was, is now under control. We have a different priority.

"Six weeks ago, two-hundred and fifty pounds of military grade Semtex went missing from the Army National Guard barracks in Hadley, Massachusetts."

Eyebrows shot up at this news. In December of 1988, Pan Am flight 103 had been brought down over Lockerbie, Scotland using just twelve ounces of the high explosive. In November of 2015, twelve Tunisian presidential guards were killed when their bus was destroyed by a suicide bomber with ties to ISIL. Less than two pounds of Semtex were used in the attack. In April of 1992, the Provisional IRA detonated a one-ton fertilizer device with one-hundred pounds of Semtex in the City of London. Three people were killed, ninety-one others were injured. The Baltic Exchange, an historic landmark in the city dating back to 1903, was completely destroyed and the immediate surroundings reduced to rubble.

"The investigation into the missing Semtex," Conlon added, "led to one Private First-Class Jaron Derome who, upon his arrest, confessed to the theft and indicated that Timothy Coleman and his group were the buyers. The case was then turned over to us at Homeland Security under the Patriot Act.

"Derome gave us the location of a storage locker in Boston where he said he'd stashed the Semtex, and the date—today—that Coleman was to retrieve it. We didn't know if the FFI was watching the unit or not, but we were pretty sure they didn't know we had Derome in custody, so it was decided we'd leave the explosives in play and grab Coleman when he picked them up.

"He and two of his associates, Travis Swingle and Alan Hrabe, left the compound late last night in a white Ford Econoline driven by Hrabe and arrived in Boston just before 5:00 a.m. this morning. We maintained satellite surveillance on the van until it left Interstate 95, when ground units began tailing them. As expected, they drove around aimlessly for about thirty minutes, looking for signs of pursuit before heading to the storage unit.

"At 5:40 a.m. we received word of the raid on the FFI compound. We had no foreknowledge of the Burlington County investigation, and by then it was too late to warn them off. At 5:42, Coleman, Swingle, and Hrabe stopped at a red light in East Cambridge. The light changed but the van didn't move. We believe someone at the compound contacted them at this point with news of the raid. Without warning, the windows of the van blew out and every vehicle within half a block was razed with gunfire. It happened so fast the men tailing them didn't have a chance to return fire. Seven people were killed, four of them DHS agents. Thirteen bystanders were injured."

"An incident like that in a heavily populated business district," ReMarr interjected, "and there was nothing on the news about it?"

"We suppressed the story," Conlon said, "in the name of national security."

"It won't stay suppressed for long," Angelica Aguilar opined.

"It won't have to," Conlon replied, "if this team gets in there and does its job."

"Which is?" Brant asked.

"We lost Coleman and his associates after they shot up the intersection," Conlon said. "The teams tailing them are dead or injured, and their backup got caught in the resulting panic and chaos. By the time the ground units got their act together, the van was six blocks away, empty, the engine still idling.

"The decision was then made that it was too dangerous to wait for Coleman to go after the Semtex, and that he'd likely abort that mission anyway. A team went in to retrieve the explosives and found nothing more than a seventy-year-old woman's used furniture."

"Derome lied," Tran said, unsurprised. "He sent you to the wrong place, wasted valuable time, and Coleman and company are now in the wind. Heavily armed, dangerous, and highly ticked off that their home was raided and that a lot of their friends are dead."

"It's worse than that," Conlon admitted. "Less than an hour after our agents lost Coleman, two women were killed while cleaning out their unit at a storage facility on the other side of Boston. The unit directly across from theirs in the complex was standing open and empty when law enforcement arrived. We sent in our lab techs. They found traces of Semtex."

"Christ," Remarr muttered, though whether as an epithet or a prayer was anyone's guess.

"This is a multi-agency operation," Conlon continued. "We've set up a base of operations in Boston and will work from that location until we either apprehend Coleman and his associates or resolve the matter through other means."

Meaning, Price thought, *kill the bastard.*

"The focus of this team should be Coleman's pathology. Where might he go? What lengths is he willing to go to? And who, if anyone, might he turn to for help? That's all for now."

Conlon turned and headed back to the cockpit. Voices rose in the cabin, questions directed at Sutherland and Decker, who remained in the corner beneath the silent TV.

Only Arianna Price heard James Remarr opine in a low voice, "With two-hundred and fifty pounds of Semtex at his disposal, *we* might be the ones who need help."

The Wheels on the Bus Go 'Round and 'Round

Art Nestir watched Billy Holloway in the wide mirror above the driver's seat as he pulled the school bus over and worked the lever that opened the boarding doors. Billy had jumped his seat and was teasing little Patty Robeson about the braids in her hair, *again*. He had a crush on the girl and meant no harm, but rules were rules, and he was going to have to have a quiet but stern conversation with the ten-year-old when they reached the school.

He watched Tammy and Tommy Faurot board from the periphery of his vision and was about to call out to Billy to ask him to stay behind for a moment after they reached Parker Grant Elementary when someone much too tall to be one of his riders boarded the bus and jammed something very cold and very hard under his jaw.

"Not a sound, old man," the man said.

Art's heart decided a three second vacation was in order when he realized what had been thrust into his throat. He couldn't have made a sound if he wanted to. He nodded instead.

Two more men followed the first, wrestling a large green box with white stenciling on the side up the narrow boarding stairs. Art turned his head to see what the stenciling read and the gun barrel moved from his jaw to his ear, the sight digging in painfully as the man holding it twisted it back and forth.

"Don't move," he growled. Art moaned and faced the windshield again. A trickle of blood ran from his ear down his cheek.

A second pair of figures entered the bus taking the seat directly behind Art. He glanced into the overhead mirror and saw that all were armed with automatic rifles and sidearms, and that at least one of them was a woman. As his stomach did a slow turn and acid burst into the back of his throat, the mirror also revealed the pair with the box moving to the back of the bus. The children looked on, a mixture of curiosity and fear on their faces.

Art shifted his gaze to the man holding the gun to his ear and was startled to find the man staring back at him. His expression was mild behind muddy brown eyes, a close shaven head, and thickly corded neck muscles. He smiled at Art, the slow and dangerous smile of a predator who has cornered its prey and is deciding which tasty bit to devour first.

"Close the doors," the man said softly, relieving the pressure on Art's ear by a fraction. "And drive."

"What are you going to do?" Art asked, not liking the tremor of fear in his voice but unable to stop it.

The pressure returned to Arts ear. Intensified. The man leaned closer and spoke in a whisper. "I will paint the walls of this bus with the blood of these children if you don't shut up and drive," he said.

Art pulled the door lever to the closed position and eased away from the curb.

THE THREE-MILE DRIVE from the private airstrip reserved for law enforcement use at Logan International Airport to the US Marshal Services offices in Boston typically takes twenty minutes in moderate traffic. The caravan of four black SUV's tearing down Interstate 90, the joint DHS/FBI task force in tow, made it in twelve.

The decision to use the USMS offices rather than the FBI field office in Chelsea was a simple one. Should Coleman and his compatriots mount a retaliatory attack in the city, One Courthouse Way was fifteen minutes closer to downtown, and nearer two likely potential targets; the Massachusetts State House, and the Boston Convention and Exhibition Center, where the Fraternal Order of Police was hosting an event in memory of fallen officers.

Mike Conlon, Howard Sutherland, and two DHS agents who'd met them at the airport were in the first vehicle. Arthur Brant and Melinda Tran rode in the second, with David Remarr behind the wheel. Angelica Aguilar drove the third vehicle with James Austin tapping away at a laptop from the shotgun seat.

Matt Decker had invited Arianna Price to join him in the last SUV. The tension in his voice and the look on his face when he'd asked told her it was an order, not a request.

Arianna remained quiet as Decker pulled the Ford Explorer onto I-90, waiting for him to speak first. Finally, after several minutes, he did:

"Was there a little trip to Gallup, New Mexico you forgot to mention, Agent Price?" His smooth baritone voice was mild and low, but Arianna knew from experience he was angry. Furthermore, he'd addressed her as *Agent*.

"I was on vacation," Arianna answered, crestfallen that Captain Goldenfeather had informed the FBI of her presence in Gallup. Not at the betrayal of her confidence, no. The captain had a duty to protect her people, the citizenry at large, her office and, by extension, the integrity of her crime scene. It was the personal betrayal that hurt. Goldenfeather had given every indication that she believed Price about her mystery unsub and had sympathized, if not agreed, with her mission.

"I wasn't aware I had to inform the BAU of my travel plans," Price said flatly.

"You do if you're going to commandeer vehicles from a local motor pool, use your credentials to access crime scenes, and question witnesses," Decker said.

"Do you have any idea who that young woman's parents are? Her father is the Mayor of Gallup, and her mother's the only living heir of one of the richest families in the state. And you questioned her. A minor. *Illegally*."

It wasn't Captain Goldenfeather who'd blown the whistle on her after all, Arianna realized. Or any of her subordinates. It was the witness, Robyn Carr. Or, more likely given the child's state of mind, her parents.

"I thought you'd given up on this shadow vigilante of yours," Decker added.

"The Carr girl was a material witness in a case—"

"A case that belongs to the McKinley County Sheriff's Department and the State of New Mexico," Decker interrupted. "*Not* the FBI. The case *you're* referring to has been closed for nine years. You have no authority to reopen or investigate it. Dammit, Price, this obsession of yours came close to ending your career once before. Are you so hell bent on proving the rest of us wrong that you'd risk it again?"

"It's not about right or wrong," Arianna protested. "It's about a serial killer."

"A serial killer with no fingerprints and no DNA," Decker responded acidly, "who impossibly escapes from multiple, unconnected crime scenes, and leaves behind no trace evidence whatsoever. A man who not only kills, but also selectively saves some innocents, while leaving others to die. That's not a serial killer, Price, that's a delusion."

Arianna turned away and looked out the window, saying nothing for fear of screaming in rage at her superior or worse, breaking into sobs. It wasn't just the comment about innocents dying, a comment he knew would cut her to the quick. It was the insinuation that her belief in the existence of this man, despite all evidence to the contrary, was delusional. That wounded her in a way she didn't know someone she cared about, and who presumably cared about her, could.

"Ari," Decker then said softly, "listen. I'm sorry." He'd regretted his words the moment he'd spoken. She now faced away from him, visibly trembling, though with sorrow or rage he couldn't tell. "I know what happened when you were a child. To you. To your family. And I know what it must have done to you. But the man that saved you would be in his fifties by now. He no longer fits the profile of the cases you've been looking into. It can't be the same man, Ari. It's just not possible."

"Of course it's not possible," she said, regaining control of her emotions and turning to face forward again. She angrily wiped a tear from her cheek. "That doesn't change the fact that it's true."

Arianna Price was one of the finest agents Decker had ever worked with, but her obsession with this...*specter* was beginning to affect her judgement to the point that Decker, for the first time, questioned her sanity. He'd known about the unsanctioned investigation for quite some time, just as he'd known that Melinda Tran was Arianna's sole confidant in the matter. Thinking it an eccentricity no different than Jimmy Austin's counting compulsion or Angelica Aguilar's shoe fetish—she owned one-hundred and nine pairs, for heaven's sake—he'd let the matter go, thinking that in time it would resolve itself. But by ignoring the conduct he'd indulged it. And now it had grown out of hand.

This time, Arianna had stuck her nose in the hornets' nest and been stung not only by an heiress, but by a public official who was threatening to take the unlawful questioning of his underage daughter by a Special Agent of the FBI before the congressional oversight committee. The man wanted Price terminated for misconduct.

Decker would do his dogged best to convince Howard Sutherland that Mayor Carr was overreacting and, in time, would agree that suspension from field work and temporary restriction to desk duty was in the best interest of all concerned. But he wasn't sure how receptive Sutherland would be in light of the growing allegations of indifference towards wrongdoing amongst the nation's various law enforcement agencies.

Decker signaled right and followed the caravan of SUVs off the Interstate. At the bottom of the exit ramp, he turned right again and merged into the heavy morning traffic.

"You didn't ask me along for a pep talk," Arianna said. "Or a bit of friendly advice. Bottom line. What are they going to do to me?"

"They want your badge," Decker told her. "And you're lucky they're not bringing you up on charges. *Yet.* I'll do everything I can to placate the bureau and Mayor Carr, but you have to be prepared, Ari. You could lose your job over this."

"I'll resign," Arianna offered. "Save everyone the trouble. I won't have you put your career on the line to save mine."

"Out of the question," Decker said. "If I gave you up without a fight, the rest of the team would never trust me again. Besides," he added, and shot her a wink, "I'm retiring in five short months, or have you forgotten? I can drag this out long enough to secure my pension and still save your sorry hide. But you have to promise me, Ari, that you'll let this vigilante, serial killer, lone savior, *whatever*—that you'll let it go. That this is the end of it. Because if you can't promise that, even if I can get you out of this mess, I won't be able to get you out of the next one."

For the first time in her career, Arianna Price knowingly lied to a superior: "Okay. I'll let it go."

"Good deal," Decker said. He signaled left and turned onto One Courthouse Way.

Ahead on the left was a security booth and gate barring entrance to the parking lot of the US Marshalls Service. The simple swing-style gate wouldn't stop a determined driver from entering the lot, but a pop-up barricade consisting of four steel posts that could be activated in under two seconds with the push of a button would stop any vehicle smaller than a tank in its tracks.

The SUV carrying Conlon and Sutherland had already passed through the checkpoint. Decker eased the Explorer in behind Aguilar and Austin, digging in his jacket pocket for his credentials.

"I have to ask you to forget all about this for now," Decker said. "We need to find and stop Coleman and his merry band before they hurt anyone else. We'll sort out the rest when this is over."

As she'd done for over twenty years, though never easily, Arianna put the vigilante out of her mind and turned her attention to the case at hand.

1994

O ne should not feel lonely at one's twentieth wedding anniversary party, not when surrounded by loving friends and family, both hers and his. But he did.

Then she walked through the door looking exquisite in a simple, strapless black dress and matching black pumps.

She returned the 'Hello's' and accepted the 'Congratulations!' that instantly ensued, extricating herself from the small talk and presentation of envelopes as politely and graciously as possible before hurrying to his side.

"I'm sorry I'm late," she whispered in his ear as he hugged her close and returned the long kiss that followed. His lips tingled where her mouth touched his. A shiver ran from his waist to his neck and back down again, following her caress. Thirty-nine was more beautiful, more stunning, than eighteen had been. That small empty part of him that opened whenever they were apart for more than a few hours closed once again. "Highway 56 was closed for construction," she whispered breathlessly in his ear. "I had to backtrack all the way to Ellinbrook and take Two-mile Road."

She turned as her mother and father approached, embracing them both and assuring them, once again, that renting out the convention center to throw this huge bash had been unnecessary. As had been the case since the idea had first come to them over a year ago, they pooh-poohed and ignored her protests.

"I have something for you," she told him as the lights dimmed and everyone took their seats. She held out a small box, four inches on a side and three deep. It was tied up with a small silver bow. "Happy Anniversary."

"Aw," he said, taking the gift. "And I didn't get you anything."

"Liar," she grinned, tossing lustrous black hair back over alabaster shoulders before presenting him with her wrist. Upon it she wore the hand beaten white gold infinity bracelet he'd left on the passenger seat of her car that morning.

He unwrapped the gift and found a Tag Heuer chronograph inside. He'd been eyeing the expensive wristwatch for months, refusing to spend that kind of money on such a frivolous item for himself. He hadn't realized she knew he wanted one.

"My love," he said simply as she fastened it to his wrist.

"As you are mine," she responded. It was their litany. Invocation, and response.

A large screen descended from the ceiling and fuzzy light burst upon it, resolving into a picture of four people, two men and two women, sitting on an expansive lawn in wing back chairs. He immediately recognized their parents.

The camera zoomed in on his father who began to speak. "This is the story of two children," his father said. The camera then cut to his mother, and she spoke. "A boy and a girl who played together."

Her father: "Grew together."

Her mother: "And fell in love together."

The camera then zoomed back out until all four were visible. His father began speaking again:

"It's a story told not in words, but in pictures." Her mother: "So, sit back."

Her father: "Relax."

His mother: "And enjoy the journey."

The scene went dark and the theme from The Banana Splits rose as an image of him as an infant filled the screen.

He took his mother's hand. "What's this?" he whispered.

"Oh, it's the newest thing for weddings and parties. It's called a montage. Your dad called around to all the photo shops looking for ideas and this was the one he settled on."

On the screen were images of first him, and then her, as infants, then toddlers, then preschoolers. An image of him naked on a blanket at age three, his bare butt in the air for all the world to see, drew titters and laughs from the audience.

"Oh, God," he groaned.

"It's a lot sexier now," his beloved whispered from his side, running an impish tongue around his earlobe.

He groaned again, for an altogether different reason, and his mother continued:

"We all got together, picked the best photos of the two of you, and sent them in. Afterwards, their cameraman came by to shoot the prologue before they put them and the music on this little disc called a DVD."

The music changed to The Beatles 'Here Comes the Sun' as their ages progressed past five or six. A picture of her grinning a silly, toothy grin minus her front teeth filled the screen and it was her turn to groan.

To thunderous applause, the photos went from solitary images of her or him to images of them together; playing on the swing set in his back yard, splashing in the pool at her house, struggling to best each other on the Atari 2600 in her basement. The photos—he hadn't realized there were so many of them together—spanned both their childhoods, at his house or hers, in parks and on vacations shared by both families.

Our life in pictures, he thought and glanced at her. The look of sheer adoration she returned brought a sensation of completeness he knew he'd never feel with anyone else.

As the images on the screen progressed past their sixteenth and into their seventeenth years, the music changed again. The discordant guitar strains prefacing the Raspberries 'Go All the Way' filled the hall and his eyes widened.

"*Did you...?*" *he asked, already knowing the answer. She was almost as close to her mother as she was to him. At some point over the years—many, many years, he hoped—she would have confided in her mother about that night. She merely smiled and took his hand tightly in her own.*

Laughter arose at an image of him at eighteen with an ill-advised and very short-lived mullet. Aaah's flourished as she sported an Ali McGraw look that she'd pull off so successfully he'd bought her a poster of the 70's icon. Him with his first car, a three-year-old red Mercury Cougar that had long ago been sold to a scrap yard, mugging from the driver's seat while she vogued from the passenger side.

Then came the wedding photos. We were so young! *he thought, as cheers arose from the fifty plus friends and family gathered in the hall.* No one thought we would make it. *She wrapped her arm around his waist and laid her head on his shoulder. He didn't have to look to know there were tears forming in her eyes. He found himself blinking back his own.*

The images continued, The Wedding March giving way to the Material Girl and Tears for Fears, who gave way to REM and The Smashing Pumpkins. Their first house, him in his John Morrell frock and hardhat from when he'd been promoted to a supervisory position at the local packing plant, her in her Keller Realty jacket, smiling proudly after she'd finalized her first sale. Their second home, the one they still lived in. Larger than the first but still comfortable and cozy enough for the two of them to never be more than a room apart.

Conspicuously absent were any images of children of their own. They'd tried. For more than a decade they'd tried. They'd seen the best doctors and specialists across Kansas, and a couple as far away as Colorado. The results, and the advice, were always the same: "There's nothing physically wrong with either of you. Everything is intact and in fine working order. You just have to keep trying."

It just hadn't happened.

He'd blamed himself. She'd blamed herself. Until there was no one to blame but each other and neither of them could find it in their hearts to do that. So, they moved past it, and put it behind them. And while the thought still came up from time to time, painful as a thorn buried deep in the flesh, their love for each other carried them through.

Whitney Houston's rousing rendition of 'I Will Always Love You' and *a present-day image of them together at her mother's 65th birthday party concluded the*—What had she called it? A montage? —*video and the lights came up.*

"I hope you liked it, son," his father said.

"I did, Dad," he said. "Thank you."

Fond memories are like a sip from a cool spring on a warm day. They revive and replenish, while making you thirst for more.

She'd left his side briefly to hug her parents. So far as he could see, there wasn't a dry eye in the house.

Shortly thereafter, wait staff began circulating amongst the table with drinks and lavish menu items for all.

Later, they were alone on the balcony. The lights of Great Bend spread out around them, mirroring a multitude of stars glittering down from the heavens.

"It's beautiful," she said. "At night, like this, when you can't see the traffic and the hurry of everyone going on with their lives as if everything has to be done right now. As if there's no time to stop. No time to wait for what comes next. As if there's no time to for each other, and no place for love."

"You're beautiful," he said, wondering at her strange and sudden melancholy, so unlike her. "You're what makes everything else beautiful. The sky, the moon, the stars. None of it would be worth looking at without you."

She pulled him close. Kissed his cheek. Laid her head on his shoulder.

"*I love you,*" she said. "*So deeply it aches, while still soothing my soul. Promise me our lives will never get so hurried, so rushed and urgent, that we forget to take time to love each other. That those images we watched are just the beginning. That years from now there'll be photos of us growing old and grey, but always together. Laughing, smiling, even fighting or crying, but always together. As one. Inseparable.*"

"*Of course,*" he agreed, pulling her closer. "*I promise.*"

They stood like that for quite some time, neither of them suspecting that the Universe loves to make fool of man and his promises, and in eighteen short months she'd be gone.

The Bullpen

The bullpen of the US Marshals Service is less spacious than the VICAP offices at Quantico, yet it was brimming with more people and more equipment. Computers, home theater size monitors, and workspaces chattered away in a seemingly incomprehensible, secret digital language. Analysts, techs, and agents of various agencies—as well as a few high-ranking officials from the Boston Police Department—rushed about, focused on various tasks, footfalls on thin institutional carpeting and tile adding to the general clamor in the room. Phones rang. Fingers typed. Voices spoke. Some quietly and softly, others urgently and insistent.

Arianna had once had business at a police precinct in the Bronx on All Hallows Eve, a notoriously demanding night for any New York precinct station. The room in front of her wasn't quite that busy. No suspects waited to be booked or released. None sat in holding cells awaiting the next day's bus to Riker's Island, adding to the ruckus by screaming, cursing, and fighting. But it was close.

A man wearing khaki shorts, a Hawaiian shirt, and with hair an alarming shade of red crossed the room to greet them:

"Directors." He shook hands with first Conlon, then Sutherland. Conlon looked him up and down icily. "Agents." The man nodded in greeting to rest of the newcomers. "I'm Deputy Director Justin Truesdale, USMS."

Initially, Arianna thought he was about twenty-five years old, and wondered how he'd reached the upper echelons of the Marshals service at such a young age. Then she looked past his clothes, garish hair color and pale, freckled face, noted the numerous age and laughter lines around his eyes and mouth, his body type and mannerisms, and placed his age closer to forty-five.

"I was expecting Director Russo," Conlon said icily, eyeing the man's clothing.

"Emergency gall bladder surgery," Truesdale explained. "I was on my annual leave. Coast Guard pulled me off a cruise ship in the Atlantic about five hours ago. I apologize for my attire. Homeland apprised me of the ongoing situation en route, and with all the catching up I have to do, not to mention the chatter, I haven't had time to change yet."

"Understandable," Conlon allowed, thawing by degrees. His eyes roamed the room, noting the large number of people crowded into the small space. "Is there somewhere Decker and his team can set up?"

"Follow me."

Truesdale led the FBI agents into a far, relatively clear corner of the room. Sutherland and Conlon were intercepted by Boston's Police Commissioner and remained behind.

"We've set up few desks back here." Truesdale pointed out an area roughly nine feet square, taken up almost entirely by four desks butted up against one another in a rectangle. Only two bore lamps, both with librarian style green shades. Behind each desk was a chair, though none matched, and one was wood, *sans* casters or armrests, that looked like it was last used by a schoolteacher during World War II. Whoever chose the desks closest to the wall would have to squeeze in to use them. There was nothing else in the space except for lighter patches on the olive-green carpeting in the shape of recently removed filing cabinets.

"There are telephone and internet jacks," Truesdale said, "but all our extra computers and monitors are tied up by the DHS and ATF agents that set up shop after the incident at the storage facility."

"That's quite all right," Brant said "we carry our own." Aguilar and Tran, the smallest members of the team, took the desks along the wall while Austin and Remarr, without a word, set up to share one of the two remaining desktops. Brant pulled out the chair of the last and gestured Arianna into it, placing his go-bag on the floor next to her seat.

"If you could get us a list of logins," Brant suggested to Truesdale.

"Sure, sure," he replied. "I'll have my assistant bring them right over."

"You mentioned chatter," Aguilar said. "What kind of chatter are we talking about?"

"We're monitoring the Boston Police bands for relevant traffic, as well as the Coast Guard. All ATF, DHS, and now FBI feeds are coming through here as well."

"What about 911?" Austin asked.

"We're working on it," Truesdale replied. "We've had some problems connecting with their new computer system but should have it up in the next ten minutes or so."

"I'm going to need access to those feeds," Austin said.

"And the logs of the feeds you've been monitoring since this started," Aguilar added.

"Consider it done," Truesdale said.

The team turned their attention to setting up their equipment as if he and the office no longer existed.

"Don't take offense," Decker told him. "This is what they do, and they're the best at it."

"Offense?" Truesdale asked, turning to scan the room for his assistant. "Not at all. I'm glad you're here. We're no slouches over here at the Marshal Service, but our primary role is protecting federal witnesses, the judiciary, and apprehending known federal fugitives. We have little experience predicting the behavior of psychopaths. That's why we rely on your BAU and VICAP units to profile our protectees and fugitives. If Director Conlon hadn't already brought you and your team in on this, I would've insisted on it. If anyone can catch these guys before they injure or kill anyone else, it's your team. If you need anything else," Truesdale finished, extending his hand, "just let me or my staff know. We'll do our best to accommodate you."

"Sir?" A young woman in a smart looking blue skirt and white top approached. "Director Conlon is asking for you."

"Thank you," Decker released Truesdale's hand as the woman whisked him away. As they moved away, reentering the flow of bodies and voices moving throughout the bullpen, Decker overheard: "The FBI needs logins to our comms and computer system."

"Yes, sir."

"See that they get that, and access to Boston 911 as soon it's online."

Then his voice was swallowed up like a single vocalist in a choir of hundreds.

"STOP YOUR SNIVELING, or I'll shoot your little boyfriend right in the face."

Art Nestir looked up in fear, scanning the mirror to see which of the hijackers was threatening his kids. Until now, they hadn't directly threatened the children. Not even when the lone woman in the group had walked around collecting electronic devices. She'd done so with a smile and each of his twenty-seven riders had quietly cooperated, dropping his or her laptop, cellphone, or iPad into the green canvas bag she held out to them. None of them had returned the smile though, and more than a few of them had shrank deep into their seatbacks at her approach.

They were scared, of course. There'd been gasps of surprise and one or two cries after the group forced their way onto the bus and ordered Nestir to start driving. But most remained relatively quiet and calm throughout. They'd been drilled monthly on school shooting scenarios since kindergarten—something Nestir himself had never had to endure when he was in school and wasn't it just a damn shame that it was common practice now? And he knew what those drills had taught them: Remain calm. Run away or hide if you can. Cooperate if you can't. Fight back as a last resort.

The mirror showed one of the gunmen, older, with greying hair tied back in a ponytail and about four days growth on his face pushing a gun into Billy Holloway's cheek. The boy's eyes had grown wide as saucers, his face pale as paper. He trembled with fear but didn't flinch away from the gun barrel digging into the flesh beneath his right eye, though if he sat any straighter in his seat he'd be standing.

Patty Robeson had crushed her face into his thin chest and was weeping. Billy was consoling her as best as a ten-year-old boy, whose most traumatic life event thus far was losing a game of Fortnite, could. He placed his left arm over her eyes.

"Leave him alone!" Nestir yelled. "He's just a boy!"

This earned him a swat on the back of the head from the gunman, who'd stayed at his side since boarding, giving him driving instructions and making sure he behaved. Nevertheless, the man Nestir had come to believe was the leader turned his head and said, "Leave the kid alone, Swingle."

"I'm tired of listening to her whine," Swingle said petulantly. "You think my Amanda's whining like this right now?" He pushed the gun deeper into Billy's face. Billy made a grunting sound but, to his credit, didn't cry out. "Hell, no, she's not. If she ain't already dead, she's with her mother, just itching for the chance to blow some fascist asshole cop away."

"I *said*, leave it alone," The leader said softly. His voice had taken on a dangerous edge that everyone on board sensed. It got very quiet, the throaty rumble of the diesel engine and tire tread on pavement the only sounds. As if thirty-three people had simultaneously decided to hold their breath. "My kids are up there too. And if we start wasting *these* kids, we'll never see ours again. Even if we make it out of this in one piece."

Swingle thought about this for a moment, his finger trembling on the trigger. Then he sighed and pulled the gun away from Billy's face and tucked it into the waistband of his jeans.

"You're right, boss," Swingle said. "Sorry." He dropped into the empty seat behind Billy and Patty and stared out the window. As the rest of the passengers took a collective breath, Billy relaxed, almost *melted*, into his own seat. Now the tears came. Hot and fast, but silent. As he visibly began to shake, Patty Robeson clung to him tighter.

"Thank you," Art Nestir said in a quiet voice.

"I could give a tin shit if he blows that overprivileged brats brains all over that girl's pretty red dress," the man hissed in Art's ear. "We wouldn't even be here if Jersey's finest hadn't gotten their panties in a twist this morning. But they did, and now fifty-two innocent kids, *our* kids, are in their custody right now. I mean to trade these little assholes for them. So, I need them alive and breathing. For now.

"But I don't need you at all, old man, so don't press your luck."

Art tried to swallow but had no spit. The tone of voice told him just how slim his chances of making it out of this alive were. He realized that his own fate mattered little to him. He'd be sixty-three years old next January. He'd never fallen in love, never married, nor had children of his own. The kids that rode his bus to and from school each day were his family. They meant as much to him as he imagined his own kids would. In that moment, he decided that if he had a chance to save any or all of them, even if it meant losing his own life, he would do so without hesitation.

"Pull over here," Art's constant companion said. He'd been directing Art on a circuitous route through middle class residential districts, where a chance encounter with the police or any of the multitude of CCTV camera's littering the downtown areas of Boston like leaves in autumn seemed unlikely.

Art pulled the bus to the curb in front of a white two-story house with green trim, a picket fence, and a dog snoozing in the yard. The dog lifted his head, yawned, and laid back down, apparently unconcerned with the new arrival.

"Hrabe," the man called, "Swingle. You ready?"

"Yes, boss," Swingle rose from his seat and headed to the front. He glared at Billy and Patty as he passed but didn't say a word.

One of the men who'd boarded the bus with the bulky green box got up from his seat at the back and moved forward. He appeared to be moving slowly, but covered the distance quickly, almost as if he were gliding instead of walking. He was of average height, weight, and build, with brown hair and sleepy brown eyes. The word *nondescript* came to mind, the kind of person you'd see but not really notice, your eyes sliding on to something visually more interesting moments after landing on him. He looked bored, indifferent. Only the gun in his waistband and the assault rifle slung over his shoulder shattered the illusion. Art suspected the man wore apathy and ennui as a disguise to hide a more vigilant, and violent, nature.

"Yeah," Hrabe said.

"Just as we discussed." The gunman told them as he pulled the handle that operated the doors, opening them. "You have twenty minutes. No more, no less."

"Yes, boss," Swingle said. Hrabe said nothing. But he smiled in a way that made Art Nestir's insides squirm.

As they descended the stairs a word from their leader stopped them: "Boys?"

The pair looked back.

"Make it *loud*."

Intersection

"Dave," Angelica Aguilar said, "take a look at this." She turned her laptop around so Remarr could see the transcripts of recent phone calls to the Boston Police Department she'd been sifting through.

"There was a call to the BPD twenty-five minutes ago. A local school—Parker Grant Elementary—one of their buses is overdue and they haven't been able to raise the driver. Dispatch sent a squad car to trace his route, thinking he'd had a flat or broken down somewhere. The officer radioed back ten minutes ago saying the bus is nowhere to be found."

"What's BPD doing?"

"Dispatch told the officer to continue searching and sent another unit to the school to see if the bus arrived and admin just forgot to call back."

Matt Decker materialized at Remarr's side:

"What do we have?"

Aguilar repeated what she'd told Remarr, adding: "I think we should call the school ourselves. If it's a false alarm, we can cross it off our list. But if there really is a missing bus full of kids out there, we should be concerned. Whether it's connected to Coleman and the FFI or not."

"But you think it *is* connected," Decker prompted.

"It's an unlikely coincidence."

"Make the call," Decker said. "But speak directly with the principal. If the bus showed, no harm, no foul. If it hasn't, I don't want the entire administration talking about it. With the shootings downtown and at the storage facility starting to hit the news, there's enough speculation about terrorism going around. We don't need the whole city in a panic."

"Yes, sir," Aguilar said. She turned her laptop back around and pulled up a directory of greater Boston before picking up the telephone.

"I have something as well," Remarr told Decker. "I've been going through the FBI transcripts of this morning's raid and found a notation about a three-second burst of static at approximately 5:41 this morning in the vicinity of the Jersey Pine Barrens. Some sort of radio signal that was powerful enough to disrupt all comms in the area. Coleman and company shot up that intersection in East Cambridge at 5:42."

"The timing is interesting. What are you thinking?" Decker asked.

"Burst transmitter," Remarr said. "Military grade. It would wash out any other radio signals for a brief period and would be untraceable unless someone was listening for it and had the equipment to decrypt it. Given Coleman's connection to Derome and the National Guard, it's well within the realm of possibility that they have one in the compound. I think someone on the inside sent out a transmission about the raid and Coleman responded by shaking the tail he already suspected was there and setting off on a new course of action."

"You think he had a plan in place for this sort of thing?" Decker asked.

Arianna, who'd been reviewing the bios and criminal histories of Coleman, Hrabe, and Swingle from the next desk, answered:

"It fits his profile. He's clever, methodical, and plans ahead. He's also extremely charismatic and manipulative. Everything we have on him indicates he typically remains one step removed from the criminal enterprises of the FFI, allowing a chosen few from his inner circle to act on his behalf rather than commit any crimes himself. In the past he persuaded others to confess to crimes known to be committed by him, to throw themselves on *his* sword so to speak, so he could avoid arrest and imprisonment. Yet, despite his remove from the criminal acts themselves, he maintains iron control over the organization while engendering loyalty in his followers similar to the devotion the Branch Davidians had for David Koresh."

"Christ," Amy Tran broke in. "Do you think that's where this is going?"

Arianna thought about it. "No. He's too narcissistic for that. If he'd been at the compound during the raid, it might have ended that way for his followers, but I'm willing to bet he has a contingency plan that would have allowed him to escape."

"So why come to Boston today?" Decker asked. "Why involve himself in what amounts to a weapons deal? Seems like a small thing to break routine over."

"Too small, given his history," Arianna agreed. "But there's no accounting for random chance. Could be he was just in the mood for a road trip. Or craved a turkey, bacon, and ranch from the original Boston Deli. Whatever the reason, he's here now. And thanks to this morning's raid, and our involvement here, he knows he's in the open and exposed. Forced to make his moves on the fly, without his support system or a solid plan."

"Which may give us the advantage," Arthur Brant said. "If we can figure out where he is before he starts killing again."

Angelica Aguilar hung up the phone and turned to the group. "The bus hasn't turned up at the school and the driver, Art Nestir, isn't responding to calls."

"What about GPS?" Brant suggested.

"The newer buses have them, but Nestir's is too old. They're supposed to retrofit the older models but won't have the new units installed until summer."

"Can we ping Nestir's phone?" Decker asked.

James Austin looked up from his laptop. "DHS got a federal judge to issue a blanket warrant for any and all electronic devices, wiretaps, cellphones, personal computers, the works. Legally speaking, I could hack the International Space Station right now if we felt it was related to this case."

"Do we have his number?" Decker asked Aguilar. She read it off her screen. Austin worked his keyboard for a few moments, then looked up again. "Nothing. Either his battery's dead, he's removed it, or the phone's been destroyed."

"What about his passengers?" Brant asked. "Every kid has a cell phone these days."

"I have a list of his riders and their tablet or cellphone numbers," Angelica said. "A few of them have both."

"Ping everything on the list," Decker told Austin. To Arianna, he said: "Run a full background on the driver. Look for anything that connects him to the FFI. It's possible he's part of this. Check out the kids, too. We could be wrong. The bus could have nothing to do with Coleman. In which case it might be a kidnap for ransom, revenge, a human trafficking grab, or anything. In that case, the more information we have on those kids and their parents, the better. Meanwhile, I'll apprise Sutherland and Conlon of the situation and see how they want us to proceed."

"Matt," Angelica said. She'd finished her call to the school and now wore a pensive expression. "The school Principal told me she can't keep this under wraps much longer. Her people already know the bus is overdue and want to notify the parents. What do I tell her?"

"Tell her...*them*, that it's in the children's best interest that this be kept quiet for now," Decker answered, "and that we'll have someone with her as soon as possible."

To Brant, he said: "See if Truesdale can send over a couple of guys in plainclothes to keep this from going public. But tell them to go easy. These are just concerned teachers. Some of them have kids of their own. If I were in their position and didn't understand the consequences of alerting all of greater Boston given the current situation, I'd want to notify the parents too."

"Yes, sir," Brant said and stepped away.

"No dice on the phones," Austin said. "Wherever that bus is, it's running silent."

THE CHILDREN WERE QUIET. *All snug in their beds,* Art Nestir's inner voice supplied inanely. *Shut up,* he told the voice, *we're a long way from bed and* very *far from snug.* Even Patty Robeson had stopped sobbing, though she still clung to Billy Holloway as if his shirt were a lifeline.

After dropping off two of the unwanted passengers—Nestir had caught the names Swingle and what sounded like *grabby* without the *g*—he'd been ordered to drive through neighborhoods whose appearance spoke of ever worsening financial situations until they'd reached an abandoned industrial complex with an underground structure. At the gunman's bidding, Nestir slowly guided the bus down a ramp littered with broken bits of wood, brick, and mortar. Overhead conduits dripped bare wires like forgotten party streamers, concrete walls covered in the graffiti scrawl of a hundred drug addicts and transients. When they reached the center of what had once been a large garage he'd been directed to park and shut off the engine.

The leader gestured to the rear of the bus and the man and woman, who'd taken the rear seats when Swingle and Hrabe exited, came forward, carrying what Art now suspected was an Army ordinance box between them. Art pulled the doors open as directed and the pair exited, clumsily maneuvering their burden over the safety rail and down the stairs.

"Two pounds on every support column," the leader instructed. "The rest around the old elevator shaft. Set yourselves up at the bottom of the entrance ramp. When they find us, and they will, they'll try to come in through there and catch us by surprise."

The woman nodded at this, and Art pulled the doors closed.

"That's C-4, isn't it?" Nestir said, risking another blow to the head. "You'll bring the whole place down on us."

"Relax, old man. It's an insurance policy. Nothing more."

"Why are you doing this?"

"Improvisation."

Nestir turned sideways in his seat to face the man. "What's that supposed to mean?"

Their captor leaned nonchalantly against the rail separating the front seats from the stairwell, arms crossed, seemingly examining his fingernails. His body language said *We're all friends here. Just hanging out.* The weapon beneath his armpit, pointed in the general direction of the children, told a different story.

"It means that today was supposed to be a simple bank job," he answered, intuiting the old man's next question. "My friends came down here to relieve some of the fine citizens of this city of their cash. Not that they stand to lose a dime since the FDIC will cover any losses. To fatten our own coffers, you understand. I tagged along to retrieve some party favors I had stashed in a storage locker.

"Before any of that could happen, the staties up in Jersey decided to stage a little home invasion. That was a big mistake, as none of my people were in the mood to go quietly. Shots were fired, feelings were hurt, the feebs and the ATF got involved. You know, shades of Ruby Ridge and Waco."

Art Nestir *did* know. And despite the man's flippant, almost humorous tone, his heart sank into the pit of his stomach. Neither of those situations had ended well for anyone involved.

"Fortunately, one of my people got the word out and apprised me of the situation. *Un*fortunately, that meant I had to change the plan. You and your little prepubescent posse here weren't supposed to be a part of this. But I need leverage to secure the release of my people up there, and so I can get out of Boston in one piece."

The fact that he hadn't included his companions in his last statement didn't go unnoticed by Art Nestir.

"And what better leverage than a bus full of snot-nosed kids?" He continued. "Rich kids, at that. The media will descend on law enforcement like a brood of harpies over the *innocent lives needlessly lost* if this doesn't go my way."

"WAIT A MINUTE," SWINGLE told Hrabe. "Hold up."

They were on a corner across the street from the First National Bank of Boston. Hrabe carried a gym bag containing an MP-4 and twelve, two-pound bricks of Semtex. Swingle also carried an MP-4 concealed under the military style jacket he wore but had a sawed off 12-gauge shotgun hanging at the ready from a lanyard at his shoulder as well. He preferred the shotgun, he said, 'for the close in wet work.'

"What?" Hrabe said. "We need to move. We're too exposed here."

"Too exposed *here*?" Swingle asked incredulously. "Just wait 'til we step out into that street." He gestured to a camera mounted on the corner of the bank near the roofline, and another atop the pole next to where they were standing. Both were angled to catch all traffic in the intersection and approaching the bank. "Every facial recognition program on the east coast is gonna start screeching once those babies catch sight of us."

Hrabe looked nervously from one camera to the next and wondered how many more there were that he couldn't see. "Maybe we should find another way in."

"There is no other way in," Swingle said. "'Sides, what'd Coleman say?"

Hrabe thought for a moment: "He said to make it loud."

"Right. And what does that mean?"

"That we're not coming back."

"Right," Swingle said.

"But our wives, our *kids*." Hrabe said.

"Our wives and kids will be fine," Swingle said. "If they're not dead already. *We* need to make a statement. Here and now. So these LEO fucks never try to invade another man's home again." He worked the lanyard under his shoulder and slid the shotgun free before turning to Hrabe. "You gonna puss out on me?"

Hrabe thought for a moment, then: "No. They need to learn a lesson."

"They do," Swingle agreed. "Which is why we're gonna wait and see if that broad over there goes inside before we cross this street, and all hell breaks loose."

Hrabe looked at the woman Swingle referred to. She had two kids in tow, a boy about fourteen with green, brush cut hair, wearing black eyeliner and a t-shirt that proclaimed '*Sorry, not everyone can be me!*' and a little red-headed girl about seven wearing sneakers, jeans, and a pullover. He knew instantly what Swingle was thinking. They'd pulled over a dozen jobs together up and down the east coast, and had gotten away free and clear, with no casualties, every time. Swingle attributed their success to a piece of advice his father, now serving a triple life sentence for multiple homicides in upstate New York, had given him as a teenager: "You can control any group of people in any situation," he'd said, "if you put a gun to the head of the youngest person in the room."

Swingle, like his father, was ruthlessly pragmatic.

The woman and her kids moved from the center of the sidewalk towards the double doors of the bank.

"You take the girl," Swingle said. "I got Mama and the boy."

Hrabe removed the MP-4 from the gym bag, checked the magazine to ensure it was secure, then pulled back the bolt with a racheting *clack!*

They entered the intersection.

Discovery

"**I**'ve found nothing remarkable about the kids or their parents," Agent Aguilar said aloud. Brant and Decker had yet to return, but agents Price, Remarr, Austin, and Tran continued with their assignments, while remaining attentive to anything their fellow agents might bring to the fore. Their ability to work separately yet together was a defining quality of their team.

"They're all from affluent homes," she continued, "as you'd expect from the neighborhood they live in and the school they attend. Three have parents working at Boston General, one's father is a dentist, and one's a stockbroker. The others include the editor of a newspaper with a small but devoted circulation, the regional manager of Flying J Truck Stops, and the owner of a small pet treat company."

"In other words," Arianna Price said, "no billionaires whose kids are likely to get grabbed for ransom."

"No," Aguilar answered, "and the few millionaires on the list have most of their money in stocks and hedge funds or tied up in their mortgages and cars. None of them really have the cash on hand that would appeal to your everyday kidnapper, though there are always those that think people with any amount of money can get more."

"Any domestic violence complaints?" Amy Tran asked. "Custody disputes?"

"Two of our couples are getting divorced," Aguliar answered. "They're both simple, no faults though, with both parents agreeing to joint custody. There *is* a domestic from five years ago. The owner of the pet treat company caught her husband cheating and went after him in the shower with a two-by-four. He lost a testicle and spent two weeks in the hospital. She spent three months on probation. He remarried last year and lives in Seattle. She's remarried as well."

"Bet *he* won't screw around on her," Remarr opined from behind his computer screen.

"What about the driver?" Price asked, ignoring the comment.

"Arthur David Nestir," Aguilar said, reading from the screen. "Sixty-two years old. Never married. No children. Inherited the house he grew up in from his mother in 1989. No mortgage. Pays his taxes. Lives within his means. No criminal history, not even a parking ticket. Good work history. Drove for UPS for thirty years, took retirement, and has been driving for Parker Grant Elementary ever since. It says here he's only taken one week of vacation time in the last fifteen years, and that was to have a pacemaker installed to control...what's this? Bradycardia?"

"An abnormally slow heartbeat, about forty or fifty beats per minute," Remarr said. "A heartrate that slow doesn't deliver enough oxygen to your body or, more importantly, your brain. You'll tire easily, and, if you're overly active, get dizzy and pass out. Not a desirable quality in a school bus driver. It's common in the elderly, and easily treatable."

"Wait." James Austin interrupted. The typically low-key agent was suddenly animated. He looked like a boy who'd won the big prize at the carnival. "Did you say Nestir has a pacemaker? When was it implanted?"

"According to this," Aguilar answered scanning the file quickly, sensing her fellow agent was on to something. "He took the vacation time four years ago."

"So, 2017." Austin said. "Perfect." His fingers danced across the keyboard. "What's his cardiologist's name?"

Aguilar read the name off the screen and got up, rounding the desk to stand behind him. His excitement was palpable, and the rest of the team soon caught it.

"When pacemakers were first introduced," Austin explained as he typed, "they had limitations. For one, they had lousy batteries. The very first—this was in 1958—lasted only three hours. The second, two days. The poor woman that received that first device had twenty-six different models installed over the next forty-three years. That problem's been resolved though, and modern batteries last anywhere from seven to ten years.

"The second problem was that they only paced at one specific rate. If your heartrate dropped below that pre-set rate, the pacemaker went to work. But there was no way to vary the pre-set rate without removing the device. Now they have rate-responsive pacemakers with breathing and activity sensors built in, that vary their pacing depending on your immediate needs.

"The third, probably worst limitation, was the frequent need to see your cardiologist. To have the generator replaced. You can't just pop a couple of triple A batteries in one and keep on trucking. The units are sealed. That, or to have the leads examined and reset if they'd worked loose from the heart muscle, which they occasionally do. But more often than not it was to retrieve data from the device or reprogram it.

"Then came the digital age."

"What's Nestir's social?" he interrupted himself.

Aguilar rattled it off from over his shoulder. He wasn't the only person on the team with a nearly eidetic memory.

"In 2009," Austin spoke again, his hands resuming their work as code scrawled across the screen, "St. Jude Medical developed a device with a built-in, low power radio transmitter that transmitted data to a receiver in the patient's home. That data was then available to their doctor via the Internet.

"In 2015, Medtronic developed a model that transmitted the data *directly* via the Internet—no more radio receivers—not only to the clinician, but also to the patient's smartphone. For the first time, patients could see the data for themselves without going to the doctor.

"Later that same year, MedAmerica developed a model with built in GPS and a gyroscope, just like a cellphone. This, along with *dedicated* wi-fi, meaning it can't be turned off and all networks are required by law to carry the signal, enabled physicians to not only communicate with and remotely reprogram the device, but to have real-time data in the event of an emergency, such as the patient's location and body position, as well as sinus and cardiac data. That and subsequent models have saved innumerable lives—"

"And it may have just saved more," he finished, leaning away from his monitor so that everyone could see the detailed map of greater Boston with the red dot flashing near its center. "I have Nestir's location."

"HOLD THE DOOR," SWINGLE said to the kid with neon green hair as he entered the right-hand door of the bank. The boy ignored him, not only letting the door shut on him and Hrabe, but on his mother and sister as well.

Fucking Gen Z, he thought, already irritated by the little shit's fashion choices and his mother's lackadaisical attitude towards discipline. *They got zero respect for anyone.*

"I'm so sorry," the woman said, offering an apologetic smile and opening the door. She stood aside, her daughter behind her, to let the two men pass. The smile vanished as Swingle stepped past her and grabbed her son roughly by the elbow.

"Hey! Ow!" The boy cried as Swingle pulled him backwards, socking the sawed off into his ribs just below his armpit.

"Hold still, you little bastard," Swingle snarled.

"*Sir!*" the mother exclaimed in surprise. She'd seen the man seize her son, but not the shotgun.

"Easy, Mom," Hrabe said quietly. He grabbed a handful of the little girl's hair and yanked her head back into the barrel of the MP-4, making sure Mom saw it. "It'd be a shame to ruin her nice top." The woman's eyes went wide at the sight of the weapon. A scream rose to her lips only to die when she saw the cold, dead look in Hrabe's eyes. She allowed her daughter and herself to be herded into the bank where Swingle was fighting to hold onto the boy. The skinny little fucker kept squirming, trying to dance away from the pain in his ribs, yelling, "*Goddamn it! Let go of me, motherfucker! Mom!*"

"Be still, Andrew," Mom said, her voice a croak of fear. She could see the shotgun nestled against her son's ribs now. The color drained from her face like water from a pitcher.

"*Fucking asshole!*" the boy raged. Swingle grunted as the boy kicked him in the shin.

"*Be still, Andrew!*" Mom screamed.

Bank patrons were starting to take note of the scuffle. A middle-aged woman filling out a deposit slip at one of three kiosks turned and looked, her mouth turning into a huge '*O*' as she saw the two heavily armed men and their hostages. A teller looked up from a stack of twenties he was counting out to a customer, eyes growing wide as he took in what was happening at the entrance. A security guard helping an elderly couple at another kiosk turned towards the ruckus and momentarily froze. His hand dipped towards his sidearm and he took a step forward.

"Fuck it," Swingle said and pulled the trigger. The sound was deafening in that small space. Buckshot tore through the kids' side, instantly destroying his heart and lungs. His mouth worked once—a little '*o*' in counterpoint to kiosk woman's—then he crumpled to the floor like a discarded wad of paper. Someone screamed.

Swingle raised the shotgun in the general direction of the lobby and the scream cut off as if someone had thrown a switch. The security guard's hand suddenly decided to move north, away from his weapon and over his head. His other hand joined its mate high in the air. Bank patrons and employees who'd witnessed the boy being cut down followed suit, some stifling groans or screams, others swallowing huge lumps that had suddenly formed in their throats.

The boy's mother screamed— "*Andreeeeew!*" —then collapsed, crawling to her son's side and sobbing, touching his face and hair gently as if he had suddenly turned to glass. Her daughter, hair firmly in Hrabe's grip, quaked with fear but made not a sound.

Over mutters of shock and dismay, gasps of horror, and more than one retch of nausea at the sight of the young boy and the blood weeping from the huge rent in his side, Swingle said: "Do I have your attention?"

PRICE FOUND BRANT AND Decker huddled around a table with Conlon, Sutherland, and a young woman she didn't know personally but recognized as a city official. The table was covered by a relief map of the greater Boston area. Pushpins had been positioned in various places. Red pins marked the intersection and the U-Store It that Coleman and his crew had shot up earlier that morning. Blue pins marked police stations, official buildings, and convention centers the FFI would likely consider targets. Yellow pins marked seemingly random areas, abandoned buildings, run-down neighborhoods, and vacant lots. Price thought the yellow pins likely marked sections of the city where local law enforcement felt the group might go to ground.

The scene was reminiscent of a war room. Generals huddled around battlefield models, plotting troop movements and devising strategies for upcoming skirmishes. In a way, Price supposed, that's exactly what it was.

"I'm sorry, Matt," Conlon was saying to Decker, "but in this situation the word *likely* sounds a bit too much like *maybe*. The missing bus is important. The lives of the driver and those kids are important. But weighed against the threat of three domestic terrorists loose in a city of seven-hundred thousand, I have to give the higher priority to tracking down Coleman and his men. I don't like it either, but unless your agents have something more substantial, I need them to stay on this case."

"Excuse me, sir," Price interrupted. To Decker and Brant, she said: "We have a location."

"You have the bus?" Brant asked.

"We have the driver," Price said. "That, and that he's alive is all we can confirm at this time."

"Where?" Decker asked.

"A parking structure on the south side of the city," Price answered. She found and pointed out the location on the map, unsurprised to see a large yellow pushpin marking the same area. "Less than a mile from the waterfront."

"That's the industrial district," the city official, a woman in her mid-thirties interjected. She wore a plain, brown skirt and had large, dark smudges of exhaustion under her eyes. "It's been largely abandoned since the nineteen nineties. There's nothing down there but decaying buildings, gangbangers, and hardcore drug addicts. Even prostitutes and the homeless avoid the area. I see no legitimate reason for the driver to take the children there."

"You're certain of this?" Sutherland broke in.

"Our tech tracked the driver's pacemaker," Price answered, silently thanking the city official for her input. "Used it's GPS to pinpoint the location. Real-time data from the device indicates his cardiac and sinus rhythms are above normal, as you'd expect if he's agitated or being held against his will, but indications are that he's otherwise unharmed."

"We need eyes in there," Brant said to Decker, "to confirm that the bus is there and determine who's responsible for seizing it."

"We have undercovers in the area," Sutherland said to Conlon. "We could divert one to the location and get confirmation before deciding how to..." He had to raise his voice at this last, as it had suddenly grown very loud in the bullpen. He let his statement trail off as he noticed the growing clamor and looked around the room curiously.

"We've got them!" Someone yelled.

Sutherland and Conlon turned in the direction of the voice as Justin Truesdale moved to the front of the room below three large monitors hanging from the ceiling. He'd changed out of the khakis and Hawaiian shirt into a suit, but his hair was still glaring and unkempt, like a wild, living animal that had had a rough day and decided to nap on his head.

"Four and a half minutes ago," he said, "Facial Rec identified Travis Swingle and Alan Hrabe as they crossed the intersection at 49th and Grand."

On the left side of the first monitor was a grainy image of two men crossing a city street. Center screen, the original images had been enlarged and sharpened, showing the profiles of the men. On the right were mugshots of Hrabe and Swingle overlaid with the green framework the facial recognition programs used to match characteristics.

"Forty seconds later," Truesdale continued, "a silent alarm was triggered at the First National Bank of Boston."

The center monitor lit up with a split screen, a picture of the bank from the opposite corner on the left, a technical floorplan of the bank on the right.

"BPD and S.W.A.T. are responding to the alarm and we're currently trying to access the bank's CCTV feeds. We have every reason to believe that Hrabe and Swingle entered that bank and are currently holding the employees and customers hostage." Truesdale looked over to a computer station at this and a young man called out, "Almost there, sir." Then, "Got it. Confirmed. They're in the bank."

The third monitor lit up with six interior views of the bank. In one, Hrabe could be seen near the front door, peering out through slats in the lowered security gate as police units filled the street. In one hand he held a weapon pressed to the back of a small hostage. Another view showed Swingle, his hands working at waist level behind a patron's back. The camera was facing the men head on, and whatever Swingle was actually up to was out of the line of sight. His shotgun was tucked within easy reach under his arm. It was likely he was securing the man's hands, but it seemed to be taking longer than necessary. Five other patrons and the bank's security guard stood side by side in a line to his left, their arms also behind their backs. Other views showed the open bank vault, the empty tellers' desks from behind and slightly above, and various angles of customers and employees sitting crossed legged on the floor, heads down, some sobbing.

The bullpen was now very quiet.

"What's that on the floor?" Conlon asked. "In view four? Can we get a better look?"

Truesdale motioned to his man working the monitors and the image went full screen. The camera zoomed in on Hrabe, holding his weapon to the back of what could now be identified as a young girl. The camera panned, then zoomed in again on a woman sitting in a large pool of blood. She cradled a dead boy in her arms, rocking back and forth, her face a mask of anguish.

"Dear God," someone in the bullpen muttered.

"Bastards!" Another hissed.

"Alright, that's enough." Sutherland spoke calmly but loud enough for all to hear. "This is what we've been waiting for. Directors, get with your team leaders and update your plans based on this information. Commissioner Simmons?" A man wearing sport coat and slacks that looked to have been hastily thrown on earlier that morning looked up from where he was standing near the communications desk. "SWAT and HRT are already on the scene?"

Don Simmons, Boston Police's Commissioner, conferred with his tech before answering, "They're two minutes out. We have units cordoning off Grand and 49th as we speak, and foot patrols blocking all entrances and exits to that building."

"Once SWAT arrives," Sutherland instructed, "have your officers fall back and set up a two-block perimeter around the bank. I want HRT to begin an evacuation of the surrounding buildings. Boston PD and the Marshals Service will coordinate with communications here to back them up. Boston SWAT will set up on adjacent rooftops. ATF and the FBI will take the lead on the ground under my direction. Once the perimeter is set, we'll contact the subjects. I'm assigning Mike Freese from ATF as our negotiator in this matter. He has twenty years of experience and I've worked with him before. Don? Is that going to ruffle any feathers?"

"I don't believe so," Commissioner Simmons said. "No, sir."

"Very well," Sutherland continued. "I want this to go smoothly, people. These guys are armed, extremely dangerous, and possibly have a large quantity of high explosives. They've already taken several lives this morning, including that of a child, and there may be more children at risk. The tiniest mistake here could have grave consequences. You have your assignments. Let's get this right."

With that Sutherland turned away from the room. The noise level returned to a dull roar immediately.

"Coleman isn't in the bank," Sutherland said to Conlon. "That means he's either in the wind or he has your bus."

"Agreed," Conlon said.

"Your agents have experience in hostage negotiation?"

"All of them have been through the training, sir," Conlon said. "But SSA Decker has the most experience."

"Good," Sutherland said. "Send Decker and his team down there to assess the situation. If it's not Coleman and the matter can be resolved quickly, do so. If it *is* Coleman, and I still have my doubts about that, fall back and hold until I can get you some backup."

Decker didn't wait for Conlon to relay the order: "You heard the man," he told Brant and Price. "Let's go."

In the Bank

R yan Shearrer was furious.
He lay prone on the floor of First National Bank, watching the man near the entrance hold a little girl by the ponytail while peering through the security gate at the activity outside. He shifted his gaze to the second man, who'd ruthlessly shot a young boy before ordering everyone else to the floor, only to order six of them, the security guard included, back to their feet. He'd disarmed the guard and lined them all up in full view of security cameras before zip-tying their hands behind their backs and attaching small blocks of what looked like white Play-Doh to their wrists.

It wasn't what the pair had done so far that had infuriated him. It was what they *hadn't* done.

The taller of the two had drawn the security gate down once inside the bank, but neither of them had attempted to disable the numerous cameras silently watching the premises. They hadn't ordered the tellers to empty their drawers before herding them from behind the desk. Nor had they made a move for the vault, despite the heavy steel door hanging in the fully open position.

Most alarming, they hadn't attempted to prevent bank personnel from pushing any of the panic buttons no doubt concealed throughout the bank. Hadn't, in fact, reacted at all when one of the tellers, a woman in her late twenties wearing a bright yellow dress, had paused at her station after being ordered out long enough to reach beneath the desk, likely triggering just such a device.

They'd made no attempt to conceal their identities. They'd immediately killed a hostage, ruling out a bargaining position for negotiations. They hadn't gone for the money. And the shorter of the two men was currently inserting a series of dull colored metal rods joined by a thin wire into the white clay blocks he'd placed on each of the standing hostages.

This wasn't a robbery.

It was a terror attack.

Ryan's left foot began to itch, which was funny because that leg was missing below the knee. He hadn't had a left foot in almost a decade.

In April of 2013, Ryan Shearrer had been a third-year law student prepping for his bar exams the following month. Early in his education he'd experienced a lack of focus in his classes that was negatively affecting his ability to concentrate on his studies. A fellow student suggested he try running before classes in order to clear his mind.

The technique had not only worked but had become so addictive that Ryan found himself not only running in the mornings before his classes, but in the evenings after. And on weekends. He'd soon extended his runs until he was covering five miles or more each day. After two years of this, he'd decided to up his game significantly and enter the Boston Marathon.

So it was that Ryan found himself one of 26,839 runners on a 26.2-mile-long course that would end in tragedy for him and hundreds of others.

It was nearing 3:00 p.m. and Ryan had been hot, bone achingly tired, and thirstier than he'd ever been in his life despite drinking dozens of spectator-offered paper and plastic cups of water and Gatorade over the last five miles. Also, his left foot had begun to itch maddeningly inside his sweat drenched sock. Still, he'd been exhilarated. He hadn't entered the race with any illusions of winning. That dream was for runners far more experienced than he. Rather, his entry had been a personal challenge. If he could cross that finish line, now within sight thanks to a large banner suspended over the end of the course, he could surely pass the bar exam and earn his degree in law.

He was passing Marathon Sports, his excitement and jubilance rising, when there was a deafening noise and a large, hot, and abrasive hand lifted him off his feet and threw him into the spectators lining the opposite side of the street. Pain, confusion, and fear followed.

It was a full day before he was cognizant enough to understand what had happened to him. Yet another to understand that the injuries to his left leg were so severe that it had been amputated below the knee. Months of rehabilitation followed, resulting in years of adjusting to various prosthetics.

He'd kept a positive attitude throughout, despite his underlying anger at the men who'd so deliberately and callously changed his life as well as the lives of others. He'd passed the bar exam, albeit three years late, and become a respected attorney at the firm he now worked for. And two years ago, thanks to advancements in prosthetics engineering, he'd begun running again. Another marathon was unlikely, as his knee became unbearable painful after more than a mile, but the exhilaration of running, along with his addiction to that fabled *runners high*, had returned.

And now it was happening again.

Years of focusing his anger into more constructive avenues had conditioned Ryan to not let his emotions overwhelm him. Years of litigation had conditioned him to be aware of his surroundings, quickly evaluate a situation, and react accordingly. These traits combined allowed Ryan to clearly see what had gone unnoticed by his fellow hostages.

The short man who'd murdered the boy and wired the five standing hostages with explosives had now moved to the front of the bank where he was wiring more white bricks, a dozen in all, to the window and door frames.

These men had no interest in the bank's money, no escape plan, and no intention of leaving the bank alive. And if something weren't done soon, none of the hostages, the innumerable people in the surrounding buildings, or the police on the street outside, would either.

THE TEAM ENCOUNTERED no resistance when they arrived at the parking garage.

From the outside, the building appeared to be deserted. An aging and condemned four-story parking garage with exposed rebar, graffiti on every surface, and ancient rust stains from innumerable storms and proximity to the salt waters of the bay. A warm, light breeze stirred debris and tossed it down the cracked and broken pavement of what had once been a busy, well-maintained city street. The only sound was that of the wind and a McDonald's cup rattling its way along the gutter.

They'd parked and descended the access ramp in pairs, weapons drawn, flashlights held beneath barrels in their subordinate hands. They moved fluidly, in unison, their behavior the product of Academy training and many years of experience, their motions as natural to them as breathing. They swept their lights back and forth, ceiling to floor, seeking out obstacles and tripwires, ever mindful that Coleman, if he were here, was in possession of two-hundred and fifty pounds of high explosive. Their lights cast harsh, chaotic shadows on the walls, the floor, and among the steel lattice crossbeams in the ceiling.

Decker and Arianna had taken the lead, followed by agents Tran and Aguilar. David Remarr and Arthur Brant brought up the rear.

James Austin had remained behind at the US Marshall's Service to guide them to their destination, monitor comms from the earwigs each team member wore, and inform them of any new information he received.

Arianna cleared the ramp and stopped a few feet into the garage proper, holding one hand up in the universal gesture to *freeze*. A dim, steady light came from beyond their position. The garage was an open parking structure. Light filtered in between floors. Not enough to make out details, but more than enough to reveal the school bus sitting in the center of the lot.

"Austin," Decker said in a low voice. "Inform Director Sutherland that we've found the missing bus."

"Copy," Austin's tinny voice replied.

A low thin whistle from Brant caught their attention. He had his flash trained on a nearby support column. A large block of Semtex fitted with a detonator had been fixed there, roughly four feet above the floor. Thin wires trailed from the detonator to the next column, similarly wired, and on to the column beyond that.

"Dear God," Agent Tran whispered.

"It's Coleman, all right," Decker said to Austin as much to the rest of the team.

Shadows moved at the front of the bus and a voice called out: "I only need one!"

Then all hell broke loose.

RYAN SHEARRER WAS WATCHING the little red-haired girl. In the past several minutes her expression had changed from one of fear when the man had ushered her into the bank by the ponytail, to one of shock and horror when her brother had been killed in front of her, to grief. Huge tears of sorrow had run down her cheeks and neck wetting the neckline of the top she wore, even as she tried to stifle the sobs wracking her thin body.

Then, peculiarly, she'd stilled, and the tears had dried up. Hectic red patches sprung up on her pale face and she balled her tiny hands into fists. At first, Ryan thought she was going into shock and was about to pass out. Then he recognized the expression on her face.

Ryan had never married and had no children of his own but had grown up with a sister two years younger than himself named Amy. A sister with flaming red hair, much like this little girl. And the attitude to match.

When Ryan was ten, he'd had some friends over to play a new video game he'd received for his birthday. When their well laid in supply of snacks ran out, Ryan left the room to replenish their supply. One of the boys, a tall, husky classmate by the name of Kevin Rummel, had taken the opportunity to tease Amy about her hair, pale skin, and abundant freckles. She'd sobbed profusely at the outset, but when Ryan returned to the room she'd grown deathly still.

"What's going on?" Ryan had asked, noting his sister's eyes locked on those of the much larger bully.

As the boy began to turn, a huge, shit eating grin on his face, Amy delivered a solid punch to his nose, breaking it, and sending the boy reeling backwards into a glass-topped coffee table that shattered on impact. Luckily, he hadn't suffered further injury from the broken glass and had gone home from the ER that very evening.

Amy, grounded for six months for her actions, had never apologized for the broken table, the boy's nose, or the constant humiliation he faced at school for being beat up by a little girl. Ryan, secretly applauding Amy's actions, had never played with Kevin Rummel again.

He now saw that same *'I'm supremely pissed off and about to blow and damn the consequences'* look on this little girl's face.

Ryan thought to warn her off somehow. This was no ten-year-old bully but a well-armed man who'd kill her just as soon as look at her. He tried to think of a gesture or a cautioning expression that would still the child, but it was already too late. She bent her right leg at the knee, lifted it as high as she could, and with a banshee shriek that would have made an Amazon warrior proud brought it down on Hrabe's instep as hard as she could. Between her shriek and Hrabe's, Ryan heard a satisfying *crunch*.

Ryan was moving before Swingle, standing near the center of the lobby and fiddling with what looked like a cell phone but Ryan thought was the detonator for the explosives he'd strung on the standing hostages, turned to see what all the fuss was about. Ryan sensed an opening, thrust his arms under his chest, shot his good right leg under his body and launched himself at Swingle just as he brought his shotgun to bear on the little girl, who continued to kick and punch at Hrabe who, amazingly, was going down amidst the onslaught.

Hrabe saw Ryan's move, ignored the girl—though she was doing a pretty good job of pummeling the hell out of him—and brought his MP-4 to bear on Ryan. He triggered off a three-round burst.

The first two rounds left holes in Ryan's pants leg, missing the thin aluminum rods of his prosthetic by millimeters. One round tore through the bun in the hair of a woman who lay on the floor beside Ryan, but otherwise did no more damage than the second, which buried itself in the counter beyond. The third round spanged off the prosthetic's ankle joint, ripping it free and sending it tumbling to the floor.

Ryan felt the tug at his pants and the pain of his prosthetic being ripped away, but ignored both as his flight brought him crashing into Swingles' thighs. The impact knocked Swingle's aim out of true and instead of hitting the little girl, the double barrel load clanged harmlessly off the security gate, the buckshot that managed to get through lodged in the bullet resistant plate glass beyond. A series of shouts went up. "Atta girl!" Ryan heard one cry. "Kill the bastards!" was another. "No! Stop! They'll kill us all!" This from one of the six standing hostages who were all too aware that they'd been wired with explosives.

Ryan tried to hold onto Swingle, to wrap his arms around his legs like a wrestler and immobilize him. He managed to bring the man down, the detonator flying out of his hand to land on the floor out of reach. Swingle recovered enough to deliver a stunning blow to the side of Ryan's face with the butt of the shotgun, then scrambled for the device just as Hrabe recovered and punched the little girl in the stomach. She crumpled to the floor.

Well, it was a good try, Ryan thought, struggling to retain his hold on the squirming terrorist and maintain consciousness at the same time. *At least we didn't go down without a fight.*

But decades of terrorist attacks around the country—the Oklahoma City bombing, the Times Square Bombing in 2008, the World Trade Center attack, and Boston's own terror attack in 2015 to name but a few—had a deeper impact than Ryan expected. *The people*, it seemed, had had enough of this sort of victimization, and his fellow hostages leapt in to finish what he and the little girl had started.

Despite knowing that he was wired with God knows what, that might go off at the slightest provocation, the security guard who'd so quickly surrendered minutes before found his courage and kicked Swingle in the side of the head as he tried to reach for the detonator. Another standee kicked the device further out of reach.

The mother of the slaughtered boy, enraged that her son had been killed and her daughter cruelly assaulted, attacked Hrabe as he tried to recover his MP-4 and cut them all down. Her banshee wail outdid that of her daughter. She clawed at his face, repeatedly kicked at his crotch, and finally ripped the automatic weapon from his hands and began beathing him senseless with the stock.

Finally, the woman whose hairdo Hrabe's stray shot had destroyed let out a howl and began beating Swingle on the head with an oddly shaped weapon that Ryan only later realized was his artificial leg. She enunciated each blow, screaming: *"Boston! Strong! Mother! Fucker!"* and didn't stop until another hostage pulled her away. By then Swingle's head was a bloody, pulpy ruin.

After several minutes of silence, interrupted only by the heavy breathing of the victorious and a telephone that had been ringing incessantly since shortly after one angry little girl had started a revolution, someone finally answered the phone.

Resolution

S omeone said: "Oh shit."
The bullpen of the US Marshall's service grew silent as all heads turned first towards the voice, a young man in khakis and a chambray shirt, then to the large, six view monitor in the center of the room his gaze was fixed upon.

James Austin, who'd guided his team to the GPS coordinates of Art Nestir's pacemaker, a parking garage as it turned out, was listening in as Decker ordered them down the ramp in standard formation. He looked up as well. *Oh shit, indeed*, he thought.

The red headed child being held by the gunman they all knew as Hrabe had done something reckless. James hadn't seen exactly what, but she was now furiously kicking and hitting the much larger man, her face contorted with an expression of hatred that lent the pixie-faced girl the appearance of a furious old crone.

She's surprised him for now, Austin thought with sad admiration for the girl's courage, *but he'll recover soon and that will be all for her. Maybe for all of them.*

Eyes then turned to a different panel in the monitor, accompanied by a simultaneous intake of breath as a man lying prone on the floor launched himself at Swingle. To Austin's astonishment, the man's leg flew off mid-flight, but he managed the leap anyway and brought Swingle down.

The bullpen grew still, the only sounds that of hard drives clicking and whirring and the overworked AC blowing through vents as the remaining agents, mostly techs coordinating with their teams like Austin and a few IT professionals, held their breath in anticipation as the scene played out.

Swingle, reaching for what could only be a detonator, was kicked in the face by the bound security guard. The little red-haired girl crumpled to the floor. A woman joined the fray, savagely beating Swingle with a prosthetic limb even as another attacked Hrabe and successfully seized his weapon. The room exploded in cheers as both terrorists were brought down.

"Get the bomb squad in there!" Austin heard Mike Conlon's voice. "And get those hostages on the phone. I don't want anyone in there to move until we've disarmed those devices."

Austin was jubilant, absurdly wondering if all of Boston's women were so ferocious. He opened his mouth to relay the good news to Decker, but Decker spoke first:

"Austin, inform Director Sutherland that we've found the missing bus."

"Copy," Austin replied.

Then, before Austin could wave the Director over: *"Dear God,"* from Agent Tran.

And: *"It's Coleman, alright,"* from Decker.

Then a staccato series of pops that Austin instantly recognized as gunfire.

THE SHOTS CAME FROM above and behind, from within the heavily shadowed recesses of steel parallel lattice beams in the ceiling that rendered their flashlights useless by casting far more shadows than they revealed.

Two well placed rounds hit Brant. The first passed through his shoulder, the second through his throat. Arianna crouched at the first report, spun around at the second. She was just in time to see

Brant's startled expression as his life's blood pumped from the side of his neck much too quickly for there to be any hope of saving him.

Melinda Tran, ahead of Brant and to his right, returned fire in the general direction the first shots came from before Brant hit the floor. David Remarr and Arianna matched her fire and had the satisfaction of seeing a woman, her face obscured by two bloody holes, tumble from the overheads before a shot from directly above Remarr drove through the top of his skull, exited his abdomen, and took his life with it.

Seconds later, the unseen weapon went fully automatic from a different position, multiple rounds tearing cleanly through Tran and Decker's vests as easily as water passes through a tap. Both went down like dominoes. Arianna realized the shooter was using Teflon coated rounds designed to pass through body armor, commonly called cop killers.

Her weapon empty, her mind reeling with the sudden deaths of her friends, her *family*, Arianna dove for cover behind the nearest column to reload.

Angelica Aguilar crossed to Trans position and crouched over her body near the ramp. She fired a volley from her backup piece, scattering her shots in a random pattern up into the steel beams in the hopes of finding a target. She was cut down from yet another position. The shooter, assuming there had been only two concealed in the steel framing above, was wilier than his dead companion, and had moved yet again.

Arianna slapped a full clip into her weapon and angrily racked the slide. Her team was down. She was alone, and the odds were against her survival. Coleman—she was sure it had been his voice she'd heard from the shadows in front of the bus—was no longer her immediate priority. The bastard, or bastards, who had just murdered the only people on Earth she gave a damn about, was. She would either kill the shooter or go down with the rest of her team.

The firing from the ceiling had stopped. The shooter must not have had a bead on her from the opposite side of the ramp. He, or they, had to be moving into a better position. But strain as she might to hear, the ringing in her ears from all the shooting and the tinny voice screaming in her ear—'*Decker, respond! Price respond! Brant, Tran, goddammit, somebody respond!*'—made it impossible. Arianna wished for night vision. Or a searchlight. A similar automatic weapon to the one the shooters had used on her team. A bazooka.

She tried to focus her senses on any movement from above or around, but her eyes kept returning to Decker's body on the concrete two yards away, blood spreading out in a wide pool around him. Brant, Remarr, Tran, Aguilar, Decker. All gone in an instant. As she soon would be.

A voice called out from the front of the bus again: "I said I needed one!"

"Got one, boss," a low voice said from behind her, in a spot that had held only empty air seconds before.

She spun to fire, too late, and something hard crashed into her skull. The world went hazy, then grey, and the floor rushed up to meet her as consciousness slipped away.

SHIT. SHIT. SHIT. FUCK. Fuck. Fuck! Austin's mind screamed. He shouted: "Director!" and the bullpen went silent again as all eyes turned to him.

"Decker, respond!" he shouted into his mic. "Price respond! Brant, Tran, goddammit, *somebody* respond!"

Sutherland heard the alarm in Austin's voice and hurried over.

"Our team is under fire," Austin said breathlessly. "They located the bus and confirmed Coleman's presence, then I heard heavy gunfire. Now, nothing."

"Easy, son," Mike Conlon said, joining Sutherland and Austin. He placed his hand on Austin's shoulder in a comforting gesture, but his face had grown pale as Austin described what he'd heard.

"Have the comms cut out?" Sutherland asked.

Austin turned up the gain on his board and listened, trying to hear above the ringing in his ears as his blood pressure increased.

"Negative," he said. "I have ambient noise."

"Put it on speaker," Conlon said.

They heard heavy, rapid breathing. Metallic sounds that may have been a gun slide being racked. A muffled, unintelligible voice in the distance. Then, much closer, deep and ominous: "Got one, boss," followed by a thud and a sound that could only be a body falling.

Conlon turned to a comm tech that had drifted closer to listen. "Get everyone not actively working on getting those people safely out of the bank over there right now. What's the location?"

Austin, his face ashen, read it off to them.

"SWAT, HRT, ATF, *everybody*." Conlon continued. "They're to approach with extreme caution. We may have agents down. But I want that entire area locked down in ten minutes and Coleman in custody within the hour."

The tech, a twenty-something kid who'd only taken his post three months prior and had already faced a year's worth of experience that day, blinked at him.

"*NOW!*" Conlon roared at him. "Move your ass!"

The tech hurried off to follow orders and Conlon turned back to Austin.

"I have dragging sounds," Austin said unnecessarily. He'd turned the volume to maximum and they could all clearly hear what sounded like something heavy being pushed or pulled across concrete.

A voice: "Where's Hayward?"

"Dead. Gook bitch back there got her. Fixed her ass, though. She won't be eatin' stray dogs no more."

Austin alternately felt grief and rage at this. Grief that his fellow agent and friend was down, that he might never again see her dazzling smile and equally dazzling clothing choices, hear her witty sarcasm, or be bested by her on the shooting range. Rage at the malicious racism directed towards one of the kindest, most free-spirited, and capable women he knew.

"Ah, no," Sutherland said quietly as he struggled with his own emotions.

"The rest?" The voice that could only be Timothy Coleman asked.

"Dead. 'Cept for this nigger."

Arianna, Austin thought, though he'd never thought of her in such ugly terms. *Price is alive!* Austin found himself elated that at least one member of his team had survived. And if that was so, it was possible others had survived as well. The anonymous shooter, obviously not a person of intellect, could be wrong and any or all of them could be injured but alive. On the heels of that thought: *But for how long?*

"You couldn't have brought me a white one?" Coleman asked. Then: "No matter. She'll do. We only need her to talk to the assholes in charge. Wake her up."

WET. COLD. HEAT. PAIN.

Arianna sputtered to consciousness, water poured onto her face from a bottle held by a man in tactical garb, his lower face covered by a black mask. Her shoulder ached from being dragged by one arm across the garage. The back of her neck was a fiery throbbing mass of flesh from being pummeled unconscious.

"Wake up, bitch," the man in black said as she threw up an arm to ward off the water that was pooling in her mouth and choking her. She spat and rolled onto her side and sat up. Pain flared at the base of her skull. Everything spun around her.

As the tilt-a-whirl in her head slowed, Arianna realized she was deeper in the garage, at the side of the school bus. An old man, his mouth covered in duct tape, hands zip tied in front of him, gazed down on her with an expression of concern. The bus driver, Art Nestir, Arianna presumed.

Coleman stood beside him, smiling, looking relaxed, casually leaning against the side of the vehicle as if attending nothing more serious than a backyard bar-be-cue. In one hand he held a Glock 9mm, in the other a cellphone. Tiny faces of children stared from the windows of the bus. Pale, frightened, confused. Coleman's associate, black hair, black mask, baleful glare in his eyes, stood at her other side.

Ari, a voice she recognized as James Austin's spoke in her ear. *If you can hear me, stall them. Help is on the way.* A pause, then: *Nine minutes out.*

"Ah," Timothy Coleman said. "There's our girl."

The man in black took one step back and said, "She ain't my girl. Fuckin' nigger."

Giving no indication she'd heard anything but the racial slur, she retorted: "And what are you supposed to be with that mask? Some kind of fucked up Winter Soldier?"

The man drew back his foot and kicked her in the face. Her head rocked back, a fine mist of blood arcing from her nose. The pain at the back of her neck flared again. Arianna recovered, hawked a wad of snot mixed with blood onto the man's boot and stared at him defiantly. The man drew back to kick her again but stopped at a single gesture from Coleman.

"Children," Coleman said warningly. "This isn't productive. Milton, go check the street. If her friends aren't already on the way, they soon will be."

The man named Milton gave Arianna a final, hateful glare, then turned and stalked off.

"You'll have to forgive Milton," Coleman said. "One of your fellow FBI agents, a fellow African American in fact, shot him in the face as he fled the scene of a homicide a few years ago. Milton escaped, but the veterinarian he went to for help couldn't put his face back together quite right. He wears the mask to cover his deformity. He hasn't been very fond of the, ah, black community, since."

"I'm sure he was the pinnacle of tolerance before that, though. Right?" Arianna said sourly.

Jesus, Ari. I said stall them. Not piss them off.

"You'd do well to remember the position you're in," Coleman said, his eyes narrowing. "The position these *children* are in—" he gestured at the frightened faces in the windows above— "before being disrespectful. I push this button—" he showed her the screen of the cellphone he was holding, a large, blinking red square lit up the center third of it— "and ten seconds later, all their happy thoughts are gone forever. Yours included."

"Why ten seconds?" Ari asked.

"What?" The question seemed to surprise Coleman.

"Why ten seconds? Why not just push the button and *poof*?"

Coleman smiled maliciously. "So we all have time to contemplate our oncoming deaths."

Seven minutes.

Price bent her knees, wrapped her arms around them, and looked curiously up at Coleman. "So, what's this all about?" she asked. "What are you doing here? Why are the kids here?"

"No, no, no," Coleman replied. "We'll get to that later. *After.*"

"After what?"

"After my friends at the bank have made their statement. You must know all about that. Your facial recognition systems would've picked them up as soon as they went in. *Then* you'll know I'm serious. *Then* I'll make my demands."

Ari, James Austin told her, *the situation at the bank was resolved five minutes ago. His men are down, the hostages are safe, and the bomb squad is clearing explosives now. The witnesses say no attempt was made to make any demands or take any money. They were there to blow the bank and everything around it. Do you hear me, Ari? That's his statement. You can't let him know his men failed. He's in a corner and has no options. His only way out now is to trigger the explosives.*

"And what's this big statement?" Price asked.

"Not what, but when," Coleman answered, "You'll know when it happens." He smiled unpleasantly. "Your associate talking to you right now will tell you all about it."

Shit, Austin said, echoing Arianna's own sentiments.

Coleman's grin widened at the look of shock that crossed Arianna's features.

"Oh. You thought I didn't know your friends can hear us?" He laughed. "Of course, I know. That's the trouble with you law enforcement types. You think everyone else is stupid. How far out are they now, agent? Ten minutes? Five? Why do you think I spared you? For your company? For negotiations?" He laughed again, his demeanor changing from that of a social acquaintance to that of a hated enemy in an instant. He leaned close to Arianna's face and screamed into her ear, *"So you fucks would hear every word I say!"*

"Not that I couldn't have just taken the earwig from your corpse," Coleman said straightening, once again the friendly acquaintance. "This way is just more fun."

Three minutes, Ari. Jesus, this guy's a loon.

"So," Coleman continued. "Wherever your friends are, they should know to hold at the perimeter. Let's say, the street outside.

Milton will have a bead on them but has orders not to fire unless they try to enter the garage. And if they do somehow get past Milton, they should be aware that I'll detonate the Semtex at the first sign of trouble. First that support will go." He pointed to a concrete pillar five yards from their position. "Then that one." He pointed to the next column in line. "Then that one, and so on. You, me, and Mcgee here," he said, pointing at Art Nestir with a grin, "will die in the first blast. But the columns are wired in series. They'll do more damage that way. And the little darlings on the bus will have time to see the building coming down around them before the souls are crushed out of them."

"So that's the plan?" Price said. "Your friends blow up the bank, kill countless people, and you demand all your psycho buddies up in Jersey go free or you'll kill more?"

Damn, Ari thought as Austin said, *Ari, no!*

"How do you know that?" Coleman demanded. He looked at his watch. "It's not time yet. They wouldn't have gone early. How do you know that?" He demanded again, his voice rising, face becoming a rictus of rage. *He's losing control*, Arianna thought as she watched his thumb hover dangerously close to the screen of his cellphone. He screamed: "What's happened? *WHAT'S HAPPENED?*"

"Boss," a voice said quietly. It was Milton. His cocky demeanor was gone, and he walked awkwardly, as if his brain wasn't guiding his feet. As he passed the concrete column Coleman had indicated was the first to blow, Arianna noticed he'd acquired a double shadow.

Coleman turned, nearly screaming: *"What?* You're supposed to be out front watching for the cops!"

Milton opened his mouth to speak but a gout of blood, bone matter, and burnt flesh came out first, accompanied by a resounding boom. His body pitched forward revealing a tall man with close cropped hair in a brown leather bomber jacket.

Oh my God! Arianna thought.

She flashed back to the frightened fourteen-year-old she'd been twenty-five years before. Victim of a home invasion, witness to the brutal slaying of her father and brother.

The two men who'd committed the crime had kicked through the bathroom door where she and her mother were hiding in the bathtub, laughing to each other about which of them they'd rape first when he appeared like a wraith behind them. He'd shot the first in the back of the head without warning, showering her mother's meticulously clean white tile with his blood, brain, and bone. The second had been faster, spinning and knocking the big gun away, slashing at the man's throat with the same large, curved knife he'd used to cut open her father's back from tailbone to neck. The man had danced away from the knife and kicked the assailant's feet out from under him. Then bludgeoned him to death with the lid from the toilet tank.

"Are you okay?" he'd asked, helping them both from the tub but directing the question at Arianna. She'd nodded and he'd gazed at her a moment, assuring himself that she was, in fact, unharmed. Then he disappeared through the doorway, moments before the police arrived.

The man that had saved her life then, twenty-five years ago, was the same man that stood before her now.

He hadn't aged a day.

"Thanks for the tip," he said to Coleman. He seized the blasting cap from the Semtex block on the column and pulled it free, ripping the trailing wires loose with the same move.

"*NO!*" Coleman screamed, mashing his thumb down on the screen of the cellphone as he raised his weapon to fire on the intruder.

He was too late on both counts. The intruder flung the blasting cap into the elevator shaft where it dropped deep into the bowels of the garage, far from any of the wired columns. He then raised his pistol and fired. The *Freiheit Fur Immer* leader's chest bloomed a huge rose of blood, his heart blown out. He was dead before he rocked back on his heels and toppled to the floor.

Deeper in the garage, the blasting cap detonated harmlessly with the sound of a small caliber weapon.

A voice was screaming in Arianna's ear: *Ari, what's going on. Talk to me! What the hell's going on?* She swiped angrily at the annoying voice, knocking the earwig from her ear, ducked her head, and rolled. Pain bloomed anew in her neck as she fetched up beside Coleman's body, seized the Glock 9mm from the floor next to his hand and aimed it at her erstwhile savior.

"Freeze!" she shouted. "Don't you fucking move!"

"You can shoot me," the man said calmly, moving to Nestir's side and producing a knife from somewhere on his waist. "Or you can help me get these kids out of harm's way." He cut through the zip-ties binding the driver's hands, then gently removed the duct tape from his mouth.

"I canvassed the area," he continued, "but there's a small chance there might be more of that guy's associates lurking around."

Arianna was torn. Here he was, finally, after decades of pursuit. She had no intention of shooting him. Wondered, in fact, if shooting him would slow him down at all. But this was her chance to arrest him, to *question* him. To get the answers she'd agonized over for more than two decades.

Why?

Why couldn't you have saved Papa and Danny, too?

A few minutes sooner, maybe only seconds, and I'd still have my family.

What was so damn special about me that you saved me and let them die?

Arianna watched as Nestir, shaking, folded into the man's arms. He was crying and thanking him over and over for saving the lives of the children.

"Did he wire the doors? Any booby traps?" The man asked Nestir, ignoring Arianna altogether.

"N-no." Nestir shook his head. "I don't think so. But he disabled the mechanism that opens the doors from the inside, to keep the children in."

"*Goddammit!*" Arianna exclaimed and dropped the weapon onto the ground. She rose and joined the men trying to force the doors from outside the bus. The children inside were clamoring to be let out.

"Fine," Arianna said, pulling at the doors with enough force to get them to crack open. She inserted her fingers in the opening and pulled. "But you're under arrest," she said, pulling harder. "There'll be a hundred federal agents around this building in under a minute. Don't even try to flee."

The doors sprung open, and, at Art Nestir's urging, the children began to file out. The girls first, by some unmentioned and seemingly unanimous decision.

When the children were all off the bus, many of them tearfully hugging their driver and Arianna as they passed, repeating *thank you, thank you*, over and over, Art began herding them towards the exit.

"Wait," Arianna said to the children, thinking of the explosives wired to the columns and the fallen members of her team. "You're safe and the authorities are on their way. Stay here until someone comes for you."

The group stopped, many of them clinging to one another.

Arianna noted the stranger had not left the side of the bus.

"You stay put," she told him warningly. "I'll be back for you."

She started towards the foot of the ramp where her colleagues lay, still in shadow.

"Sorry," the man said from directly behind her. She had neither seen nor heard him move. Before she could react, she felt pressure on her neck and consciousness, like a small bird, fled yet again.

1995

Four a.m. brought wind and autumn leaves that danced joyously in the wake of the Pontiac Grand Am, as if delighted to be free of the branches that had held them prisoner throughout the long, hot summer.

His shift at the John Morrell plant in Great Bend had begun at six p.m. the previous evening and ended at three-thirty, just a half hour ago. Second shift, or, if you prefer, the graveyard shift. He'd taken the promotion to Night Manager after the death of his wife, for the smaller crew and quieter hours, and not for the salary increase and twenty cent an hour shift differential as some had believed.

The evenings were the hardest, after the sun fell and the moon rose up to watch over the landscape, its solitary silver eye casting purple black shade beneath trees, along buildings, and deep into dark corners. Without the work, he'd lay awake in his bed in the dark, missing the feel of her next to him, the warmth of her skin against his, the breath of her soft snores in his ears or on his chest, pulling him closer to sleep.

Instead, he'd had only the ticking of a bedside clock and his own heartbeat to listen to, the persistent lub-dubbing in his chest, itself a clock of sorts. Each beat a reminder of a moment he'd lived on without her. Alone. Empty. With no reason to continue living other than the genetic imperative to do so.

It had gone on this way for months, as winter turned to spring, spring to summer, and summer now to fall. Until he'd decided that God, the Universe, or whatever or whomever was in control of fate, wasn't going to let him just lay down and die. He'd returned to work months earlier, taken the second shift, and now slept with the curtains drawn *and the stereo at full volume to drown out the lumbering timpani of his heart.*

He did not listen to the Raspberries.

It was an existence. Certainly not a life. That *had ended the moment her hand had gone limp in his as he'd sat at her bedside. He hadn't needed to hear the steady tone of the heart monitor to know that she'd passed. She'd been as beautiful to him on that day as the day he'd first met her, despite the loss of her hair to the chemo, the wasting of her body to the malignancy. She'd taken the best parts of him—his love, his passion, his will—with her. He'd felt it go. His soul stripped from his body, leaving an emptiness behind that had blossomed in his chest like a rose. He'd found a niche he could exist in, because that was what one did in the wake of such a tremendous loss. Hadn't his family and friends told him so? His pastor? His colleagues?* In time it will all be better, *they'd assured him.* In time it will pass. *He listened because it was expected of him. Nodded in all the right places, agreed aloud when pressed.*

His heart told him differently. Life as he'd known it was over. His love had moved on. His mother had seen the truth of it, the depth of his loss, in his eyes on the day they had laid her to rest. She'd recognized that she'd lost not just a daughter, but her son as well, and had openly wept. There was nothing left for him in this world. He was just marking time until he could be with his beloved again.

Had he known death was, at that very moment, coming to wrap him in its icy embrace, he might have wept himself. Not in sorrow or fear, but with joy.

Two-Mile road, technically Southeast 20 Road, but so referred to by locals for its starting point exactly two miles outside of Great Bend, Kansas, rolled out beneath the Michelin all weather radials as the grey Pontiac Grand Am chased its headlights east towards Ellinbrook and a home that was now so still where once there had been so much life. So empty where once it had brimmed to overflowing with love. So solemn where once there had been joy. The sun sat beneath the horizon, slowly casting pinkish orange arms across the earth to chase away the shadows, drawing out deer, voles, and other crepuscular creatures that forage at dusk and dawn for their meals.

A half mile away, traveling west, was a black Ford F-150 belonging to one Donald Prescott of Great Bend, now being piloted by his seventeen-year-old daughter Fallon. Fallon, like talon with an 'F' she'd tell those who asked, had spent the night with her boyfriend Tommy again despite strict orders from her parents to the contrary. This usually wasn't a problem. Her mother, a Navy Lieutenant, was stationed on the U.S.S. Abraham Lincoln, which was currently somewhere in the vicinity of the Cape Horn, carrying out Big Daddy Bush's orders. Her father worked the night shift at the salt plant in Lyons and didn't get home most mornings until well after six.

Except for Thursdays. On Thursday mornings his shift ended at three. And how she'd forgotten that fact she couldn't say. It might have had something to do with the Chivas Regal and the pot, both of which flowed like water at Tommy's house.

The clock on the dash informed her it was now 4:17 in the morning. With a travel time of roughly forty-five minutes between Lyons and Great Bend she could still beat her father home and be in bed, by all appearances as innocent as a lamb, by a good fifteen minutes.

If she hurried.

Approaching the only hill on Two-Mile significant enough to have double yellow lines painted down the center, Fallon pushed hard on the accelerator, bringing the aging truck up to seventy miles an hour.

Death, ever the opportunist, reached out in that moment in the form of an eight-point buck that wandered casually out into her lane at the top of the hill.

Fallon, who didn't know the difference between nocturnal, diurnal, or crepuscular, and wouldn't have cared in any event, swung the truck into the left-hand lane to avoid the majestic animal and hit a grey Pontiac traveling in the opposite direction head on, crushing the front *end of the smaller vehicle, violently shoving the engine block into the passenger compartment and killing the driver on impact.*

Fallon wasn't as fortunate. Her habit of fastening the seatbelt and sitting on it rather than wearing it, so as not to wrinkle her blouse, coupled with a faulty steering wheel adjustment lever that dropped the wheel to its lowest position on impact, threw her forward. The airbag deployed uselessly between her legs as she catapulted through the windshield, over the Pontiac, and landed face first on the pavement beyond.

She skidded, twenty feet of pavement grinding her chin and portions of her upper chest away as efficiently as a file removes rough metal.

As the shrieking steel meets steel, glass shattering, hot engines cooling noise of the crash faded away into the early morning, the buck continued across Two-Mile and into the ditch on the other side. If he'd been startled by the appearance of either vehicle or what had followed, he showed no sign of it, so intent he was on the tasty shoots of grass hidden beneath autumns blanket in the fields beyond.

Miraculously still conscious, Fallon placed a bracing hand to either side and pushed herself first to her knees, then her feet. An ugly swath of blood, bruise purple in the gloaming, trailed out behind where she'd been lying, gobbets of flesh and teeth strewn throughout like rice thrown after a macabre and bloody wedding. The tip of her nose, her chin, and lower jaw were gone, as were most of her upper teeth. What remained of her tongue lolled against her neck like a flaccid piece of taffy. Her blouse hung in tatters. White bone showed through at her shoulder, ribs gleamed dully through a bloody hole where her right breast had been.

The trauma had been so fast, so severe, that her nerves—those that hadn't been peeled away like cheese through a grater—hadn't reported in yet and she wasn't aware of the copious amounts of blood rushing down her torso and legs from the rents in her flesh, carrying her life away with it. She felt no pain as she turned, surveyed the scene of the accident, then spied an errant lock of hair as the wind stirred briefly and lifted it across her field of vision.

It had blood in it. Now, *she thought in her confusion*, I'll have to shower before Daddy gets home.

She took three steps towards the side of the road and collapsed as her brain redirected blood flow away from her extremities in a vain attempt to stay alive. Her legs twitched twice, and she stared at the grey Pontiac, so far gone that she no longer recognized it for what it was, or knew where it had come from.

A bright light blossomed over the vehicle and slowly descended, coming to rest briefly on the roof before passing through the dented and accordioned metal. Inside the vehicle it grew brighter, a beautiful and horrible light, flashing from yellow to red to green to blue so rapidly, with such intensity, that her optic nerves overloaded and burned away.

She was left to die in darkness.

In the Air

"Isn't she beautiful?"

"She certainly is. How old is she?"

"She'll be eight months tomorrow."

The baby, nestled in a sling carrier on her mother's lap, screwed her eyes up tight, her forehead wrinkling as if in deep concentration. Tiny hands clenched into fists and shook as tremors passed throughout the pint-size body like an old woman with delirium tremens.

"Oh, look!" The infant's mother cried proudly. "She's going to poo!"

A loud sound like icing forced through a pastry bag came from the woman's lap, rousing a startled *Dear Lord!* from an elderly woman in the next row.

Lonnie Schultz smile never wavered, not even when the putrid smell hit him. Other passengers groaned and made sounds of revulsion, but Lonnie only continued to smile, *beam* even, allowing no indication of the irrepressible urge to seize the infant from its mothers' arms cross his features. His fingers trembled imperceptibly as he internalized the desire to throttle the foul thing until it's face turned purple and its eyes popped from their sockets, shake it until the delicate bones in its neck snapped like small twigs beneath his fingers, drop kick the stinking corpse down the aisle of the plane, as opening a window and chucking it from thirty-thousand feet wasn't possible. Then he would turn his attention on the wretched things mother, who'd likely be shitting her own pants by then.

"Such a good girl!" The baby's mother crooned.

"Healthy, too," Lonnie said, wanting to punch the vapid bitch in the face.

"I'd better clean her up, though" the mother said and rose. She worked her way towards the back of the plane and the bathroom, oblivious to the pained expressions on the faces of passengers she passed.

Lonnie sighed. *Maybe she'll accidentally drop the nasty thing in the toilet, and it'll drown before they can land this heap and pull it from the septic tank.* The thought of the baby being pulled from the tank, blue from asphyxia as well as the dye they put in airplane sewage systems, never to cry, or shake, or spew bacteria and disease from every orifice again, put a smile on his face. The first genuine smile to cross his features since leaving the Mount Nasak facility.

Getting his hands on the GT-16 had been easy once he'd eliminated Sergeant McAfee at the duty station. Killing Marshall, Quagliarella, and Maze hadn't been entirely necessary. They'd have been busy in their lab for another six hours at a minimum, and unable to raise the alarm about the murders or theft in any event. He'd seen to it that all but one line of communication to or from the base had been severed before he put his plan in motion, and it was a grueling five-hour trek across the permafrost, by Sno-Cat or snowmobile, to the closest human habitation in Point Hope. He'd taken care of the snowmobiles and all but one of the Sno-Cats too. *Yes, indeedy.* But killing McMillan's team had been as satisfying as killing all the rest, and left him with no worries whatsoever that someone might happen along unexpectedly and foul up his plans.

The containment system for the many viruses, toxins, and super bacterium had been designed to be infallible. The vault in the east wing of the facility's underground complex was protected by a retinal scanner as well as an hourly shifting ten-digit access code that could only be retrieved from Sergeant McAfee's duty station. The code itself had been easy to obtain, as Lonnie's earlier hack had given him full access to all computer stations in the facility. It took him less than a minute to call up the code and jot it down on a piece of paper.

Fooling the retinal scanner had been more difficult. While he'd have been more than happy to pop one of McAfee's eyeballs out of his head and use that to access the vault, it wouldn't have worked. The scanner read vascular activity in the multitude of arteries and veins within the eye. The eye of a corpse would have set off the facilities safety protocols, sounding an internal alarm and locking every secure door in the facility, including all exits, for seventy-two hours; the length of time it would take whoever was running this macabre show to send in a team to apprehend and terminate whoever was responsible. The facility safety protocols were the one line of communication he *couldn't* cut. Merely attempting to do so would have triggered the lockdown.

The retinal scanner was also sensitive enough that bopping ol' Fred over the head and rendering him unconscious would have had the same result. In this case, the half-dead Fred trick was as useless as the old eyeball on a pen trick.

It had cost Lonnie twenty-thousand dollars and an exquisitely uncomfortable thirty minutes under a high-resolution camera, his right eye forcibly held open with a speculum, to have his own retinal scan made by a high-tech black-market identity forger in Anchorage. It was money well spent. And if the mustached, heavy-set, forty-something-year-old woman who had taken the scan and placed it on a mini disc for him had known what it was for, she'd have spent the money quickly. It had been a small matter after that to add the scan to the computer database.

The serums themselves were housed in any one of seventy-two temperature and humidity-controlled carousels locked inside the vault. Each carousel contained twelve racks housing twelve vials of man-made, or man-*altered*, pestilence. The vials bore no names, only random coded numbers that the lead researcher in each lab was privy to. Again, Lonnie's hacking skills had served him well. The GT-16 had been in carousel nine, rack two, vials seven through twelve.

The true genius was in the device he'd constructed to transport the genotoxin. Quagliarella had confided in him that the toxin had a narrow range of survivability. He'd double checked her numbers against Dr. McMillan's private digital notes, and she'd been correct. Anything less than one-hundred and two-degrees Fahrenheit, or greater than one-hundred and six, and he'd be left with an inert liquid less dangerous than salt water. With this in mind, he'd constructed a miniature heater and micro-thermostat that would maintain 2 milliliters of the toxin—double the amount Quagliarella indicated had the potential to wipe out humanity—at a constant one-hundred and four degrees for up to forty-eight hours, and cleverly concealed it within the lithium-ion battery of a DLSR camera.

The battery was the ideal hiding place. No one looked twice at someone carrying a camera on board an airplane and, thanks to a thin layer of lead lining the plastic case, the rig would remain invisible even if a TSA agent insisted on passing the camera through an x-ray machine. The single drawback was that the heater kept the battery slightly warmer than Lonnie would have liked, about as warm as the forehead of someone with a moderate fever. He was confident, however, that the small temperature variance would be written off as one of the typical characteristics of Li-Ion batteries.

He'd donned a pressure suit for the task of transferring the toxin from the ten milliliter vials to his modified heater. He was unconcerned about being infected with GT-16. It would find his body's natural ninety-eight point six degrees inhospitable and die before it could do any damage. But there were many other viruses and bacterium housed in the vault, some fatal, or worse, on contact. Though the fail safes were sound and the possibility infinitesimal, any number of them could be airborne within those porcelain lined titanium walls.

He hummed as he selected one of the six vials, plunged a syringe into its stopper, and removed just over two milliliters from it. He quickly transferred the contents through a self-sealing injection port hidden under a false terminal of the battery, then tossed the syringe over his shoulder. Any remaining toxin would be inert within seconds of the syringe cooling.

He considered opening or breaking other vials at random. Surely *something* would survive and escape the facility. But had decided against it. Such an action might trigger the vault's safety protocols and initiate a lockdown, trapping him inside.

He whistled as he exited the vault, removed the pressure suit, and returned to the main floor of the facility. He broke into song—*Oh, what a beautiful morning!*—as he packed the few items he would be taking along, dressed himself in all-weather gear, and drove away in the only operational Sno-Cat.

The singing dried up an hour outside of Mt. Nasak as heavy snow began to fall. Turned to curses after another three hours of bumping and jostling over snow drifts and ice mounds. Became a dead still and quiet rage when he realized he'd missed the due West turn he'd needed to take him onto the thin peninsula the Point Hope airport sat on, and he would have to waste another hour backtracking. Finally, nearly two hours late for the last flight out to Kotzebue that evening, he made Point Hope, where he'd had to rent a room at a local Inn until morning.

After an inept examination of his belongings by Point Hope's sole underpaid TSA agent, Lonnie had boarded a Piper light aircraft, setting down at the Ralph Wein Memorial Airport fifty-five minutes later. After a two-hour layover, he boarded a sparsely populated Boeing 737-300 for the ninety-minute flight to Anchorage. After yet another fifty-minute layover, an Alaska Airlines 737 ferried him from Anchorage to Seattle, Washington. That flight had been overbooked and he spent the entire time ignoring the rancid, dead meat smell—he recognized it as ketoacidosis—emanating from the morbidly obese man sitting next to him. He'd barely restrained himself from vomiting when the man had first squeezed past him, then lifted the armrest between their seats without asking to make more room for his huge ass. Lonnie had resisted the urge to scream and spit in the man's face as he'd dutifully exchanged idle chit-chat with him throughout the three-and-a-half-hour flight.

The TSA agents at Tacoma-Seattle International Airport were more thorough than they'd been in Alaska. They dug through the contents of his bag; extra batteries, SD cards, various lenses and cleaning supplies, all dutifully removed, and the lining of the bag thoroughly searched. Neither of the pair, a middle-aged man and a girl of about twenty, did more than remove the lens cover from the camera itself, let alone open the battery compartment.

After the longest layover yet, seven hours and twenty minutes, he was little more than halfway through the last leg of his journey. Time was his enemy now. He regretted not waiting until he had the toxin within his grasp before activating the heater. In his haste, he'd unnecessarily burned ninety minutes of its forty-eight-hour lifespan.

It had taken nine hours to reach Point Hope, another twelve were wasted waiting for a flight. Now, with an additional twenty hours of layover and flight time behind him, and another two and a half still ahead, he would have less than four hours to reach his intended target site before his heater failed and the toxin became inert. If that happened, he'd be just another mass murderer on the run instead of the savior of the planet he'd known since the age of four he was destined to become.

The woman, he hadn't paid enough attention to remember her name, was returning from the bathroom, cooing and muttering nonsensical words to her baby. She hadn't dropped the loathsome thing in the toilet after all.

Brrraaaaap!

"Good grief," one passenger muttered.

"Lady, are you kidding me?" said another.

"Whoops!" The proud mother said, turned on her heel, and went back the way she came.

Lonnie smiled again as a mixture of quiet laughter and sounds of revulsion reverberated through the cabin. Fate, it seemed, would have a second chance to end the child's life, however unlikely it seemed.

And where fate might fail, there was Lonnie Schultz.

Taken

E xquisite pain shot up Arianna's leg, waking her.
Cramp, she thought, gritting her teeth against it. *Have to move. Have to put weight on it.*

She extended her legs to get up, to swing them over the side of the bed and get them on the floor, but her feet hit something solid, and she couldn't get enough leverage to turn from her side. She pushed harder, then realized her legs were bound at the ankles. She turned her head and opened her eyes, receiving a harsh reminder that she'd recently taken a severe blow to the base of her skull and another to her face. It joined the pain clamoring in her calf, making her eyes water. She focused on her surroundings.

Dim light. A rocking sensation. This was no bed. Too small. A couch? She moved her arm to push herself into a sitting position, but her wrists were bound as well.

The hell? she thought, pain biting into her calf, a deep throbbing in her skull. She worked her left ankle as much as the restraints allowed to quiet it. *The fuck is going on?*

The last vestiges of sleep cleared, and she remembered:

The bank had been secured; the hostages were safe. Coleman had been shot. She'd seen the life drain from his face before his body had fallen. The known remainder of his merry band were, according to James Austin, dead or in custody. The children had gotten off the bus safely and she'd turned to her team, all down and by every indication deceased, her motivation unclear even to herself. With the immediate danger past, her mind reeled with the events of the past day. Her emotions were far too confusing to quantify her intent.

Perhaps she'd turned to see if she could do anything. Help in some way, or just be with them. Feel them. Begin to process their passing, though she knew that would take more than a few moments at their sides, or hours at their funerals, or months spent in mourning.

My family is gone.

Again.

And then *he* whispered in her ear, and it all went black.

She now found herself bound in the cramped backseat of a car, going God knows where for God knows what reason. Darkness enveloped the vehicle like a shroud. And rain, as indicated by streamers of water trailing across windows occasionally lit by passing vehicles. She pushed again with her feet. They fetched up short against the armrest of the rear driver's side door.

Taken, she thought incredulously as a mixture of disbelief, confusion, fear (and beneath it all, a nagging sensation of curiosity) washed over her. *I've been kidnapped.*

Had someone from Coleman's group survived? Had he more accomplices they'd failed to identify, as they had the three at the garage? Was she now *their* hostage? A bargaining chip in their bid for freedom?

Despite the pain in her calf and neck she stilled herself. Best not to let her abductors know she was awake until she knew more about her situation.

The dashboard and instrument cluster were visible between the bucket seats, the large digital numbers of the speedometer read 105. Jesus, they were really moving. The glow from the dash illuminated an empty passenger seat. On the center console lay her service weapon, in its holster, and a familiar wallet that she knew contained her credentials.

That has to be a trick, she thought. No self-respecting kidnapper would leave a handgun in full view and within easy reach of their victim. It had to be a lure. To see if she would cooperate when she awakened or go for the gun. Why they'd taken the time to retrieve it from where she'd been struck unconscious in the first place escaped her.

The dash lights also illuminated the driver. Her heart thumped so hard she could feel it rise into her throat. The driver was her unsub. The vigilante. Her one-time savior.

Anger pushed aside her confusion and fear, numbed the pain in her calf and neck. *Bastard!* Questions flooded her mind. *Who the hell did he think he was? What the hell was he doing? Where was he taking her? Why? And why, after decades of her searching for him, had he shown up again, now?*

"You'd be more comfortable if you sat up," he said conversationally. As if they were old friends on a road trip and not captor and prey. "You've been sacked out back there for almost twelve hours. Your muscles need to move, or you'll cramp up."

Twelve hours? At over a hundred miles an hour? Even allowing for rest stops and up to an hour to secure her in the car, that put them a thousand or more miles from Boston. *Where the hell is he taking me?*

Conceding that the sleep ruse had failed, she said: "I'm a federal agent. Kidnapping me is a federal offense that carries up to a twenty-year sentence. Harming me in any way in the course of a kidnapping carries the death penalty. Pull the car over now, surrender, and we'll see what we can do about those charges."

He said nothing for a moment, then: "Sit up, Ari. There's a lap belt around your waist. I didn't want you rolling off the seat. That's why you couldn't sit up the first time you tried. You can reach the latch."

She felt for the belt and buckle and depressed the button. The belt fell away, and she swung her legs onto the floorboard, pushing herself up with her hands. The cramp in her calf intensified, then began to back off as she worked her feet as much as her bonds would allow. She tilted her head side to side and rotated it to alleviate the pain there as well. She realized she was now sitting directly behind her captor. She could throw her arms over his head and pin his neck to the headrest, force him to stop the vehicle or choke him unconscious and risk wrecking it.

"Move to the other side, please," he said calmly. He met her eyes in the rearview mirror. There was no trace of impatience or anger in his gaze, just a cool tranquility. A self-controlled poise, bordering on serenity. "At this speed you'll kill a lot of people if you try anything rash."

She considered defying him and strangling him anyway. Not just unconscious, but wrenching his head back against the headrest until his neck snapped and to hell with the consequences. He was a multiple murderer. A serial killer who'd operated in the shadows for decades, with a long and convoluted history of victims that no one, not even herself, knew the true extent of. The world would certainly be better off without him. And if the act killed her as well, and it most certainly would, she realized, noting the windshield wipers working against the rain, the wet pavement beneath the tires, and the multiple vehicles they were passing as if they stood still, then so be it. Her team was gone. She had no other friends besides those she worked with. Her mother, the last of her biological family, had been taken by cancer when she was nineteen. She was most likely out of a job and had nothing to fall back on. Hell, her own cat didn't even like her. What did it matter?

"There's a lot more at stake here than just you and I, Ari," he said.

She looked out the rain-streaked window, at the lights beyond the highway (*four lanes, divided; an Interstate*, the ever-present analytical part of her mind informed her) at vehicles they passed. Cars, trucks, a semi, a van with children in the back, their faces lit up by monitors set into the headrests, a flash of Timon and Pumba cavorting on the screen the little boy closest to her was watching as they passed. She assumed he meant that these lives were at stake too. This vehicle careening out of control, flipping at these speeds and in these weather conditions, hurtling down the highway like an unguided missile, would do untold damage before it finally came to rest, potentially killing dozens of innocent people.

She grudgingly decided he was right and moved to the passenger side of the vehicle.

"Don't call me Ari," she said, further working her left foot. The cramp there was finally easing. The throbbing in her neck receded to a dull ache. "Only my friends call me that."

"WHERE ARE WE GOING?" Arianna asked. Neither of them had spoken for several minutes and, had he not adjusted the rearview mirror so that he could better see her, she might have thought he'd forgotten about her for all the attention he'd shown. He wasn't behaving like a kidnapper. He hadn't questioned her. Made no demands other than asking her to change seats. He'd *advised* her to sit up. That hadn't seemed like a demand either, but rather a change in position for her benefit. There had been no threats of violence. No explanation of why she'd been abducted. It was as if he were waiting for something. As if he himself were unsure of what was going on and was relying on some external source (*A partner?* she thought) to guide him. In the meantime, she was simply along for the ride.

"I don't know," he responded.

Great, she thought. *I'm right. He's just a pawn and I'm at the mercy of someone I can't see, don't know, and whose intentions aren't clear. The great mystery of my life is no more than an errand boy.*

"Southeast," he added needlessly. She'd seen the I-59 markers for the last few miles and knew it ran the Northwest/Southeast corridor.

"Look," she said, "whoever you're working for, whatever they want, this isn't the way to achieve any sort of worthwhile goal. Whatever they're paying you—"

He met her eyes in the rearview, silencing her.

"I don't work for anyone," he said in that same, casual, *maddening* voice. "At least not anyone who pays me."

"And what does that mean?" she asked.

She had him talking. Good. Her training included hostage negotiations, in which the first step was to open a dialogue and listen. She remembered her instructor's words:

"You must remember that you can't get someone to see things your way until they believe that you see things their way. Instinct will tell you to attempt to modify the other person's behavior and thinking by convincing them that you're right and they're wrong. This is a mistake. The more you try to win that person over, the more they'll convince themselves that they're right, and you're wrong. The reason for that is simple. While you're spending all your time talking and convincing the other person, he or she just isn't hearing a word of it. They're taking that time to reinforce their own perspective while you position yourself as an adversary. The key isn't to convince them of anything, but instead to start by understanding them. Which means, no matter how ridiculous you think their perspective, how wrong you believe their thinking, you shut up and listen."

He met her eyes in the mirror again.

"I know what you do for a living, Ms. Price," he said. "And I know you've spent the better part of your adulthood trying to find me. I also know your training. Weapons, combat, psychological conditioning, *and* hostage resolution. You're wasting your time. Understanding me won't help with what's coming. Only *you* can. Your Bureau approved five-step negotiations process is of no value whatsoever."

How the hell does he know what I'm thinking?

"Besides," he added. "you're not my hostage."

"You *abducted* me from a crime scene," she said indignantly, "tied me up and threw me in the back of this car. If I'm not a hostage, pull over now and let me go."

Her eyes widened in fear and surprise as he downshifted, hitting the brakes hard and cutting across three lanes of traffic to squealing tires and honking horns. The van with the children in it shot by, both kids staring wide-eyed at the car as the van overtook and passed them. He guided the vehicle down an exit ramp lit by a single overhead light at the bottom, cut the engine, and got out.

Oh, shit, shit, shit! She thought frantically, her eyes darting about the interior of the car. They landed on her service weapon on the console. She lunged forward to grab it, calculating how long it would take her to jam her finger through the trigger guard and fire it while it was still in the holster—*please be loaded, please!* –but he was already opening her door and reaching inside, a huge knife in his hands. She tried to swing her arms at his head, but he ducked the blow, cut the zip-ties from her ankles, then caught her arms as she tried to deliver a blow to the back of his neck. He cut the zip-ties there as well, before pulling her from the car as if she were light as paper. He set her on her feet at the side of the road. Rain poured down on them both.

Breathing heavily, she turned to face him.

"Huntville's about twelve miles that way," he said, pointing north up a dark and deserted feeder road. "You should be able to make it by dawn."

Huntsville? Alabama? He brought me all the way to Alabama?

He turned, closed the rear passenger door of the car, and walked back to the driver's side without another word. Arianna stood watching him, wet, surprised, and more than a little nonplussed.

"Wait," she said, not knowing why.

"I'm as confused and angry as you are," he told her. "But I've lived with both for a very long time. You just have to believe that I don't have a choice here. Neither of us do."

He began to get back into the car. To drive off, leaving her cold, alone, and without any of the answers she'd so desperately sought for most of her life.

"Why did you take me?" she blurted out before he could seat himself. "Why come back into my life after all this time?"

He paused and straightened, looking at her over the roof of the car. His hesitance and demeanor told her that this was a man unaccustomed to explaining himself to anyone. A man who felt himself alone and wholly apart from other human beings.

"I was led to understand that I need you," he said. "Not anyone else, but specifically you. That's never happened before."

"By who?"

He grinned at this. A perfectly innocent and charming grin that prompted a smile in return. Until she remembered that Ted Bundy and Ed Gein had also been remarkably charming.

"I've been asking myself that for a long time," he answered. "My guide. My mentor. My muse. Call it whatever you like, it hasn't been wrong so far. I won't doubt it this time. It says I need you to do this, that I won't succeed without you. But I'm no longer willing to drag you into this against your will."

He got in the car.

Arianna's mind reeled.

She was free. She could run for a house. There had to be dozens of them between here and Huntsville. Or go back up to the Interstate and flag down a passing car. State troopers frequented every Interstate in the nation, this one would be no different.

Then why didn't he get pulled over doing better than a hundred miles an hour for the last twelve hours? Dumb luck? Or something else?

She knew what direction he was travelling, if not his intended destination. With a little luck she could have a significant law enforcement presence in place further south to intercept him. There'd be nowhere for him to flee in the middle of the Interstate.

There'd been nowhere for him to flee to in Albuquerque last year. Or Manhattan two years before that. Or the Chicago Hotel that had been teeming with SWAT members five years ago.

How many times has he eluded law enforcement? Vanished without a trace, only to turn up at another location at another time, only to vanish yet again?

He started the car.

And what about that, Ari? She argued with herself. *How does he do that? And why does he look the same now as he did twenty-five years ago? Not just similar, but* exactly *the same.*

He's a murderer.

Is he? You've been investigating him for years. There's probably no one on earth who knows his history better than you. He's a killer to be sure, but are you aware of a single instance where he didn't kill in defense of others? That his actions didn't prevent a larger tragedy?

And what, after all he's done, the ruin he's averted, could be so important that he needs your help now?

He averted no tragedy in my case.

He saved you, Ari.

And let Papa and Danny die.

Did he let *them die? Or was he powerless to prevent it?*

She had no answer for that. Consumed by her grief and loss, the thought had never occurred to her.

What is it you really want, Ari?

I want to prevent this man from escaping to kill again.

No, Ari. What do you really want?

I want to bring this man to justice.

Twenty-five years, Ari. Thousands of hours of research, footwork, and investigation, all the while forsaking a normal life, normal friendships, love, a chance at raising a family of your own. Tortured by ridicule for your beliefs, your own self-doubt, insecurities, and uncertainty. He's right in front of you. Right now. What do you really *want?*

I want answers.

The car—she could see now that it was a late model Camaro in dark blue or black—started to pull away and Arianna grabbed the passenger door handle, opened it, and plunged inside before it could pick up speed. She sat, hair dripping rainwater on the passenger seat, as surprised by her actions as the raised eyebrows of her former captor indicated he was. She plucked her wallet from the console and pocketed it, her weapon she snapped to her waist without bothering to check the clip. He made no move to stop her, upshifted, and pulled back onto the Interstate.

"I'm not saying I buy any of this," she said as the vehicle accelerated to over one-hundred miles an hour. "That you're on some divine mission or whatever you want to call it, guided by some mystic force that claims you need my help to fulfill it. But I'm willing to listen. For now. No negotiation tactics, no Bureau training, no law enforcement mind set. Just two people, riding along, having a conversation.

"You can start by telling me just who the hell you are."

Who Are You?

I t was a fair enough question. One he'd heard repeatedly.
Who are you?

It most often came from those about to die at his hands. Asked, sometimes *screamed*, out of anger, pain, and fear. He heard it less often from those he saved, so quick was he to vanish once the task was complete. On those occasions the simple, rote question was asked out of curiosity, gratitude, and on more than one occasion, a sense of wonder.

He had no answer for the woman staring intently at him from the passenger seat, her arms crossed, eyes slightly widened in anticipation, her wet clothes slowly drying as they traveled south along the I-59 corridor. He had no memory of his past, or his name if he'd ever had one. If he had, he certainly couldn't remember it. Couldn't remember being a child, with parents who'd raised and loved him, or despised and neglected him. Had no memory of being a teenager, or becoming an adult, of having a job, buying a car, being married or single, owning a home, or any of the other things that defined manhood.

His first memory was becoming aware that he was cold and naked and alone on a dark city street. He'd awakened, crumpled uncomfortably on his side against the curb, as if tossed there like an empty paper cup or used candy wrapper by some careless passerby. A single spot of light shone from an alley off to his right, where, no more than a dozen yards in, he'd seen a man and young girl struggling. The man had a knife to the girl's belly and was trying to unfasten his belt. Her blouse was torn, her skirt rucked up around her thighs, and she'd been pleading with him not to do this, she was only fifteen, it was late, her mother would be worried, and she just wanted to go home. *Please!*

He'd thrust himself to his feet and waded in, ignoring the girl's widening eyes at his nakedness and her scream, part relief and part terror, as he'd wrapped one arm around the man's neck and pushed sideways with the other until it cracked loudly. The man had gone limp in his arms. The girl ran off, still wailing and not looking back. If she had, she'd have only seen him helping himself to the would-be rapist's clothes, the wallet stuffed with cash he'd had in his jacket pocket, and the dead man's boots. He'd left the knife where it was.

He'd found the rapists vehicle, a brand-new grey '97 Dodge custom van with red leather interior and darkened windows, parked two blocks away with the keys in the ignition. He didn't know, or care, how he knew who the vehicle belonged to. He got in and pulled away from the curb, unnoticed by the cop in the cruiser with *Great Bend Police* stenciled on the side as he sped past, red and blue lights flashing chaotically from twin bubblegum's mounted atop the Crown Vic.

Two days later he'd found himself at a pawnshop in Ft. Myers, Florida, where he killed a man high on methamphetamines who'd taken it into his head that the pawnshop owner and his family across the street were aliens, bent on cooking his brain with microwaves shot from a hidden emitter in their second story apartment above their store.

He'd been too late to save the owner and her son, an eighteen-year-old who'd just graduated high school a month before. He *had* saved the father and his young daughter, a wispy, blonde haired six-year-old who'd been crouching in a corner, crying and hugging a stuffed Pooh Bear so tightly to her thin chest that the seams along Pooh's pudgy belly had burst.

A week after that he found himself in up-state New York, the gun he'd taken off the body of the meth head in Florida in his hand barking sharp rejoinders to the fireworks exploding in bright and festive fashion overhead in honor of the nation's birthday. The rounds smashed through the torso of a serial killer who'd already murdered seven girls between the ages of ten and twenty-three. He'd saved another child, this one a raven-haired teen still wearing braces.

He'd then stopped the kidnapping of a young boy in Kennebunkport, Maine.

Pulled three from a house fire in Toronto.

Stopped a robbery in Atlanta.

A homicide in Dallas.

It had gone on like that ever since.

That was who he was.

How was he to explain that to her? Did he even want to?

"I'm Nobody," he said.

"Nobody isn't a name," she said. "Start with that. Everybody has a name."

"I don't," he said. "No name. No social security number. No identity. But you already know that."

"Just because it's not in a database somewhere doesn't mean it doesn't exist," she said. "Look, we agreed to a conversation—"

"I agreed to nothing," he said. "I told you to go. *You* got back in the car."

She sat quietly for a moment. He was right. She'd debated doing so but had gotten back in the vehicle of her own accord. She looked around the interior, wondering if that had been such a wise decision, after all.

"Where'd you get it?" she asked, motioning around her. "Steal it? Jack someone for it? Is there a dead owner lying on the street somewhere back in Boston?"

"The keys were in it," he said. "It happens. I prefer to think of it as borrowing."

"Right," she said, snorting air through her nostrils. He said nothing for several minutes. Then, apropos of nothing:

"New Orleans."

"What?" she asked, confused.

"You wanted to know where we're going," he said. "New Orleans."

"Why didn't you say so before?"

"I didn't know before," he answered.

"But now you do," she said derisively. "You've been driving for half a day, through nine states and over twelve-hundred miles on an Interstate that practically *ends* in New Orleans, but you didn't know until just now that that is where you were going?"

"That's how it works," he said.

"That's how *what* works?" she spat in frustration.

He took his eyes off the road and looked at her. *Really* looked at her. On the surface she was Arianna Price, Special Agent of the FBI. An attractive, proud, African American woman defined by neither sex nor race who'd devoted her life to helping others. Who sought justice for the vulnerable by stopping those who would make victims of them. Who lived her life not only by the laws and codes taught her, but also by an innate sense of right and wrong, guided by a recognizably strong moral compass. This was an intelligent, capable woman, he realized, who would readily meet violence with violence. And kill when necessary. But only to ensure the survival of others.

Beneath the tough cop exterior, however, he could see the confused and frightened teen he'd once plucked from a bathtub, covered in her father and brother's blood, crying and shaking in terror, grief-stricken by loss.

Twice, he thought. *I've never been sent to the same person twice before. What does that mean?*

"She says I need you," he said, breaking the silence. "That I can't do this alone."

Arianna looked at him. He'd said something similar back at the side of the road.

"Who is *she*?" she asked.

"I don't know," he said, taking one hand off the wheel and holding it out in a placating gesture to forestall a reaction to yet another non-answer. "She comes most often and most clearly in my sleep. In my dreams. But since I don't sleep much, a lot of what I receive just comes to me as intuition. Like 'New Orleans' just came to me a few minutes ago. The thoughts just form in my mind."

"You don't sleep?" she asked.

"I do," he said. "Just not often. It doesn't seem necessary, except when I'm a little too slow and someone gets off a shot, or I miss another threat. A knife, a pipe, a baseball bat, and I'm injured. I chased a guy up on the roof of a twelve-story building once. Caught up to him as he scaled a water tower feeding apartments below. I twisted his arm away from the ladder and threw him off the side of the building. It was a one-hundred and fifty-foot drop. But he grabbed my jacket and we both fell. I walked, *limped*, away. In pain. Bloodied and bruised. My right arm useless and a huge welt on the left side of my head. I knew my skull was fractured. I was amazed I was still alive. The other guy died on impact. But that was a long time ago. Near the beginning. Before I realized I could take much more that the average man and still stand upright afterwards."

"What does that have to do with—?"

He held out his hand again. *Wait.*

"My body's a roadmap of scars," he continued. "Knife wounds, gunshot wounds, burns, you name it. I have a scar on the right side of my chest from a bullet. The exit wound is under my shoulder blade. Given the trajectory of the round and the excruciating pain I was in after, the slug that passed through me destroyed my lung and should've left me lying on the ground, gasping for breath as my chest filled with blood and I suffocated. Instead, I lurched away, returned to the motel room I'd rented earlier that evening, and fell face first across the bed. I slept for forty-six hours. Woke up feeling vital and refreshed, as if I'd just taken a nap. The scars on my chest and back had already formed and appeared to be months old."

"You sleep to heal," she said, not believing that she was taking any of this ridiculous explanation seriously.

"And when I sleep," he said, "sometimes I dream."

If they are dreams, he added to himself.

He was as uncertain of the images and visions he perceived while sleeping as he was about himself. Long, tall, man-shaped shadows lurking in corners and dark places, watching, studying, as if observing humanity to seek out the weak, those easy to influence. Biding time until their malevolent schemes could be brought to fruition. He thought these beings, if they existed and weren't just random manifestations of his subconscious mind, to be malignant. As malicious and cruel as a hateful child who ties cans to a cat's paws or sets fire to the tail of a dog just to watch it run screaming from fear and pain.

There were other presences as well. Beings of light so pure it hurt the eyes to look at them, pained the ears to hear them when, and if, they spoke. Beings of such energy and virtue they could only be considered just and moral. Righteous.

He often got the sense that these two forces were in turmoil. Struggling, constantly battling each other, as if waging a timeless war. But for what cause and to what end he did not know.

If any of it were real.

What seemed more real to him, more *substantial,* was the reoccurring image of a female.

"She appears to me at various ages," he said. "Sometimes as old as her mid-thirties, sometimes as young as seven. But always with the same lustrous black hair, green eyes, and porcelain skin." *Skin so smooth and unblemished*, he thought, *that it might have been poured from a pitcher like cream.* Hers was an exquisite beauty he'd never seen in any of the living women, or girls for that matter, in whose fates he'd intervened. She was all the more real to him because of it. To Arianna he said:

"She seems so real in those dreams. Is she, was she, a real person? Did I know her before? In the life I assume I once had? Or is she a phantom of my mind? An apparition that haunts my dreams? I don't know the answer to that any more than I know if I *had* a life before all this. If I did, I can't remember it."

He's had a psychotic break, Arianna thought. *What else could it be? Delusions, hallucinations, voices in his head, violent and deadly outbursts.* He was describing psychotic episodes and just didn't know it. Or couldn't accept it.

Come on, Ari, that nagging voice spoke up in her head again. *A twenty-five-year long psychotic episode? Extreme psychosis last days, maybe weeks. Not years. You're trying to jump from point A to point C without considering point B. The fact that no one could operate in such a state for so long without destroying themselves. There's more to this than a man with a mental disease. You said it yourself. It's not possible. But that doesn't change the fact that it's true.*

"And this woman, or girl, is the one who tells you what to do?" she asked, pushing the internal debate aside. "Like voices in your head?"

He looked at her then. Not in frustration or anger as she would expect from someone so pointedly challenged with reference to schizophrenia, but with disappointment and sadness.

"No," he said, looking back at the road. "She doesn't speak to me. But I understand her intentions all the same. She's just there. In my dreams. As some sort of, I don't know, representative. Sometimes she shows me things.

"To answer your question, no one gives me instructions. Not in any direct way. I act out of intuition. Compulsion. Who, where, and when just come to me. As if from the ether. As if whoever issues my marching orders isn't here in this plane of existence. As if they're...elsewhere. I've come to believe that this is an effort to preserve life, but, given the fact that I'm only given enough information to save *certain* lives, I believe something more is going on. Something beyond preserving lives. Something more akin to maintaining some sort of balance."

"Balance for what?" she mocked. "Humanity? The Earth? The Universe?"

He sighed, the sound loud in the enclosed space. Despite her contemptuous tone, he realized he'd asked himself the same question hundreds, if not thousands of times before, and had yet to reach any satisfying conclusions. In the end he was left with the mere fact of his existence.

Am I even a man at all? Was I ever? Or did I spring forth, whole and breathing, from somewhere else?

That question, too, went unanswered. No great and booming voice offered new insight. No celestial light sprang forth to clarify his purpose.

"I only know that the incidents are becoming more violent," he continued. "More prevalent. That there are many more perpetrators committing far more heinous acts with multiple casualties than I've ever encountered before.

"Four in New Mexico, with at least a dozen dead. Some of them children. And I was there to save *one* of them. A teenage girl, outwardly no different than the others. Why her and her alone?" The fact that his actions had cut short what was sure to be a prolonged siege, with scores more wounded and dead had he not interfered, did little to soothe the sorrow he felt over the lost lives of those other innocents.

"Another two last week," he continued, "planning to set off a pressure-cooker bomb outside a schoolhouse in El Paso."

"That was you?" she asked. A friend in data analysis saw to it that Arianna received daily briefings of any unusual reports involving crimes by an unknown subject whose actions averted a larger crime. A report had crossed her desk the week before. Two rich, bored, and stupid teens had been rammed off the road by persons unknown, causing them to crash into a nearby aqueduct. The report hadn't been notable for the incident itself, but for the explosive device that had been found when first responders arrived to pull them from the wreckage. The police had been notified and the pair taken into custody.

"There'd been two to save there," he continued, "twin brothers who looked as ordinary as any of the other eighteen children who could have died."

That happened three days before the incident in New Mexico, Arianna thought. *And wasn't there something about a serial child killer that had been killed in Ohio two days later, his victim delivered to a nearby hospital by persons unknown?*

Three incidents, including Boston, in under a week. If he's correct—*come on, you're not taking this seriously, are you?* –and the frequency was increasing, would an escalation to a larger, more terrifying event be inevitable?

"But you did save them," she thought out loud. "All of them. Just like you saved those children back at the garage."

But you didn't save my team.

Or Danny and my dad.

"I'm sorry about your team, Ms. Price," he said, intuiting her thoughts again. She could hear genuine regret in his voice. "And that I was too late to help them. But I wasn't there for them. Or the children. I was there for you."

"You would have let those kids die?" she asked, incredulously.

"If necessary, to save your life, yes."

She stared at him in horror.

Two Begat Eight Billion

One-hundred and twenty thousand pounds of aluminum, plastics, flesh, and blood defied gravity in the sky above Louis Armstrong International Airport in the form of a Boeing 737-300, carrying 119 passengers from Seattle, Washington to New Orleans, Louisiana.

Not as wondrous as one might imagine, Lonnie Schultz thought, if one knew that the storm the plane was about to descend through weighed more than that by a factor of ten. The combined weight of the clouds alone, each made up of water droplets, particulates, and hail at higher altitudes, could be millions of pounds. Few ever thought about all that weight cruising through the sky above their heads, or the fact that if all of it fell to Earth in one instant, the damage would be far greater than that of a single aircraft crash.

Still, as Flight AS 788 descended into the dark grey clouds and turbulence began to affect the airframe, those who had thus far ignored the pilots standard hail to fasten their seatbelts for approach found themselves reaching for the straps and hastening to buckle themselves in.

The woman carrying the loathsome infant—Marjorie Kinkle, she'd told Lonnie her name before adding that the child's name was McKenna and isn't she just the most precious thing and she's already taking a bottle and she's already rolling over on her own and on and on until the grin he'd plastered to his face had begun a cramp in his cheeks and a buzzing between his ears that made him feel as if his head would explode—winced and uttered a little yelp as the aircraft suddenly dropped hundreds of feet before its twin CFM56 turbofans, shrieking with strain, could return it to its proper altitude and heading. The frightened murmurs of other passengers echoed throughout the fuselage.

The intercom dinged and the pilot's voice again filled the cabin:

"Sorry about that, folks," he said, his voice calm and natural, as if the aircraft hadn't just plunged the height of a medium-sized building. "We seem to have a bit of wind shear up here, but ground control assures me that conditions are much smoother below the ceiling. Please remain seated, with seatbelts securely fastened and seatbacks and trays in their upright and locked position, and we'll have you safely on the ground in about ten minutes. And, once again, thank you for flying with us today."

Amazingly, little McKenna had slept through the whole thing. Lonnie looked at her now, wrapped in a blanket in her mothers' arms, only her face and one tiny fist resting against her cheek visible amongst the swaddling.

That's how she'll look when she's dead.

Lonnie was comforted by the thought.

That's how they'll all look. Peaceful. At rest. No more sadness. No more hatred. No more violence. No more noise. No more spewing bacteria and viruses and pestilence from every pore and orifice, infecting everyone and everything they come into contact with. And they'll stay that way, for a time. No bacteria will cause their bodies to swell and bloat with gasses, there'll be no decomposition. No decay. They'll stay pure until the wind and rain and heat reduce them to withered husks, until time reduces them to dust. In thirty years, fifty at the most, all of them will be gone, and the Earth will finally be cleansed. Fresh. Renewed.

Of course, not *all* of them would die peacefully. Some would be in aircraft like this one when GT-16 hit them. Or on buses, trains, or cars careening down the Interstate at seventy-five miles an hour. The drivers or pilots of those vehicles, gone in mere seconds, wouldn't live to see their planes crash into homes, buildings, mountainsides. Drivers wouldn't be aware of hitting other motorists or pedestrians, train engineers wouldn't be conscious of derailments. The carnage would be incredible. Bodies smashed, burned, strewn about like burst pumpkins. Spreading the genotoxin even further as once living and now mutated cells took to the wind.

Dr. McMillan had written about the event in a daily summary, one of hundreds of long-winded and overly verbose reports he'd authored on the subject of his nasty little bug. He'd dubbed it the *collateral effect*, and estimated that once the genotoxin had mutated enough to break the *thermal barrier*—another pretentious term the good doctor, who was now little more than a pile of ash to be swept up and dumped in the nearest trash bin had felt obligated to coin—several million deaths would be attributable to non-genotoxic causes alone.

Of more interest to Lonnie, however, were the thousands of hours of video that had been shot inside the lab. Rather than plodding through line after line of grandiose verbiage and diction inside a word processing program, he'd been able to fast forward through the more banal aspects of the trials. The innocuous banter of the team, the tedious preparations for each test, the explanations of the difficulties of inducing the correct temperature range in the test subjects—accomplished beforehand by injection with common cold viruses and far easier in the primate subjects than in the rodents—and get directly to the good stuff.

Time and again he'd watched the direct injections of GT-16 in the single rodent trials. Those within the temperature range simply dropped over, dead, while those outside the range continued to lick their little paws and smooth their furry little faces and do all the other things that rats in a cage do. Then they injected single rats in the presence of another. Again, those within the correct temperature range dropped dead while their companions remained unconcerned.

Then came the multiple subject trials. Four rats, all in the proper temperature range, were placed under the fume hoods. Two were injected, two were not. The injected rats died within a minute, the 'clean' rats a few minutes later, thus proving that GT-16 was transmissible in rodents with body temperatures in the proper range.

Things really got interesting when they switched to primate trials.

They'd repeated the same tests with the primates—in this case, Rhesus Macaques—as with the rodents. With the same results. GT-16 killed those in the effective temperature range, while leaving those outside the range alone.

Then, Dr. McMillan and his team conceived a ridiculously elaborate test at a cost of several million dollars, in which a sixty-by-sixty-foot habitat was built, secured, and insulated against any possible contagion leak. Earth was moved in, as was a water supply in the form of a stream. Trees and other plants were added, all allowed to take root and grow over the course of six months. The entire habitat was held at a comfortable temperature controlled seventy-two degrees, as it would be for the duration of the experiment. Finally, in the seventh month, twenty-four Rhesus monkeys were moved to the habitat and allowed to thrive. For three months Dr. McMillan and his team tended what they referred to as their *real-world scenario*, feeding the primates, playing with them, encouraging social behavior and bonding. It had looked to Lonnie as near an actual society, albeit of monkeys and not humans, as one would see in a laboratory environment. And in his opinion, the Macaques were far superior in their social skills, far kinder and more loving to one another, than any human had ever been.

Ten months to the day after the habitat had begun construction, twelve of the Rhesus monkeys were injected with the common cold virus. After seventy-two hours, all twelve had fevers that ranged between one-hundred and three and one-hundred and five degrees.

They were then fitted with specially designed collars that would inject all twelve, at two-minute intervals, with GT-16.

The results were spectacular. Anyone else would have been terrified. Lonnie Schultz was filled with glee.

At 1200 hours the first collar activated. At 1201 a furry brown Rhesus monkey Bobby Maze had dubbed Gumbo toppled out of the tree where he'd been sitting, contentedly munching on a mango. Three others moved in to investigate, nudging the still form with concern, and two minutes later, a gray named Lucius went down, face first into the artificial stream. A large, reddish female named Gracie rushed to his side and began to haul him away from the current that was trying to drag his lifeless body downstream. Then Gracie went down. Then all nine of the remaining 'hot' monkeys, regardless of their whereabouts inside the habitat, dropped simultaneously, long before their collars could infect them.

The remaining uninfected and 'cold' subjects were, by this time, running frantically about the habitat, some clutching one another in fear, others shrieking and climbing the trees, jumping limb from limb, throwing fruit and small branches in what could only be described as terror and despair. No unconcerned rodents here. These intelligent creatures had just witnessed the sudden and inexplicable death of half their number and were acting out emotionally. That fact may have been of interest to a psychologist studying the effect of trauma on a troop of primates, but Lonnie Schultz hadn't given a tin shit. He was waiting for the bigger payoff.

It came less than ninety seconds later. The troops patriarch, a large black and white named Oreo, came crashing down through a baobab tree he'd been scaling, landing on a large rock with a bone shattering crash. Oreo had been injected with neither the cold virus nor GT-16. A glance at a status panel that had remained in the upper lefthand corner of the video frame confirmed that the habitat had remained at seventy-two degrees. The remaining Rhesus Macaques fell within the next sixty seconds.

Seventy-two hours later the video resumed.

The Rhesus habitat was markedly changed. Where before the plant life had been vibrant with greens and yellows and reddish pinks, it was now a sickly brown, and in the case of the grass, an odd, dead gray. The toxin had, indeed, crossed into the plant life, infecting and destroying its RNA. The Macaques remained where they'd fallen, save Lucius, whose body had fetched up at the end of the 'stream' where a grate held him in place as the water emptied into a trough and was recirculated by a pump to the opposite end through of the habitat. The water moving through the closed system and Lucius' hair were the only motion.

A triple-sealed airlock at the rear of the habitat opened and four more Rhesus monkeys cautiously entered the habitat. Three made it inside, warily sniffing the air before toppling like dominoes on a tabletop. The fourth didn't make it past the airlock threshold.

The test was repeated once more, seven days later, with the same result. The airlock, now jammed with tiny corpses, was sealed off, the entire habitat burned with Dicyanoacetylene, then filled with and covered to a depth of twelve feet by concrete. If any of the GT-16 used in the experiment had survived the burn, it was forever lost under the weight of ten-thousand cubic yards of concrete.

Once its effectiveness had been proven, research had turned to modifying the toxin. As it directly and quite efficiently attacked the DNA of a host, surely it could be modified to attack specific DNA traits and characteristics while leaving others unharmed. *In other words*, Lonnie had thought, *specific ethnic and racial groups. Wipe out the Arabs. Then the kikes. Then the wetbacks and niggers. But why stop there? Was being poor a genetic trait? How about homosexuality? What about those predisposed to commit crimes? Whittle the world down all you want, until only one race remains standing, and that's still one race too many.*

He'd lost interest in the research at that point. As far as he was concerned the GT-16 variant that had annihilated all life inside the habitat had been the engine of destruction he swas looking for. It was perfection. And they wanted to dilute it down into a mere weapon of genocide. As with Adolph Hitler, a man he both admired and disdained in turns, they lacked vision and understanding.

In the beginning, it had all begun with one man and woman. Purportedly, Adam and Eve. Whether you wanted to believe the biblical version or not, it took one member of each sex to start the ball rolling, no matter their names, the abilities of modern science notwithstanding. And just those two had begat eight billion whining, puling, self-absorbed, morally repugnant beings.

Not that he believed in the biblical account. He thought the human race was the result of dumb luck on the part of genetics. *Bad* dumb luck, at that. He would see to it that none of them were left to repeat the process.

AS 788 descended beneath the unimaginable weight of the storm and into smoother, albeit rain and windswept air. The landing gear unfolded with a thump. Lonnie Schultz looked at his watch, noting the time. He allowed a smile to cross his features. By his reckoning, the homemade battery he'd designed had three and a half hours of charge left. He calculated a half hour for the plane to land, taxi, and disgorge its passengers, and another half hour, maybe forty-five minutes, for him to locate a rental counter and acquire a vehicle. His destination was only fifteen miles away, but across a busy New Orleans in severe weather. He added another thirty to forty minutes for travel time. That was two hours, two and a half at the outside, if he allowed for unexpected delays on Interstate 10. That still gave him a comfortable one-hour margin to select four subjects to infect.

Lonnie Schultz smiled.

Margeaux Quagriella had theorized it would require a dozen or so 'hot' hosts for GT-16 to mutate into an airborne version of itself that could defeat the thermal barrier. Lonnie had watched with his own eyes as the genotoxin became airborne after only three hosts, killing every other hot host before moving on to the clean hosts, and then the vegetation, and presumably everything else. Where Lonnie Schultz planned to replicate the habitat experiment, there would be *dozens* of hot hosts. Plural.

His smile broadened until he was practically beaming.

"Someone must have a pretty girl waiting for them down there," Marjorie Kinkle's voice cut across his thoughts. "A smile like that, you must be thinking of making one of these for yourself," she added, holding little McKenna up closer to him.

The baby still slept, despite the rise in conversation and noise around them. A tiny trail of snot from her nose began growing into a bubble.

Lonnie's smile faltered a fraction at the thought of reproduction and the sloppy, sickening act that it required. It resurfaced in full force with the thought of wiping the snot bubble from baby McKenna's nose with a hammer.

"That's definitely the smile of someone about to have the greatest night of his life," Marjorie said.

"That's the plan," Lonnie said, still smiling.

Disappointment

The Camaro moved through the night, out of the rain and onto a drier stretch of Interstate. Stubborn, errant flashes of lightning ignited the sky to the south as if a more violent storm festered there. Arianna stared out the passenger window, uncertain of what to say in response to the revelation that he felt her survival was more important than that of twenty-seven innocent children.

A sign at the side of the Interstate announced that they had just crossed the state line into Mississippi. A few miles beyond that another read:

Meridian 15
Laurel 68
Hattiesburg 100
New Orleans 208

Beneath the sign sat a Mississippi State Trooper vehicle, interior lights on, the glow of brake lights illuminating exhaust gases resembling smoke from a cigarette. Arianna glanced at the speedometer, tensing when she saw that they were still traveling in excess of one-hundred miles an hour.

Here we go, she thought. *This little road trip is about to get a lot more interesting. Either he'll pull over and stop this charade, or, more likely, we're both going to die at the end of a short and ugly pursuit.*

She considered drawing her service weapon and ordering him to the side of the road but by then they were abreast of the state vehicle. She looked out the window again, noting that the trooper was looking directly at them. His eyes met hers briefly, then they were past.

She looked in the side mirror in anticipation, again mulling over whether or not to pull her weapon. Emergency beacons on the Troopers vehicle didn't flare into life. Tires didn't spin, spitting out wet sand and mud with sudden acceleration. The vehicle's reflection receded to a pinpoint, then was lost in the darkness.

"He won't follow," he said.

"Of course he will," Arianna said, still looking in the sideview, expecting to see blue flashers at any moment. "We're speeding. And he looked right at me."

"Doesn't matter," he answered. "He won't react. They never do."

"His radar," she stammered. "His dashcam—"

"He'll ignore them," he finished for her. "If they recorded anything at all."

"Impossible," she repeated.

His next words, as if he'd read her thoughts and pulled her own argument from them, chilled her:

"That doesn't mean it isn't true."

"CAN YOU DIE?" SHE ASKED later.

She found herself slipping. Away from what she knew to be reality and further towards belief. In the man. In his unknown mission. In the new reality unfolding around her. Or was it insanity? Part of her insisted this must be true. Delusions and hallucinations could be transmitted between two people. It was called folie à deux, or shared delusional disorder.

Doesn't quite fit the criteria though, does it, Ari?

SDD, she knew, was typically diagnosed when two or more individuals who lived in proximity were socially or physically isolated and had little interaction with other people, usually arising in couples or close siblings. Arianna couldn't speak for him, but she interacted with others on a daily basis. Sometimes a lot more than she wished.

And you've been with him for mere hours, Ari. Not for the months or years it takes SDD to develop.

"What do you mean?" he asked, flashing that casual smile once again. She wondered if he'd been smiling like that when he blew the back of her masked assailant's throat out.

"You said you heal when you sleep," she answered.

"Mmm," he said in agreement. "That seems to be the case. Why?"

"You haven't aged a day in twenty-five years," she said. "Not that I can see. And you said it yourself, you overcame what should have been a fatal injury while sleeping. So, I'm curious if you think you can die."

He was silent for a moment, guiding the Camaro ever southward towards a city that had seen its share of sin long before Las Vegas existed.

"What makes you so certain *you're* alive?" he asked.

"What?' she said, confused. "I breathe. I grow. I reproduce. That's the basic definition of life."

"Fire breathes," he said. "It grows. Reproduces. So do bacteria and viruses."

"Fire's a chemical reaction," she said. "It may mimic life, but it's not alive. And bacteria and viruses are living things. They're just not organized, higher life forms."

He was quiet for a moment, and she was about to repeat her question when he said:

"I've seen no evidence that humanity is a higher life form."

"That's...what are you talking about?" She was suddenly defensive. "I'm a sentient being. We're *all* sentient beings. The only sentient beings science has definitively proven to exist."

"How?"

"What?"

"How has science proved that human beings are sentient?"

She contemplated her answer before responding: "Well, we're self-aware for one thing."

"Are you?"

"What do you mean, '*Are you?*'" she asked hotly. "Of course we are. I'm aware of my existence in the world, just as everyone else is. I have a *self.* I. Me. I'm an individual."

"Are you?" he asked, his voice maddeningly neutral in the face of her growing anger.

"Damn it, stop that!" she demanded. "Of course I am. I have my own likes, dislikes, prejudices. I love and hate and can feel happiness, sadness, joy, anger. I'm feeling a lot of that one right now," she added. "I make my own decisions. I'm an individual."

"Do you own a dog?"

"What? What does that have to do with..."

"Do you have one?" he insisted.

"No," she answered. "I have a cat. Or rather, a cat has me. I don't think any of us really *has* an animal. There are just some that tolerate our presence."

"And does your cat have likes and dislikes?" he asked. "Can it love and hate? Does it feel sadness and joy? Maybe happiness when you get home after a long day? Anger when you're away for too long?"

She sighed, exasperated. "I know what you're getting at. And yes, I do believe animals can feel basic emotions. But they aren't capable of the same sort of higher thought processes humans are."

"Did you invent echolocation?"

"Echo what?" she said, becoming more and more confused—and frustrated—with this...this *interrogation.*

"Echolocation. It's the same principle behind radar. You send out a burst of sound and, based on how and when it bounces back, you can construct a three-dimensional image of things that are too far away or too far to see."

"Okay, yes," she said. "I get it. And no, I didn't invent it. It was invented in the thirties, I think. During World War Two."

"No, it wasn't," he countered. "Humans just figured out how to reproduce an existing technology during World War Two. Dolphins, whales, and bats have been using echolocation for centuries. Millennia."

"Well that just proves my point," she said, seizing on the fact. "Humans figured out how to reproduce an inherent trait. That's a higher thought process. Animals aren't capable of that."

"Sure they are. Dolphins and whales *developed* the ability to echolocate, over time, in order to see better in murky waters and to feed more efficiently. Bats for much the same reason. Their vision is poor, and they feed at dusk and dawn, when their prey is hard to distinguish, so they developed a sense to allow them to 'see' it. I think that's a fair example of a higher thought process."

He continued: "It's not just those species, either. Simian species: apes, baboons, chimpanzees, have learned to fashion and use tools for hunting and defense, even for building. Otters use rocks to open shells. Beavers build elaborate dams. And complex thinking isn't confined to mammals. Fire ants build wondrous, elaborate constructions with spires and tunnels that no human construction could hope to match. Other insects, bees for instance, exhibit ordered and logical thought processes throughout their existence. And some species of plants have developed chemical and biological warfare to combat being consumed by insects and other predators."

"Those are examples of an order of intelligence, I'll grant you," she countered, "but a dog will never hold a steady job, or learn to read a floorplan, and cats will never adapt to build houses."

"Why should they when they can just purr or wag their tails and some human will do it for them? Which is the more intelligent species in that equation?"

"I don't understand what any of this has to do with—" she began.

"You asked me if I could die," he explained. 'My answer is, 'How can I die if neither of us can explain how I'm alive?'"

They were both silent as the miles rolled out behind them.

"Ever heard of the Immortal Jellyfish?" he suddenly asked.

"The *what?*" she asked, tiring of confusing questions.

"Turritopsis dohrnii," he said. "What science considers the only immortal creature on the planet. After reproduction, instead of getting old and dying off as most other living things do, it reverts to a juvenile state. Tentacles retract, it shrinks in size, and then sinks back to the ocean floor as a juvenile. Then it repeats the process. Over and over again."

"Where the hell did you learn that?" she asked, surprised by such an obscure reference. "That just pop into your head, too? Like New Orleans?"

"I read," he said, matter of factly.

Which made sense when she thought about it. Even vigilantes, psychotic or not, had to take a day off now and again.

"So, at some time or another, you got younger again? So you could go on killing?"

Stop baiting him, Ari.

"Nothing like that, I'm afraid," he said, ignoring the jibe. "Assuming I am, indeed, alive, I haven't woken up a ten-year-old boy and had to wait out adolescence. I don't remember ever being an adolescent in the first place. I just don't age. Or, if I do, it's extremely subtle. The immortal jellyfish is just as close as I can come to an explanation."

"And my actions don't always result in death, Ms. Price. Often, I'm sad to say, yes. But killing isn't always required."

"So, you're immortal," she said.

"I hope not," he said quietly. "I'd hate to think this punishment could last forever."

"Punishment?"

"What would you call it?" he asked, taking his eyes off the road long enough to meet her gaze. "Do you think I welcome this existence? That I enjoy being the agent of destruction for reasons unknown, for some being or force I don't understand? That I find killing desirable under any circumstances?" He looked back at the windshield. "Besides, it makes as much sense as anything else. And if that's the case, I must have been a cruel person, led a terrible life, to be condemned to this existence as penance."

"How do you know it's not the opposite?" she said.

"What do you mean?"

"How do you know you didn't live a charmed life?" she asked, indulging an impulse to play devil's advocate. "A rare lifetime of joy and happiness, devoid of the darkness or sadness most of us endure."

"That makes no sense," he said, his brow furrowed. "Why would I be punished for that?"

"Who says it's punishment?" she asked.

"Everything has a cost."

THEY LEFT LAUREL, MISSISSIPPI, behind and were approaching the first exit for Hattiesburg before either of them spoke again.

"Go ahead, Ms. Price" he said, "Ask."

How does he do that? she wondered. *It's as if he knows what I'm thinking even as I'm thinking it. Can he read my mind? Or am I just that transparent?*

He'd startled her from thoughts of her father and Danny, their lives before that fateful night. Her father, who'd seemed so tall and strong, falling to the slash of a knife. Her brother Danny, so sweet and kind, who'd just won a scholarship to attend UC Berkley and had an incredible future laid out in front of him, mercilessly cut down, that future unrealized. And *his* involvement.

On the heels of that: *Ask, Ari. You've waited twenty-five years for the answer. For a chance to understand. There may not be time later.*

"Why didn't you save them?" she asked, hating that she sounded more like the fourteen-year-old girl she'd been then than the thirty-nine-year-old woman she'd become. "Why just me and my mom?"

"It wasn't my choice to make," he said. "I've tried, time and again, to save more. And failed. Either because I'm too slow or because I missed some opportunity due to a lack of knowledge. In your case, just like Boston, I got there too late to save anyone else. I would have saved your team if I could, believe me. It just wasn't part of the design."

"You're blaming fate," she said, deciding the answer was insufficient. "As if my dad and brother dying like that, in that apartment, was their destiny."

"Maybe I am," he said. "Maybe it *is* destiny. If that's the case, I'm meddling in it. Changing it somehow. On behalf of someone or some*thing* else. *You* were supposed to die there, too."

"I don't believe that," she said. "And I don't believe in fate. That we're destined to follow a predetermined course throughout our lives. We make our own paths. We're not animals relying on instinct. We have a choice. *You* have a choice."

"Some choice," he muttered.

"What? You don't believe you have a choice? Have you ever considered ignoring your intuition, compulsion, whatever you call it? Simply saying *'fuck all'* to the visions or whatever the hell they are?"

"I have," he answered, his expression grim. "Years ago. In Colorado. I saw a man working in his basement, assembling something on a workbench. Everything was so clear; it was as if I were in the room with him. I could see his face, the objects he was fiddling with. I even got his name off a utility bill on the desk behind him," he paused, as if back in that moment. "Dennis LeHayne."

The name struck a chord in Arianna's memory, but she couldn't pin it down.

"Then," he continued, "I got the image of an airplane. Air Canada Flight 551 to Quebec, out of Denver International."

Arianna got the feeling she'd heard that flight number before. Some dim and faded memory that was tucked away in the recesses of her mind. *Dennis Lahayne. Flight 551. Where have I heard that?*

"I was questioning everything I was doing at the time. The images, the voices, the information I was being given. Wondering who I was. *What* I was. If what I was doing was actually making a difference or if it was all in my head and I was delusional. A lunatic, a psychopath, hell bent on murder. I was rebelling, I suppose, and decided I'd had enough of the killing and wasn't going to do it anymore. I made a choice to ignore the intuition."

He fell into silence, his expression bleak.

"And?" she prompted.

"Dennis Lehayne committed suicide on that flight," he said. "He put a ten-pound bomb in his baggage and detonated it over the Great Lakes. Two-hundred-and eleven people died."

Arianna remembered the story now. She'd still been at the Academy when it happened. Two years prior to the destruction of Flight 551, LeHayne had embezzled close to a million dollars from his employers, a stock and securities firm in Vale, Colorado. He'd subsequently been convicted of fraud. While he'd been serving eighteen months of a two-year sentence at the federal prison at Englewood, his wife had closed what was left of their bank accounts, packed up the house, the kids, the family dog, and lit out for parts unknown. Six months later he'd carried out his suicide plan at thirty-five thousand feet. The plane had broken apart before plummeting into Lake Superior. Seventeen of the two-hundred and eleven people on board had never been found.

"You can't blame yourself for the actions of a madman," Arianna said.

"Can't I?" he asked. "I was given all the information I needed, and I chose to ignore it. It wouldn't have taken much. A bomb threat called in to the airline would have done the trick. TSA didn't exist back then, but planes were routinely grounded for less. I could have helped those people. I *want* to help people. What's one man's life, a *suicidal* man's life, when compared to the lives of so many others?

"That's why I couldn't save your family," he said softly. "I didn't see your dad or your mother and brother. I only saw you."

"Saw me how?" she asked. "Dead? Alive? Before the attack of after?"

"I don't think you want to—" he began.

"Saw me *how*?" she insisted.

"Dead. In your bedroom. You'd been beaten and raped repeatedly, your throat cut wide."

Arianna shivered at the brutal description of events that had never happened. Because *he* had intervened.

"By the time I got there," he continued, "your brother and dad were already gone. There was nothing I could do."

I was an answer, of sorts. If not the all illuminating answer she'd been hoping for.

Learning To Fly

Ｉ t was as if a switch had been thrown.

They'd fallen into silence again as Arianna had digested the all-too complicated answer before moving on to a more pressing matter: What, if anything, did he think her role in this was?

He'd said that he needed her for this—*what*? Task? Intervention? Rather, that he'd been *told* he needed her. For what? To what end?

He certainly didn't need her authority or credentials to gain access to a location. If that were the case, he simply could have stolen her ID back in Boston. Few people, even those responsible for security, gave her shield more than a cursory glance when she presented it. Fewer still bothered to look at the identification card attached to it. It was unlikely he'd need to do more than flash the badge to gain access to anything other than a federal or ultra-secure building. Besides, he was a wraith. Able to move about at will, even in the presence of armed and trained law enforcement officers. He'd operated invisibly in multiple police jurisdictions over the past two-and-a half decades, once eluding a SWAT team seeking the murderer of a pedophile in a sealed building, had evaded the Bureau on so many occasions that they considered him a myth, had stymied her own ongoing investigation for years, and had, moments ago, gone unnoticed by a State Trooper who'd been looking directly at them.

Equally unlikely was the notion that he needed her skills as an agent of the FBI. He was a crack shot, as evidenced by three well placed rounds at over ten yards in a crowded restaurant in New

Mexico. His analytical skills, what he called intuition, were above reproach. She herself had thought him capable of reading minds. And who needed deductive reasoning when you had a handy spirit girl/woman telling you everything you needed to know?

She could think of no knowledge she possessed, either of him, their destination, or the situation at hand—of which she knew nothing—that would be to his advantage. Outside of her duties as a field agent she'd been to New Orleans only twice in her life, both times during Mardi Gras, the last time on a long weekend with Melinda Tran. That memory brought about a sharp pang of heartache that she forced away and placed on a high mental shelf for later contemplation. She had little familiarity with the city, its qualities, or its topography.

So, unless they faced a force so overwhelming that he'd need her to call in the cavalry, she could think of no logical reason why her presence, specifically *her* presence, was required.

And I can't believe I'm entertaining this as more than an abduction by a delusional murderer, a voice spoke up in her mind.

And then it happened. As if a circuit had been broken—or engaged—he was gone from the car.

His body was still there. His hand still gripped the steering wheel, his eyes remained on the Interstate, his foot still pressed the accelerator. But his cognizant mind was gone. As if he'd gone to sleep at one-hundred-and five miles an hour but remained aware enough to safely guide the vehicle along the blacktop. The shift in consciousness was so profound that she'd actually felt it, as if a burst of static electricity had moved through the Camaro's interior.

Panic gripped Arianna's heart in a vise. She was riding with an empty shell, an automaton, at the mercy of whatever had gripped him.

He gasped lightly and muttered "Oh," or what might have been *no*, and his hand shifted slightly on the wheel. The car drifted to the left with the motion but didn't leave the lane. His foot remained solid on the accelerator.

It, whatever *it* was, was over in a matter of seconds. She felt his consciousness return like an ocean wave crashing along a shore.

He looked at her, an expression of anguish stamped upon his visage like the specter of death.

"What the hell just happened?" she demanded as her heart slowly returned to something akin to a normal heartbeat.

"This is taking too long," he said, his usual placid—maddening! –demeanor had returned. "We'll be there in an hour."

"What's taking too long?" she cried. "We'll be where? What the fuck does this have to do with me?"

"She said you should sleep," he said.

"She—. *Who*? You said she doesn't speak to you!"

"I'm sorry," he said and reached for her.

She was drawn into darkness.

ARIANNA KNEW SHE WAS dreaming because it was only in her dreams that she could fly.

She hovered above a shoreline buffeted by cresting waves so transparent they were almost crystalline in nature, leaving little in the way of foam along the craggy rocks they collapsed upon. She cast her eyes out over the ocean, noting the reflection of a sun that seemed too hot even for this time of day on the clear marine surface. *Too* clear, she thought, then moved, or was moved, farther out to sea, towards a speck on the horizon that gradually took shape the closer she got to it, first appearing as a four-legged behemoth standing in shallows, then a free-standing dais strewn with debris, before resolving into the familiar shape of an oil rig of advanced design with gantries, cranes, and helipads.

She paused here. A metal-on-metal sound came to her from above. A gantry hook swinging in the breeze. A creaking, settling sound from below. No mechanical sounds. No pumps or motors, no chains snapping around lengths of drill pipe, no cranes lifting and shifting pipe into position. No human sounds either. No grunts of labor, no good-natured banter, no cursing, no footfalls on steel. No gulls crying as they rode air currents above, hoping some tidbit of food or tasty garbage would be dropped on the deck plates below, fair game for scavenging. All she could hear was wind, waves, and the ticking of the gantry hook.

The rig was abandoned. Long forgotten. A derelict, rusting in the too hot sun.

She moved then, much faster than before though she felt no velocity.

Down. Into the ocean depths. She fought a momentary fear of drowning before she remembered she was dreaming. Deeper and deeper she moved until she paused again, mere meters above the ocean floor.

She could see far in the clear, cloudless water. Much farther than expected despite what she knew must be a great depth. Nothing moved. No sea bass, no yellowtail, no jack mackerel or shy harbor seals. No kelp forests teeming with Bat, Manta, or Torpedo Rays. No purple hydrocoral, hiding angel sharks stealthily stalking mola-mola and butterfly fish. No evidence of dolphins or whales. Not even shrimp, plankton, or krill. Just sand, a vast and unbroken expanse of it, as far as the eye could see.

She rose from the depths without so much as a ripple and headed inland. Her heart began to pound at what he saw.

No sea grass separated the shore from the highway below. No bushes, no trees. She could see no vegetation as she moved over a small city.

Welcome to the City of Monterey, a faded green sign set in stone announced.

She passed over vacant, crumbling homes with lawns of rock and sand, businesses with blank windows, a deteriorating Spanish-style church, and an empty large-scale aquarium. All were barren. Devoid of life down to their empty flowerpots and gardens. She touched down softly on yellow lined asphalt cracked with age and neglect but free of overgrowth. The wind came again to her ears. A sign declaring this area Cannery Row creaked back and forth on rusted eyebolts. A loose piece of sheet metal siding ticked against a rusty screw. There was no sound of traffic, near or distant. No children's voices carried by the breeze. No thump of closing doors or the rattle of windows being opened. No hum of power in the lines overhead and, again, no gulls crying out, in hunger or joy, a constant sound in any coastal city.

What happened here? She asked herself, then was whisked away again, farther inland, like a mote of dust in the wind.

Buildings and roads gave way to a great expanse of sand, and she knew she'd crossed into Nevada. The desert stretched out beneath her, unbroken from horizon to horizon, littered by neither roads nor small towns, no oasis nor sage. Then, a flash of sunlight off metal. A highway brushed bare by the wind, leading to a once great metropolis now drifted in sand. Choking with it. Buried beneath it, as ancient Egyptian cities had been, and every bit as dead. She descended towards a once wide thoroughfare, the source of the reflection. A highway sign, once solid green but now worn by wind and erosion said *Wel to La egas!* Then she hurtled upwards again before continuing East.

Her chest tightened and she struggled to breathe as she rose higher and higher. Not from a lack of oxygen. That remained constant. But from horror at what she saw below. Vast expanses of sand, dirt, and rock broken only by the half-buried remains of what had once been great cities. Wichita, Kansas City, St. Louis.

Indianapolis, Pittsburg, and finally, New York City. All empty, devoid of any form of life. Slowly being reclaimed by the dirt and stone they'd been built upon.

She flew higher still and faster, across the Atlantic to London, Berlin, Moscow. All empty and eroding, without a trace of human life, animals, or vegetation.

Finally, she achieved orbit and the Earth turned slowly beneath her. A world of dull browns, stark whites, and gloomy blue waters. No vibrant green rainforests, no purple mountain majesties, no amber waves of grain. The planet was dead. Absolutely and finally, nothing more than the third rock from the sun.

As Arianna's soul cried out in anguish North America rotated into view beneath her. There was a flash of light in the south, a reflection of motion. Once. Twice. Then gone. What, she asked herself, could cast a reflection large enough to be visible from space? She willed herself closer—if such a thing were possible, she was uncertain who or what had control—and began to descend. If there was motion, she reasoned, there might be life. And where there was life, there was hope.

She descended faster than a meteor in freefall. Faster than a rocket. Vertigo gripped her in a chilling embrace as the Earth loomed close, features becoming larger and larger, more distinguishable, as if she were watching Google Earth zoom in on a selected coordinate.

Despite her speed and what must have been incredible velocity, she touched down softly on a barren city street paved with bricks. Crumbling buildings in the French style surrounded her, rusted ironwork fronted the balconies that remained. Quaint carriage lamps lined the street, looking as if they'd been installed in the early 1900's. A street sign of baroque design hung from one near the corner. Rust had all but eaten it away but enough remained to make out the name: 'Bourbon.'

New Orleans, she realized. *The French Quarter.*

A sound came to her on the wind, from the direction of Dauphine Street. A rumbling, grunting sound that was out of place in the barren landscape. It was followed by shifting noises, as if a great mound of rubble had been displaced.

Arianna wanted to go up and soon found herself rising. She cleared the buildings on Bourbon and her heart seized in her chest. Dauphine was gone. As was Burgundy. A nine-block area with North Rampart to the north and Canal and Conti to the west and east had been blasted out as if struck by a giant fist. At the center of the crater was an enormous snake, far too large for Arianna's mind to adequately comprehend. *No*, she corrected herself. *It's not a snake. It's a damn dragon.* But that description was equally inadequate because no dragon she'd ever heard of had gold scales, and horns that looked as if they'd been forged from stainless steel. Also, the thing had no wings. Only forelegs that ended in steel talons and a mouth—*the size of a football stadium!* her mind screamed at her—lined with hundreds of razor-sharp teeth that gleamed metallically in its maw as it fed on the carcass of an equally large and fantastic creature that had once been a majestic, multi-colored bird.

"*You seek* Biitei," a voice spoke from her memory. "*A ghost. The spirit of* Bha'a, *the Thunderbird. The Great Protector who is always at odds with Hinncebiit, a monster with metal horns and glittering eyes who seeks to destroy mankind.*"

Arianna fled. But not before the snake/dragon thing took notice of her. It stared at her, alien light flashing in its eyes, as if sizing her up. An all-consuming terror she'd never before experienced took her and she expected it to pounce, to devour her as easily as one swallows a small pill. Instead, it opened its great maw and laughed. A maniacal, booming, all too human laugh. Its rancid breath washed over her in a gale. She raced northward thinking, "*That's what hell smells like.*"

The creature did not, as she expected, pursue her. Perhaps it felt no need. Found her insignificant, a mere bug too tiny to be swatted away. Or perhaps it sensed she wasn't really there, just a remnant consciousness from another time. After all, its battles were over. Humanity had been destroyed once and for all, along with everything it had created and cherished, and all it saw in front of it was a ghost.

She wanted to wake up now. This dream, vision, whatever it was, was too much. Her mind was overloaded, her emotions dancing on the ragged edge of sanity. Was this what her unsub experienced in his dreams? These sorts of images, sounds, smells? Is this what he went through when he, as he'd put it, *intuited* what was to come? If so, she pitied him. Murderer or not. His was a living torment, madness his constant companion, with no end or reward in sight.

Despite her desire to wake it appeared that, unlike the quasi control she'd found in her ability to fly, she had no control over that. That whatever had drawn her to this place and time had more in store for her.

She touched down in a large, concrete, open air area next to stainless steel sculpture that resembled a huge kidney bean. Its once highly polished surface was now mottled with patina like an antique mirror that hadn't aged well. *Cloud Gate*, she remembered, was the name of the sculpture. It had been the centerpiece of Millennium Park in Chicago, Illinois, since 2006.

Why am I here? She wondered. *What else is there to see? More mythical monsters running around loose on a planet once ruled by humans?*

She caught movement from the corner of her eye and spun around, the part of her mind that was well beyond panic insisting that she would indeed see another visage of hell, or someone's legendary version of it anyway.

What, or rather *who* she saw, was Matthew Decker.

He looked younger than when she'd last seen him, the age he'd been when they'd first met back at Quantico. Instead of his usual suit and tie he wore jeans and a buff-colored rag wool half-zip sweater, just the kind of thing she'd seen him wear a hundred times before on evenings after work, or on his days off. Joy shoved aside the sick feelings in her heart at the sight of him and she took a step forward, to embrace him, or just to be closer. He receded from her without taking a step. Smiled, and shook his head '*No*.'

She took another step towards him anyway and he receded again, just as before. Intuition told her she could take another twenty steps at a full out run and he'd remain just as far away, just as unreachable, with every step she took.

"You're not him, are you?" she asked. He shrugged and spread his arms. Looked at them. Looked at her. "Or if you are him," she continued, "you're a different version of him. A *higher* version of him."

He simply smiled.

"You're my version of *his* little girl," she said, referring to her unsub. "My guide in this—what is this anyway? A dream? A vision?"

He shrugged. Then smiled that warm and frustrating smile again.

"This is all going to happen if I don't help him, isn't it?" she asked.

He nodded.

"Not a dream," she continued, "not the delusions of a shattered mind. Except maybe for that beastie back there. I can't wrap my head around that one yet. This is a prophecy. Whatever we're facing is honest to God reality and will destroy all of humanity if we lose. But how? What could possibly be so devastating that it wipes out every living thing, right down to grass and plankton, on the entire planet?"

By the time she finished the question Matt Decker had vanished. So, it seemed, had Millennium Park. Startled by the rapid and fluid transition, she realized she was no longer outside, no longer on a lifeless planet. She was in a room in a building, with sounds of life all around.

The lighting was poor, and she couldn't see much, but she could hear footfalls in the hall beyond the room. Soft, crepe-soled shoes on polished tile. Closer, breathing. Not the normal breaths of a person at rest. Rather, the mechanical click and wheeze of a machine. There was a regular, insistent beeping coming from off to the right that seemed to be coming from a monitor full of squiggly lines and other information she couldn't readily understand. An antiseptic odor filled the room. Pungent astringents and sanitizers, used as cleaning agents.

Then the onslaught of sensory information coalesced, and she realized she was in a medical suite. In a hospital. And she was not alone.

There was a patient in the rooms only bed, but she couldn't make out whether the patient was a man or a woman because another man, a nurse or doctor, was leaning over them, examining them intently. He wore a yellow gown, sterile gloves, and when he turned his head to the side, she could see he also wore an N95 surgical mask that was tied at his neck and at the back of his head amidst longish, greasy, and unkempt jet-black hair. His garb seemed appropriate, especially if she were in an ICU or isolation unit. His hair didn't. It seemed unlikely to her that a hospital worker, even a janitor, would be allowed to interact with patients while wearing such a contamination risk as filthy hair.

The man drew back, withdrew a syringe and a small black box from the pocket of his gown, and plunged the needle into what looked to her like a lithium-ion battery. He withdrew a small amount of a clear liquid into the needle and then began injecting it into a catheter line near the patient's elbow.

Arianna yelled, "No!" and reached out to stay his hand—whatever he'd drawn into that syringe hadn't been prescribed by any physician, she'd bet her life on it—but her arm passed through him. Either she wasn't there, or he wasn't, or neither of them were—*yet*—but her effort had no effect. The man stood back and crossed his arms, seeming very pleased with himself.

The heart monitor on the wall began beeping erratically and an alarm went off. Then the line indicating the heartbeat went flat. As Arianna's heart was gripped with icy terror anew, the man chuckled and left the room, just before it filled with nurses bearing a crash cart.

Arianna was pulled sideways as if on a string. She passed through two nurses and medical equipment—

The crash cart. Something about it. Something red—

before passing through the wall into the room next door. The same man was there, injecting another patient with his witch's brew while medical staff was distracted by the code in the room next door. Again, the heart monitor went flat. Again, alarms brayed. Again, the man moved on to another room as Arianna uselessly screamed for help.

The string pulled again, this time backwards and up and she was outside, rapidly being pulled away from the building. This time she felt the motion. It pulled at her insides like being on a crazy backwards rollercoaster. Nausea filled her throat with bile, and she began to black out. Before she lost consciousness she focused on the front of the building and a bronze sculpture of three children playing on stilts that sat in front of it. Large blue lettering covered a low, white brick wall surrounding the sculpture. The last comprehensible thought she had as she was yanked faster and faster, farther and farther away, was what those letters spelled.

CHILDREN'S HOSPITAL

Jack

"D"on't you *ever* fucking do that again!" Arianna screamed, yanking on the sleeve of his leather coat so hard the seam at his shoulder popped.

"If you keep that up," he said, his voice as maddeningly calm and neutral as ever, "we'll end up in the ditch. Or worse."

She'd come back to the car—she didn't think of it as waking because she was now convinced it hadn't been a dream—screaming, crying, and laughing at the same time. Screaming at the horror of it. Crying at the sorrow of it. Laughing at the wonder of it. She could still feel that extraordinarily fresh air on her body, hear that odd stillness in the air, smell the putrid breath of that *thing*. She'd been holding onto the sleeve of his jacket when she 'arrived,' and had lashed out in fear and rage. She let go now, noting the deep rents her fingernails left behind in the supple leather. She imagined she'd left similar marks on his arm through the material and regretted it.

"How long?" she said, wiping tears from her face and trying to still the shaking in her limbs. "How long was I gone?"

"A few seconds," he said. "No more."

"Christ, it felt like hours," she said, willing her racing heart back to a more normal pace. "Is it always like that?"

"That short a time span?" he answered. "Sure. But the imagery was different this time. Far clearer, far worse, far more urgent than any I've experienced before."

"You saw what I saw?" she asked.

"A dead Earth. Yes."

"And the man who causes it?"

"Yellow gown, face mask, greasy black hair. A syringe full of death and a hospital in New Orleans. But I don't know which one."

"Children's Hospital," she said. "I saw it when I got pulled out of there, before I blacked out and ended up back here. Those are some friends you've got there; you know?" she added sarcastically. "They show you the most wonderful things."

"I wouldn't exactly call them friends," he said. "*She* seems benevolent, at least. But she's always out of reach. As for some of the other things I've seen, I try not to think about them too much."

"What is that place, anyway?" she asked. "It seemed like a dream at first, but it was too real for that. It felt more like the future. Or another reality altogether."

"I believe it's all of that and more," he said. "Past, present, future. Alternate timelines. Alternate realities. Heaven. Hell. All wrapped up in one. I think it's a kind of nexus. Where everything, everywhere, every possibility, is not only real, but happens in the same instance."

"And these spirits, or guides as you call them? What's their place in all of this? Who's guiding *them*?"

"I don't know," he said. "I probably wouldn't be able to understand the answer. I get the feeling it's too much for a human mind to comprehend. And even if it's not, no one, or nothing, has ever bothered to answer the question."

"And the snake thingy?" she asked. "Any idea where it fits into all this?"

"Snake thingy?" he asked, his brow furrowing.

"The big ass metal dragon that wrecked half the French Quarter?" she prompted. "It was munching on a giant bird when I interrupted it. I thought it would eat me too, but it just laughed at me, and I got the hell out of there."

He shook his head: "I didn't see anything like that. Just a dead world, up close and in detail. But I've seen spooky stuff before. Twelve-foot-tall shadow people and figures of light. Something that looked like an Aztec God. Once, a dog that turned out not to be a dog at all but a thing with eyes all over its body and several sets of wings. No metal dragons or giant birds, though."

She sat back and contemplated this. They'd had similar, but not the same, experiences. She'd seen no woman-child and assumed he'd not seen Matt Decker. It made sense that he'd have a different, more familiar guide. But why hadn't he seen the creatures in New Orleans or the devastation one or both had wrought? Was it even significant, compared to what they faced? What the planet faced? And ultimately, what did she care?

She was finished with her pursuit of this man. Her need to bring him in. If he were an agent of some supernatural presence or divine influence, it was beyond her ability to control. She would leave justice up to them. Her questions were answered, if poorly, and she wanted nothing more to do with him. Once this endeavor had ended, for better or worse, she was going back to whatever remained of her life and hoped to never see or think about that place, or *him*, again.

She dug in the pockets of her coat. Muttered under her breath when she didn't find what she was looking for.

"What is it?" he asked.

"My cellphone," she answered. "I was hoping I hadn't lost it. I could look up the address of the hospital, save us some time. Or were you planning to intuit its location?"

"I thought we'd stop for dinner," he answered, "ask someone for directions."

She gazed at him in disbelief. He threw back that charming grin of his and winked.

"Lord, help me," she said, but not without kindness, "the supernatural assassin's a smart-ass."

"The glovebox," he said, and pointed.

She sprung the latch and discovered her cellphone. It was out of its case, it's battery laying alongside. She retrieved all three, wondering again at his intuition. Or was it just common sense? Had he thought she might need the phone and kept it? But since leaving the battery in meant law enforcement in general, and specifically James Austin, could track her, had taken it apart before putting it in the glovebox? Or had he just swept it up and kept it on impulse?

"Okay, Jack," she said. She'd opened the back of the phone and was holding the battery above its slot. "Once I put this in, my tech guy's going to know exactly where we are. And since I went MIA with my whole team down—she swallowed hard at the thought—the entire Bureau, and probably a couple of other agencies, are sure to drop on us like a starving hawk on a fat mouse. Any last words?"

"Jack?" he asked.

"Well," she answered, "Since we're obviously in this together, I have to call you something. The 'unsub' or 'suspect' no longer seem right. Besides, Jack Kerouac is my favorite author. Also, Jack is almost as anonymous as John, but has a bit more style. Is there something else you'd prefer I call you? Steve Rogers? Or maybe Bruce Wayne?"

"Jack it is," he said, having no idea who the other two men could be. Jack Kerouac, he was familiar with. While he'd read all his novels and most of his poetry, the novel *Book of Dreams*, with its intertwining plots of characters from his other works, it's theme of life and events continuing long after the story has ended, and its spontaneous and flowing style, had struck a rich chord somewhere within him, making it his favorite. He nodded at the phone. "Go ahead."

Arianna replaced the battery in the phone, closed the cover, and steeled herself against what she knew was about to happen.

IT TOOK ALL OF EIGHT seconds. Arianna turned the phone on, entered the Google site, typed in 'Children's Hospital, New Orleans,' when the screen shifted to an incoming call. She didn't need to see the name on the screen to recognize the caller, the Pac-Man theme she'd downloaded to his contact information said it all. Jack—she wondered if anyone had ever named him before and how he felt about it now—shot her a glance and raised an eyebrow at the tones. She shrugged and answered, silencing the *wacka-wacka-wacka* sound of the Pacster gobbling up ghosts.

"Jimmy," she said. "I need you to listen to me very carefully."

"Ari?" James Austin's voice screamed from the speaker. "Are you okay? What the hell's going on? And why are you in Louisiana for God's sake?"

THE RAIN CAME AGAIN as I-59 merged with I-10 and they crossed Lake Ponchartrain. Large, heavy drops that suicidally flung themselves from the heavens and splashed into lifeless puddles against the windshield before being carelessly swiped away by the wipers. Lightning intermittently turned the false night of heavy cloud cover back to daylight, lighting up the rapidly approaching city, the lake beneath them, and the steadily increasing traffic around them. Thunder roared back, shaking the frame of the car as it sped southwest, its engine howling as tires threw up twin fantails of runoff. It was as if the old Gods had gathered above, the city an arena, and each bellowed and roared in turn, cheering their respective champions on in the battle that was about to take place below.

"They'll be coming for us," Arianna said needlessly, as if he hadn't heard every word of the heated conversation she'd just had with her associate through the external speaker of her phone. She removed the battery from the device and shoved it angrily into the pocket of her coat.

"*I'm* a person of interest now," she continued. "A witness saw me walk out of that garage with an unknown male, my entire team down, apparently of my own free will," she eyed him questioningly, accusingly. "An *accomplice,* they think. They're tearing my place apart right now. Looking for connections to Coleman, the FFI, and clues to your identity and what our plans are. For now, they're operating under the assumption that *you* were behind Coleman, pulling the FFI's strings. And that you betrayed him back in Boston as a part of a much grander scheme. And that I've been in league with you all along."

"I'm sorry, Ms. Price," he said. There was nothing else to say.

"Call me Ari," she said with a sigh. "My family is dead. My friends are dead. My career is over, along with life as I knew it. The FBI, ATF, US Marshal Service, and God knows how many other agencies are hunting me. *If* I come out of this alive, I'll be facing months if not years of questions, investigations, hearings, and possible imprisonment. You and this fucking crusade are all I have left now. You may as well call me Ari."

"You can call me Jack," he said, that charming grin of his lighting up his face and her mood. "I was recently advised that's my name."

Despite herself, she returned the grin.

"Well, Jack," she said, putting her self-pity on the same high shelf she'd placed her grief on earlier, "the bad news is that Jimmy is the best tech the FBI has, which means he undoubtedly accessed and downloaded my phone log while we were talking and knows the address I was searching for. Which means there are probably a dozen or more agents on their way to the Children's Hospital right now. The good news is that helicopters can't safely fly in this weather, so they're stuck with ground travel just like us. It's a race, now, to see which of us gets there first."

She paused as Jack rapidly maneuvered the Camaro around a mini-van only to find the lane ahead blocked by an open-air auto carrier hauling eight brand new Ford F-150 pickup trucks. A Freightliner Cascadia, hauling a fifty-three-foot double drop trailer with a modular home resting on it blocked the other. The remaining lanes were choked with passenger vehicles. Instead of slowing as she expected, Jack goosed the accelerator and they shot through a narrow gap between the two big rigs before slaloming left into the carpool lane, which was now clear ahead for a good quarter of a mile. Arianna swallowed her stomach back into its normal position and willed the hair on her arms and neck to lay back down before continuing:

"A race I have no doubt we'll win," she added dryly.

"Won't your friend relay the information you gave him about this dark-haired man," Jack asked, "and the toxin he's carrying?"

"He will," Arianna said, assuring herself that her seatbelt was still firmly buckled. "Jimmy's a good agent, and he'll take the information seriously whether he believes it or not. But others in the Agency will focus on what is known and what they can act on. And right now, what they know is that five of their fellow agents are dead and that I've apparently gone rogue with the man who killed their murderers. Apprehending us, *stopping* us, is the only action they'll pursue. They'll worry about the whys and wherefores later."

"Then we won't be apprehended," he said.

"Easy for you to say," Arianna said. "We don't even know *where* in the hospital our perp plans to inject his victims. It's a big place. Their website boasts over a thousand beds on a two-hundred-and-fifty-thousand square foot campus. That's a lot of ground to cover."

"Unless your spirit guide or whatever has already told you," she added.

He was silent as he guided the car through the I-10 to State Route 90 interchange. Arianna looked south, thinking she might catch a glimpse of the newly constructed Caesars Superdome, but the stadium was shrouded in rain.

"Jack?" she prompted.

"Our visions were different," he finally answered. "Mine ended after I saw *him*. I didn't see what hospital. I didn't see your mechanical monster. And I didn't see *her*." The latter point seemed to concern him. "Maybe that's how it works when they're communicating with two of us. I don't know. There's never been more than just me." He glanced at her, and she felt something more was bothering him, something he hadn't yet told her, but he continued before she could ask: "For whatever reason, they chose to give you more information. Think back on what you saw, what you felt. The answer must be in there somewhere."

She considered this.

She dismissed her journey across a barren Earth and her encounter with Matt Decker, focusing on what she'd experienced inside the hospital. Inside the suite where she'd seen the man with the filthy hair.

Tile floors, polished to a high gloss, the repetitive wheeze of a ventilator. Quiet footsteps in the hall outside, the odor of sanitizer, the crinkle of fabric as the man straightened, crossed his arms, and uttered a contented sigh.

Again, Arianna tried to focus on the man's face. Again, she failed. As alarms blared throughout the room and at the nurses' station down the hall, she was pulled backwards towards a wall, through nurses bearing a crash cart with a large red placard on the side.

It was the same sort of label placed on all medical equipment in large hospitals, so that it's returned to the proper unit if it needs maintenance or is borrowed. This one read IDU400.

"Any idea what it means?" she asked after describing the vison.

"Four hundred could mean the fourth floor," he suggested. "Are you sure it wasn't ICU? The Intensive Care Unit?"

"No. It was definitely IDU," she said, concentrating on her limited knowledge of medical jargon.

Jack blew past two cars waiting at a red light and cut the next corner through a gas station parking lot, putting them on Hank Aaron Boulevard. They were seconds away from Children's Hospital. As they neared the entrance to the vast parking area surrounding the five-story building, he slowed the vehicle, reducing the roar of the engine to a contented purr.

"Well," he said. "This should be interesting."

Arianna, her attention focused on deciphering the riddle of what, if anything, the placard in her vision meant, looked up and gasped.

Entry

P andemonium.

That was the word that popped into Arianna's mind when they pulled into parking lot E of the New Orleans Children's Hospital. To her, the sight was reminiscent of the scene in Gallup, New Mexico, only twofold. *And had that only been days ago?* she thought. *It feels like forever.*

The campus was, indeed, a sprawling affair. With five buildings spread out over gracefully sweeping lawns, all connected by well-lit paths and two-lane avenues leading to large parking lots. A city within a city. Separate, yet integrated. Like a college campus.

The main building was four stories tall, made of glass that would reflect green in daylight and shaped like a capital D, with the curved surface facing forwards. In the center of the curve was a single-story covered entrance with a wide, circular drive for dropping off patients or visitors. The words CHILDRENS HOSPITAL glowed bluish green in four-foot-tall letters set on the edge of the roof, declaring it the main entrance. Illuminated red letters spelled out EMERGENCY above a portico with a similarly broad driveway several hundred feet to the right.

Both entrances, a hundred yards from where Jack allowed the vehicle to roll to a stop before shutting off the engine, were teeming with law enforcement. Black and blue clad bodies in vinyl rain slickers hurried this way and that, taking up what appeared to be defensive positions. Vehicles, hospital security, blue over white New Orleans Police cars, red over white Louisiana State Police vehicles, and even a few plain—but obviously official—sedans surrounded the building as if in preparation to repel a siege.

Police flashers split the darkness. Red, blue, and white, in counterpoint to the lightning flashing intermittently through the sky. The steady rain added multicolored prisms of chaos to the scene.

It was more than she had expected. More than she'd *imagined.*

"All this for us?" she mused aloud.

"A rogue federal agent in league with the mastermind of a major domestic terrorism organization?" Jack answered, scanning the scene. "I'm surprised they didn't send more."

"We can't pass through all that," Arianna said. "By now they'll have my photo and a description of you from Art Nestir and the children. They'll see us coming a mile away. How the hell are we going to get in there?"

"I plan to walk," Jack said, opening the car door to step out.

"Wait," Arianna laid her hand on his arm again, pulled him back. He reluctantly closed the door.

"Maybe we don't have to," she said. "I mean, look out there. They've locked the place down. Do you think our guy could have gotten through all that? That he could move about freely, do what he plans to do in there with all those cops running around? This wasn't part of my vision. There weren't any cops roaming the halls when he was injecting those patients. Just hospital staff. And the place wasn't surrounded by all these vehicles when I was pulled outside, either. Maybe it's all over. Maybe Jimmy unwittingly stopped it when he alerted my superiors that we were coming here and set all this in motion."

He paused for a moment.

"Was it raining in your vision?" he asked.

"No. The sun was out, or I probably wouldn't have noticed the sign."

"And I didn't see everything you saw," he reminded her. "Like the snake thing. Or the destruction you said it caused. That place I see in my visions, that existence, is always changing, always in flux. But the events I'm shown there always happen. Unless I intervene."

She thought about it.

"So, it's not over."

"Does it feel over?" he asked.

She searched her feelings.

"No," she said finally. "It feels like we're running out of time."

They opened the Camaro's doors and stepped out into the rain.

Instinct and training compelled Arianna to go low and slow. Use the vehicles between the Camaro and the building for cover. Then the waste bins, benches set up around the perimeter of the circular main drive, and the large ornamental planters filled with flowers and trees when the cars ran out.

Jack had no such compulsion. He strode quickly, purposefully through the rain, the shirt beneath his jacket soaked through in minutes, blue jeans darkening with moisture, shoes kicking up sprays of water with each step. Arianna hurried to catch up.

"So that's the trick to being invisible?" She asked as she matched his speed and gait, trying to emulate his air of confidence. "Act like you know what you're doing? Like you belong in places you don't?"

"Not at all," he said. "To them, we're just shapes in the rain. Those slickers they're wearing limit their vision and drown out sound. Unless we get too close, they'll assume we're just other cops out here securing the perimeter."

Twenty yards from the driveway he took her arm and guided her to the left, away from the main entrance. There were police officers everywhere. Four covered the main entrance, six covered the emergency doors around to the right. Another two were headed directly towards them, close enough that Arianna could hear their radios crackling with traffic. She tried to look everywhere at once, without looking like she was looking everywhere at once. Nothing screamed *Suspicious!* to law enforcement like someone rubbernecking their way through a scene.

They passed between two parked cruisers, lights flashing idiotically in the rain, and onto the drive. The windows were cranked up, engines running, windows fogged over. A sure sign that both vehicles were occupied. The officers that had been approaching passed behind them and got into the back of one of the cruisers, seeking shelter. One of them muttered something about catching this sort of bullshit duty in the rain.

Arianna let out a breath she hadn't realized she'd been holding as they turned the corner of the building, out of the sightline of the vehicles.

"How the hell did that just happen?" she mused aloud. Despite Jack's assurances, she'd expected screams of *Halt!* with every step. *Freeze! Get on the ground!* Followed by being wrestled down by a dozen or more officers, cuffed, and unceremoniously dumped in the back of a cruiser. Instead, they'd passed by unnoticed.

Jack didn't answer. Simply kept his pace and pointed ahead.

A cruiser was parked at the curb opposite an open maintenance door halfway down the length of the building, its roof rack casting blue and white staccato bursts of light against the earthen colored walls. It appeared empty. No interior shadows broke the light coming from the unit's onboard computer screen. The windows were clear, rain washing down them in tiny rivers. A rectangle of light shone out onto the wet sidewalk from inside the open doorway. Jack slowed and reached for his shoulder holster.

"Hold it, cowboy," Arianna said in a low voice, stilling his hand. "He's probably right inside the door, having a cigarette. Or just down the hall, keeping out of the rain."

Jack shook his head, gestured to the empty rectangle of light. "If he was inside the door, we'd see his shadow. Something's wrong here." He drew his gun.

Despite herself, Arianna drew her weapon. He was right. This seemed too convenient. She could still hear the activity at the hospital's entrances, over the rain, over the occasional thunder. Why was it so quiet here, at this inexplicably open door? Was it a trap? Had they been spotted crossing the parking lot? Skirting the building? It seemed like a lot of trouble to go to when they simply could have been overwhelmed by force and arrested at any point since leaving the Camaro.

"We'll find another way in," she suggested.

Jack shook his head, pointed out past the parking lot. A line of black Chevy Suburban's was making its way down Hank Aaron Boulevard. She counted six, through the pouring rain.

"Your friends are here."

"Shit," she muttered. "What—"

do you think? she'd been about to say, but Jack was already gone. He darted through the rectangle of light to the opposite side of the door and took up an entry position, his weapon pointed at the sky. He nodded and Arianna took position opposite him, her weapon aimed at concrete.

"It's a service hallway," he said in a low voice. "I didn't see anyone."

Arianna nodded her understanding and they pivoted into the doorway simultaneously, flawlessly, Arianna covering the low angles, Jack covering high. As if they'd done so dozens of times. As if they were partners who'd trained together.

The hallway was empty, roughly twenty feet long. Harsh light from above revealed a closed door at the opposite end and one on each side. Rain had blown in the open door and puddled on the yellow tile flooring. Two sets of wet footprints led deeper into the hall, becoming smaller as they dried.

Arianna checked their six, noted that all six Chevy Suburban's had exited Hank Aaron Boulevard and were presumably taking up positions in front of the building. She closed the outer door before turning back.

Jack checked the knob on the door to the right, found it unlocked, and eased it open. He pushed it the last few inches with the barrel of his gun before turning:

"A stairwell. Leads to the basement."

"Our guy wouldn't go down there," Arianna said, shaking her head. "I saw him in a medical suite. He needs access to the patients."

She tried the door opposite. Faint wet shoe impressions led inside. It was marked UTILITY and she expected to see nothing more than a small closet containing a large sink, some mops and cleaning rags, chemicals, and some of those little yellow signs they put out when a floor is wet, so people who fall on their asses can't sue. In fact, she did see all of that, if not in the exact layout she had imagined. But what she also saw as the door swung slowly inward was a thin, middle-aged man in a red shirt and shorts, sitting in the sink with his legs crossed, grinning at her. *Leering* at her maniacally from the shadows within.

Arianna raised her weapon and clicked the light switch before her conscious mind could process that she had done so, bathing the room in LED radiance.

The man in the sink wasn't grinning at her. And his shirt hadn't started out red.

His throat was split open from ear to ear, head lolled back, resting between the HOT and COLD handles of the faucet. Arterial spray was splashed across the walls of the closet. The ceiling. The floor. More blood had run down his chest, staining his undershirt and boxers. He'd been placed in the sink, presumably while his killer had undressed him.

"Our missing cop?" Jack suggested from behind her.

"Or somebody else that got in our guy's way," Arianna answered, her momentary dread fleeing in the cold, harsh light of the closet. She noted a wadded rain slicker, pink with blood, tossed in a corner. Relatively clean slacks, a button-down shirt, and a pair of black dress shoes had been discarded in the same corner. Slowly congealing blood had pooled and been tracked all over the floor.

"Either way," Jack said, "He's already here."

"And we're out of time."

Fox in the Henhouse

After killing the cop, Lonnie had flipped the pig over and boosted him into the sink to get his shoes and pants off. His physique had been a near match, so the uniform fit well enough, but he'd had the feet of an eleven-year-old girl and Lonnie had been forced to wear his own sodden loafers. He prayed they wouldn't squeak on the polished tile floor, drawing attention to the incongruous footwear.

He abandoned the rain slicker. It kept most of the cops' blood from soiling the uniform, save a few crimson stains on the collar and one on the right trouser knee, but red against black was barely noticeable and Lonnie had taken pains to keep the pooled and coagulating mess from spreading as he'd changed. The slicker itself, however, was too stained to consider wearing.

Satisfied that his overall appearance was suitable, Lonnie thought: *Just like a fox in the henhouse.* He exited the maintenance hallway and headed for the elevators.

The shoes didn't squeak.

He turned left onto a large corridor, following the handy signs posted at every intersection indicating the direction of the elevators. Past the financial aid offices, dark at this hour, and a lounge.

Two patrolmen, lapel pins informing him they were from the fifth precinct, passed in the opposite direction without looking up. They were discussing the merits of gun control, each quietly arguing his point as they ignored his presence.

Even if they'd bothered to look up, had bothered to meet his eyes, Lonnie doubted they would have done more than nod and continue their banal conversation. The NOPD had over nineteen-hundred police officers spread out over eight precincts. It was unlikely he'd be spotted for an impostor in the few minutes it would take him to reach his destination.

The officers posted at the main entrance were more alert than those roaming the halls, but their attention was focused outward rather than in. He passed four in tactical garb, carrying mean looking MP5K's, their vests proudly bearing the SWAT logo. Then three more in patrol uniforms, too busy chatting up the girl at the reception desk to give him more than a passing glance.

He followed the signs past reception, into a small cul de sac that housed two elevators and pushed the UP button. After what seemed like forever but was only a few minutes—the damn things were stopping at *every* floor—the bell dinged, signaling the car's arrival. He had to step back, allowing no trace of surprise or apprehension to show on his face as the doors parted and disgorged four uniformed officers and a man in a business suit that Lonnie took for an administrator of some sort. Three of the officers continued into the lobby but the administrator type and one officer, an overweight, grey-haired man with Captain's bars on his collar, stopped just outside the door.

"We have three-hundred and ninety-seven sick children in this building alone," the administrator type explained. "Some of them *very* sick. I understand your need to thoroughly search the grounds, I'm just asking that it be done with a modicum of empathy for the children and their families. Two of your men burst onto the oncology unit and scared several of our patients. They don't need that sort of stress on top of everything else they're dealing with."

"You would prefer they endure the stress of a domestic terrorist attack?" the captain retorted.

The administrator ran his hands through his hair and took a deep, calming breath. Lonnie squeezed past the pair and boarded the elevator. The captain's eyes swung to follow. He locked eyes with Lonnie.

"Of course not—" the administrator began, but the captain waved him off, still looking Lonnie up and down.

"I'll tell my men to finish clearing the building," the captain promised, turning towards the elevator and putting his arm out to trip the door sensor. "They won't disturb your patients unnecessarily again."

The administrator, duly dismissed, headed towards the entrance as the doors opened and the lobby began filling up with men and women in dark suits and rain gear.

"Officer Weiss," the captain read Lonnie's name tag and collar in a glance, "You're out of uniform."

Lonnie feigned respect and deference while wanting to gouge the man's eyes out with his thumbs.

"Sir?"

"Your headcover," the captain said.

Lonnie placed his hand on his head as if feeling for the standard issue black police cap. He mentally kicked himself. Weiss, which had to be the name of the cop he'd killed in the maintenance closet, hadn't been wearing one. In his haste, Lonnie hadn't considered it.

"Must've left it in the car, sir," Lonnie said, projecting embarrassment. "My apologies."

"Well," the captain retorted, "I don't know how your Captain feels about these things over in the third, but here in the second we take our dress code seriously. Get your head covered, or I'll be speaking with your Sergeant. And wash your damn hair."

"Uh, yessir," Lonnie said, throwing the man a half-hearted salute with a look of chagrin thrown in for good measure.

One member of the group that had entered the lobby separated himself from the others and approached.

"Captain," he said, "I'm Special Agent in Charge Mark Belflour, FBI. It seems we may not be just looking for two suspects here. There may be a third. If you'll join us in the atrium?" An order. Not a request. The man turned and walked away without another word.

The captain sighed and let the elevator door go. As it closed, Lonnie secured the blade on the buck knife he'd opened one handed and held at the ready behind his back. He'd have been delighted to plunge the blade into the cops' neck and drag him backwards into the elevator, silencing that officious voice forever, but had doubted he could do so without being seen. He refolded the knife and placed it back on the cop's duty belt. From beyond the closed door, before the elevator began to rise, he heard the captain mutter: "*Fucking feds.*"

"WE CAN'T JUST STROLL on out there," Arianna said.

They'd followed more shoe impressions to the door at the end of the hall, but Jack had hesitated to open it. It undoubtedly led to the main corridor, and it was a good bet that *he'd* taken that route. Now dressed in a dead man's clothes he could pass unnoticed through the heavy foot traffic they could hear on the other side with ease. But a pair of soaked and sodden fugitives was sure to raise an alarm.

"Every cop in this building is already looking for us. And now that the FBI is here, every door and stairwell will be covered in a matter of minutes. It's dumb luck that we made it this far. We go out there we won't make it a hundred feet."

He nodded for her to continue.

"If we're assuming what I saw in my vision means anything, we want the fourth floor." She pointed to the door behind them. "We go down to get back up."

"The basement?"

"I've been in a lot of hospitals, Jack," she said, retracing their steps. "One thing they all have in common is dozens of people everywhere, at all hours of the day or night. People in the patient's rooms, in waiting rooms, at nurse's stations. Some just walking the halls. Doctors, nurses, lab techs, all coming from somewhere and going somewhere else. And that's without the added police traffic," she opened the door on the stairwell leading down before continuing, "Another thing they all have in common is the basement." Sensing no one on the stairs or waiting at the bottom, she started down. Heard his footsteps as he followed. She briefly wondered if he'd ever followed before, rather than led. Probably not, she decided, as he'd told her that having to rely on someone else was unexpected.

She also wondered at his hesitation. He'd seemed confident and self-assured thus far. It was uncharacteristic of the man she'd pursued for decades, the man who'd boldly put an end to the schemes of dozens, perhaps hundreds of lowlife scumbags while saving the lives of others, to hesitate for even a moment. Hadn't he fearlessly walked into a firestorm in Gallup, New Mexico, less than a week ago, thwarting what was sure to be a long and deadly siege? And valiantly rid the world of a serial child killer just days later?

Hadn't he pulled *her*, terrified and covered in blood, from a bathtub two decades ago, gently reassuring her that it was all over now, and, despite her loss, things would work out as the universe had designed?

He'd told her that the incidents were becoming more frequent, more violent. Four events in one week, if you counted the attempted pipe bombing in El Paso and the events in Boston. All leading to an even more terrifying event—*this* event, she believed—the destruction of mankind.

How much can one man, even one possessed of supernatural abilities, take? At what point does he break? Physically? Mentally? At what point does he lose his conviction?

She pushed the thought aside in favor of their current situation and, still sensing no one in the area, continued down the stairs.

Their feet rang loudly on the steel treads, and she softened her steps and voice.

"Every hospital basement is similar. With mechanical rooms, a laundry, a morgue," they reached the bottom, scanned the area, and took positions on either side of the hallway. "And a loading dock with a service elevator. I doubt anyone's making deliveries in this weather, during a lockdown, so there shouldn't be too many people around. That's our way up."

Jack said nothing, only nodded, drew his weapon, and started forward.

THE HALLWAY TURNED to the right after a dozen feet, then left again, following the outside wall of the building. Pipes led overhead, branching off in different directions and upwards as they traveled. Steam and water along the left-hand wall, oxygen, painted bright red to be easily identifiable, down the middle. Gas, and a conduit that branched off far more frequently than the others, likely containing power lines of various voltages, on the right-hand side. Their progress was slower than Jack would have liked. Rooms opened up on their left and there was little choice but to take the time to clear them, stepping into doorways a degree at a time, searching each new angle before moving on to the next. Like sectioning a pie. Scanning each new opening for anyone that might see them or, improbably, their suspect.

The first room they came to, as she'd predicted, was a vast laundry room. It was empty and quiet, which made perfect sense, considering. NOPD would have started clearing the building in two squads, one working from top to bottom, the other from bottom to top. All workers not essential to the operation of the hospital would have been screened, cleared, and sent home. The laundry would have been deemed non-essential in the short term. As would the morgue, the loading dock, and any other facilities housed on this level. Other than police, they might encounter a maintenance man or two, but even their movements would likely be restricted.

Despite the absence of personnel—*obstacles*, Jack's mind insisted—and the slow speed of their progress, he let Arianna set the pace. He didn't trust his instincts at this point. His intuition had failed him.

Arianna was right. The fact that they'd made it this far was dumb luck. His confident stroll across the parking lot, through the law enforcement presence there, had been based on the rain, the distraction of flashing lights and thunder crashing all around, and the human tendency to ignore things that appear to belong. It had had nothing to do with prescience, his ability to remain unobserved, or his connection to whatever force guided him.

The problem had begun in the Camaro, shortly after they'd entered the parking lot.

Usually, he needn't look for guidance. There'd be a brief sensation akin to climbing a stair, a lifting of the mind rather than the body. Typically, he'd see or hear something, a brief vision of a direction to take, a door to walk through, or not. An object or face to recognize, an ambient noise that would lead him onward. They were fleeting glimpses, and never in complete detail. Just clear enough that he could recognize his next move.

But if he *did* search for it, it came. Same sensations, same result. Until now.

Now, the sensation was of taking a step up and finding nothing there. As when climbing an unfamiliar staircase in the dark, reaching the top, and thinking there's one more step when there isn't. The body expects another step, the brain expects another step, but there's nothing there to push up from and the body lurches awkwardly. It takes but a moment to recover physically, but the mind remains off balance for several seconds afterwards.

That was what Jack was feeling. Off balance and awkward. As if the connection he had with the force that guided him had been severed.

No, he thought, *not severed. Interfered with.*

Because there was *something* in that moment. Something like but unlike static. Something like but unlike snow on a TV screen. Something similar to signal degradation of the sort you get when two powerful, but opposing electromagnetic fields come into proximity of one another.

He'd reached the door leading to the main concourse of the hospital and, receiving nothing but static, had been about to proceed until Arianna stopped him and pointed out something he should have thought of himself.

He was, for the first time in his memory, questioning his own judgement.

Is this what she meant when she said that I couldn't do this alone? he asked himself. *That something would interfere with her ability to communicate with me? Or is it something else?*

He'd learned long ago that he'd receive no answers to his questions and set the matter aside. There was a man to stop here. A world to save. Looking inward to find only a snowy screen—he envisioned a television test pattern with the words TECHNICAL DIFFICULTIES PLEASE STAND BY emblazoned across it—and an oddly oscillating hum of static that was beginning more and more to sound like mocking laughter, would bring him no closer to that goal.

For now, until his clarity returned, he would follow Arianna.

IT IS A TRICK OF THE human mind that travel to a destination through unfamiliar surroundings seems to take far longer than it does. Just as the return trip home seems to go much faster.

The eight minutes it took Jack and Arianna to traverse the basement, clearing doors, rooms, and obstacles in the corridor before proceeding, using the large, round overhead mirrors placed more for preventing those with large food and laundry carts or gurneys from running into other personnel than for the sake of security, seemed to take much longer.

The corridor branched to the right ahead of them, the noise of the rain growing louder as it rang off metal rather than concrete.

Arianna held up her hand, a stilling motion. Jack stopped. He could hear voices ahead and to the right. He looked into the overhead mirrors and saw what Arianna could already see from her position. An area thirty-feet wide and twenty-feet long that protruded out from the rest of the building, a steel roof that amplified the sound of the rain overhead. Two eight-foot by twelve steel roll-up doors comprised the outer wall, closed against the rain that nevertheless found its way inside, leaving puddles on the floor of the large loading dock.

Two New Orleans police officers stood well inside the doors, either to have a better view, to stay out of the water, or both. They had the relaxed pose of two men, familiar with each other and currently bored with their duties, casually conversing about their jobs, their wives, their kids. Behind them and to the right was a stairwell leading upwards. To the left were the open doors of a service elevator.

"Molly's cast comes off next Monday," the taller one said, "and I'll save about twenty bucks a week in corn starch. She's dumped so much of that crap down her leg to stop the itching that her mother suggested just cutting it off and frying it up 'cause it's already battered."

"I thought people used baby powder for that," said the other.

"That shit causes cancer," the first replied.

Jack thought hard. Hoped for a flash of intuition, guidance, anything. Nothing came and he only received a brief twinkling of static when he sought it out. Arianna was looking at him:

What now?

He scanned the area again. The wet floor. The overhead piping. A long, low cart in the corner against the wall beside the farthest roll-up door bearing a dozen or more tall cylinders marked OXYGEN. The mirrors. If either officer looked up, they'd see Jack's reflection, weapon in hand, and this situation would unravel in a matter of seconds.

His eyes were drawn back to the piping. If he fired a round into the steam line it might cause enough of a distraction for him and Arianna to rush the officers and render them unconscious before they could draw their weapons or send up an alarm. It was a risky proposition, but at the moment it was all he had.

He signaled his intentions by pointing at the overhead lines and his gun, then at the officers, making a punching motion. She nodded reluctantly, pointing at the closer of the two officers—*I'll take him*—and holstered her weapon. She wasn't about to shoot an innocent man just doing his job. Not even to save the world.

Jack took aim. His finger tightened on the trigger. Both officers' radios burst to life.

"*Officer down. Officer down,*" a tinny voice frantically exclaimed through the speakers. "*I have an officer down in maintenance hallway two, first floor!*"

The officers looked at each other with a mixture of surprise of dread and, conversation of casts and cancer forgotten, took off running down the adjacent corridor.

Jack relaxed his finger on the trigger and looked over to where Arianna had been standing. She was gone. Already crossing the loading dock for the elevator beyond.

"Let's go," she said, gesturing for him to follow. "I doubt we'll get another chance."

Dissonance

"That was convenient," Arianna said.

They boarded the elevator and Jack drew down the barrier. The outer doors closed, and, by unspoken mutual consent, Arianna pushed the button for the fourth floor. They ascended at an agonizingly slow pace.

"The way that call came through just as you were about to shoot the steam lines. I'm not sure it would have worked. That it would have been enough or that we would have come out on top."

"It wasn't so convenient for the guy in that closet," Jack said, "but I've gotten used to that sort of thing."

They were quiet for a moment as the elevator crept upwards. Arianna took in his appearance under the fluorescents, the first good lighting she'd seen him in since the maintenance hallway. His condition had deteriorated, even in that short span of time. He looked weary. His shoulders slumped a bit where before they had been square and confident. His legs bent slightly at the knees where before they had been strong and locked. They were subtle differences, differences that would likely go unnoticed by an untrained eye. The dark circles that had taken up residence beneath his eyes, however, would be apparent even to a casual observer.

The car shuddered, hesitated at the second floor as if deciding whether to stop and open the doors for additional passengers before continuing. The floor beneath them groaned but the car did not stop.

"What's going on with you, Jack?"

When he didn't answer she continued.

"You hesitated back there. In the service hallway. Almost walked us into a situation we wouldn't have gotten out of without hurting a lot of people. And you look exhausted. Like you need a vacation, or one of those forty-hour naps you told me about."

"Dissonance," he said softly, watching the floor numbers above the door change. Then he met her eyes, smiled a dry, dispirited smile.

"What does that mean?"

"It means something's stopping me from seeing the usual cues. Where to go, what to do, what path to follow. There's interference. Like when two amplified signals come together and drown each other out. Each is distinct yet distorted. Until it clears, I'm guessing. And I don't like to guess."

"You can't unravel on me, Jack," Arianna said. "Not now. Not before we stop this guy. When this is over, you can disappear back into the shadows. Have a rest. Read a book. Do whatever it is you do.

"I'm through pursuing you, if that's what's bothering you. It's not as if I'll have a career in law enforcement after tonight anyway. And no one else believes you exist.

"I'm through with these guides of yours, too," she continued, voicing her decision. "These directors, or Gods. They can keep their visions and their tasks. This is your calling, not mine, and you're welcome to it. I just want to go back to my life and pick up whatever pieces are left. Feed my damn cat. Try to live a normal life. One without places and creatures that shouldn't exist, people hell-bent on destruction, and preternatural hit men.

"But before I can do that, I have to survive this. *We* have to survive this. Or nobody else will."

The car groaned beneath their feet again, then settled into place. A bell outside the car signaled their arrival and the doors creaked open on the fourth floor. Jack lifted the interior grate, then paused, staring at the far wall, one arm still raised against the underside of the barrier.

"Son of a bitch," he breathed.

Arianna looked where he was looking. Understood.

"Dissonance, huh?" she said stepping past him. A corridor ran off to the right and vanished around a lefthand curve that would take them back to the front of the building. "Looks like you're still getting help. Cues, or no cues."

Jack left the gate in the up position. Safety features wouldn't allow the outer doors to close on the open gate and the car would remain where it was. Handy, if they found themselves needing to beat a hasty retreat.

A series of multi-colored signs were attached to the opposite wall. The second from the top was red, with an arrow pointing down the corridor. It read:

INFECTIOUS DISEASE UNIT Rms 400–416.

LONNIE SCHULTZ TRIED to ignore the ticking growing louder in his head, filling him with white hot rage.

The ticking wasn't real, he knew that. The heater he'd designed to keep the GT-16 genotoxin viable had no timer, and thus couldn't tick. He heard it anyway, as time ran short and delay after delay cost him precious time. He estimated he now had less than twenty minutes to find suitable hosts before the heater, snugged neatly in his right pants pocket, dropped below one-hundred and two degrees and rendered the genotoxin inert.

tick tick

Two of New Orleans finest had boarded the elevator on the second floor. They chatted briefly, about what Lonnie did not care, sparing him no more than a glance as they exited on three where two more boarded. Lonnie waited for the doors to rattle closed and for the car to carry him to the fourth floor, where his destiny awaited.

"Hold the door, please," a voice sang out.

tick tick

The officer nearest the doors slipped a friendly hand out over the safety bar and waited. Lonnie wanted to shoot him in the stomach.

"Thanks," said a twenty-something nurse pushing a med cart full of pills and potions, all locked away in various drawers. She had blonde hair pulled back in a ponytail and a smooth figure beneath her crisp white uniform. Lonnie supposed she'd be considered pretty by most male standards. He thought she'd be prettier covered in blood.

"Sorry," she said, as one of the carts wheels got stuck in the gap between the elevator car and the floor. Officer friendly, no doubt thinking she'd be prettier covered in nothing at all, grabbed the front of the cart and lifted it physically into the car.

"Thanks again," she said, offering an apologetic smile to each of them in turn. Lonnie, thinking he'd have saved time if he'd taken the stairs, resisted the urge to bare his teeth at her.

Tick Tick

The elevator swept upwards, and the doors parted on the fourth floor. Officer Friendly and the nurse struggled to get the med cart back out of the elevator before turning right, in the direction of Cardiology and Electrophysiology according to signs posted on the wall. Once they were out of sight, Lonnie walked straight ahead down a short hallway. A set of double doors at the end of the hall bore the legend Infectious Disease Unit. Smiling, Lonnie pushed on the right-hand door. Nothing. He pushed on the left. Again, nothing. His smile faded as he looked around for a latch or a doorknob. There was only a keypad with a speaker set into it, a call button beneath.

Lonnie pushed the button. Waited.

Tick Tick

"Can I help you?" a tired, feminine voice squawked from the speaker.

"Police," Lonnie said simply. He peered through the glass set into the doors. Another hallway, a cart of drawers like a portable dresser, and, on the left-hand wall about six feet down, a large silver button.

"Thought you guys had already cleared this unit," the voice said.

"It *is* a locked ward. No one could have gotten in here without my knowing it."

"Captain ordered another sweep, ma'am," Lonnie said, struggling to keep the anger out of his voice. He added, "I'm just doing my job."

"Alright." A sigh. "I'll be there in a moment."

Tick. Tick.

A moment lasted three minutes, and by the end of it, Lonnie was seething. He considered kicking the doors in or breaking out the glass and crawling through the hole before killing anyone that got between him and the children waiting in the rooms beyond. It wasn't as if the IDU was a psychiatric or prisoner holding unit. Locking it was more a precaution against visitors wandering in and spreading contagions around the ward than keeping dangerous patients in. All his preparations would be for naught if he didn't get inside quickly.

He'd insinuated himself at the Mt. Nasak facility seven years before, patiently waiting for the vermin there to create the instrument of their own destruction, to then understand that instrument, and decide how best to distribute it. In the end, he'd decided it should be these children.

As had been done time and time again, generation after generation, the most vulnerable and innocent of a population had been cast aside. Their needs ignored in favor of those who sought stability, progress, and cold, hard cash.

Lonnie had watched for three years as the world changed in the wake of COVID-19. At the outset, the virus had targeted the elderly and adults with preexisting medical conditions. At that time, governments worldwide had told the people there was little, if anything, to fear. Only when the virus moved on to working adults, those with no reason to succumb to what amounted to a common respiratory illness known to exist since 1965 that had only recently managed to jump the animal/human barrier, did governments react with mask mandates, mandatory lockdowns, and social distancing guidelines.

Lonnie had watched the television accounts of mass panic, terror, and the rising death tolls with glee. Unfortunately, though it had mutated several times and wiped-out portions of the population, largely in third world countries, the virus had lacked the potency to do so quickly enough to offset humanity's irritating ability to rally behind a cause. Vaccines had been developed. Distributed. Dispensed. Lockdowns had ended. Masks, once required anywhere beyond your front door, were no longer required. Not because the threat had passed, Lonnie surmised, but because all those working adults needed to get back to work. Because their governments, and those that pulled *their* strings, were losing billions of dollars.

Now that the virus had mutated to target children specifically, no one cared. There was a vaccine for those over the age of five, though its effectiveness was still unknown, but no mask mandates, no lockdowns, few guidelines. Once again, society had left its children defenseless. Either to defeat the virus and live to become so-called productive members of society, or to succumb and die on their own.

It was fitting, therefore, that the virus be introduced here, amongst the cast offs in New Orleans, where, despite the rain, the forecast was for temperatures to remain in the low one-hundreds for the next two days. He didn't think the ambient temperature would be a factor once the toxin got going but, better safe than sorry.

"And the children shall lead them," he misquoted, "to their own demise."

Tick. Tick.

A nurse in her mid-fifties wearing a mask, cap, and gown over blue scrubs finally entered Lonnie's field of vision. She might have weighed three-hundred pounds, and walked as if every step were an inconvenience, the task of pushing the button that activated the door a burden.

"Thanks," Lonnie said, offering her a thousand-watt smile as the doors whooshed open before him.

"Uh-huh," she said, noncommittally.

Lonnie started past her, and she put a meaty hand on his shoulder. It felt like spiders crawling on his skin.

"Hold it, cowboy," she said.

TICK. TICK.

"You can't go in dressed like that. Do you have any idea how many pathogens you're carrying around? How sick these kids are?" She gestured at the cart against the wall. "You gotta be masked, gloved, suited, and booted before you go in there. And if you find it necessary to enter any of the rooms, which you shouldn't, you need to change it all again. Before, and after."

Shoot her! a voice screamed in Lonnie's mind. *Shoot the fat bitch and get on with it! TICK FUCKING TICK!*

"Yes, of course," Lonnie responded mildly. As much as he would have liked to gun the woman down where she stood, perhaps putting a round or two in the mask covering that nagging mouth for good measure, it would only serve as an impediment, summoning other nurses or doctors assigned to this unit. And likely more cops from other units on this floor. Even with a locked door between them he doubted it would take long for them to gain entry. He moved to the cart and opened the top drawer, removing a hairnet from the assortment within.

The nurse grunted in satisfaction. "I'll be at the duty desk around the corner if you need anything," she stated in a tone that clearly said

Don't need anything. She then plodded back in the direction she'd come from.

Lonnie slipped the net over his hair and moved on to the next drawer. It was full of yellow gowns.

"Thank you," he said to the empty air where she'd been standing.

He was going to need a syringe.

Tick Tick.

UNBELIEVABLE, Arianna thought as she and Jack moved down a gently curving hallway that would bring them back to the front of the building. They weren't quite running. It took precious seconds to check doorways, waiting areas, and the corridor ahead for police, visitors, and hospital staff. The corridor was particularly worrisome because though the curvature was slight, anyone could come around it at any moment. But they weren't walking along leisurely, either. Arianna thought of it as a tactical jog.

Their caution was unwarranted, however, as there was no one about. No doctors or nurses hustling here and there, dispensing medicines, pushing carts from point A to point B, or even taking a break from the routine of their day. No patients or visitors walked the halls or waited in uncomfortable chairs, watching television with the volume blaring as they always seemed to do in hospital waiting rooms. Most distressing, no police were standing guard or on sweeps, keeping an eye out for the terrorists that were supposed to be launching an attack against the building.

She'd participated in no less than a dozen domestic terrorism drills during her career with the FBI and had never experienced a scenario this grim. A failure of this magnitude. At the very least, every elevator, stairwell, and doorway on every floor should have been covered by a team of two officers, with an additional two roaming teams per floor.

Thus far, she and Jack had crossed the entirety of the basement, boarded an elevator and ridden it four floors, before traversing this hallway, completely unobserved, unmolested, and without challenge. Early in her Quantico days, she'd dated a fellow student who'd been an avid fan of horror movies. She had no taste for such films. Had, in fact, lived enough horror for one lifetime, thank you very much. But she'd genuinely enjoyed the young man's company and had agreed to view what he referred to as *classic* horror, on VHS no less, in his dorm room one evening.

The plot was laughable. A masked psychopath was stalking a young woman through a hospital late at night, killing anyone who got in his way. The killer had been creepy enough, and Arianna had found the soundtrack brilliant, but in typical 80's slasher film fashion the movie had been more blood and gore than plot, the premise ridiculous. No hospital operated with a mere three nurses, one doctor, two EMT's, and a single, overweight and lonely—and certainly doomed—security guard on hand. Not even through the darkest hours of the morning.

It just didn't happen.

Yet here they were, swiftly moving along a deserted corridor in a functioning hospital that should have been crawling with not only medical personnel and civilians, but federal agents and police officers as well.

Only this time *they* were stalking the masked man. And he'd come not just for one victim, but for the entire world.

LONNIE SKETCHED A WAVE at the man and three women, one of them the Large Marge who had let him onto the unit, as he passed the duty station. All wore the prerequisite yellow gowns and masks and, save the male nurse who waved back noncommittally, uniformly ignored him. Their faces were glued to monitors and computer screens relaying information from the patient rooms to the desk. Lonnie supposed the setup minimized the need for interaction and reduced the potential of spreading contagions.

He whistled.

Hi-ho. Hi-ho. It's off to work I go.

The unit was shaped like a flat-bottomed teardrop. He'd entered near the top and passed a large storage area before passing the duty station on the left. The bottom of the area housed bathrooms, another storage area, and a fire door leading to a hallway outside.

There were eight patient suites on each side, all within view of the duty station, each with large observation windows and glass doors revealing one bed, various monitors, ventilators, and IV infusion pumps. Each held a single small sleeping or unconscious form, most breathing with the assistance of the machines. Each suite also had a red sharps disposal box complete with biohazard labels attached to the wall. The boxes would be full of used syringes. It would be a small, if potentially noisy matter, to break one open to get to the needles inside.

None of the rooms had windows facing the outside of the building. The air from the rooms was drawn out, passed through a scrubber housing a large number of increasingly finer HEPA filters, then recirculated throughout the unit and the rest of the building. This posed no problem whatsoever. While some of the GT-16 would be lost to the filters once it mutated to an airborne state, enough of the genotoxin would attach itself to the clothing and persons of those attending the patients to spread it beyond the reach of the scrubbers.

Lonnie passed the bathrooms and custodian's closet and began his way back up the opposite side of the teardrop, scanning each room as if looking for anything inappropriate or out of place. His real focus was on the monitors displaying vital signs. Pulse, breathing, oxygen saturation, blood pressure. And body temperature. Of the nine suites he'd scanned so far, six of the patients had temperatures within the optimal range.

He was pleased to find a nurse in the next suite, her back to him, punching buttons on a computer-controlled infusion machine connected to a nine- or ten-year-old boy through a Peripherally Inserted Central Catheter in his upper arm. His nose and cheeks were covered in small bruises, scrapes, and surgical tape, the result of the barbaric looking headpiece the likes of which were never shown on any television or film screen, no matter how realistic the drama, necessary to hold a breathing tube steady in his throat. She'd placed a tray on the bed beside him containing an empty IV bag, two injection vials, and several syringes. The boy was unconscious. She could have placed the tray directly on his face and he'd have been none the wiser. A glance at the monitor displaying his vitals revealed that his body temperature was one-hundred and three degrees.

Jackpot.

Lonnie looked towards the duty station to see if he was being observed. He needn't have bothered. None of the four nurses was looking in his direction.

He opened the door and stepped inside.

Confrontation

"Here," Jack said, turning left down a hallway. Arianna followed, noting the red sign with an arrow pointing them in the same direction.

They reached a set of double doors informing them their destination lay beyond. Jack pushed on the right-hand side. Nothing. Tried the left with the same result.

Arianna looked around, noted the keypad, speaker, and call button. Jack peered through the glass and saw the door release button on the other side.

"It's a locked ward," Arianna told him. "We'll have to ring for the nurse unless your friends on high gave you the code."

"I have my own code," Jack said.

He shot her a wicked smile, raised his foot and kicked in the doors.

The electromagnetic seal holding the double doors closed broke under the weight of Jack's boot and the doors crashed inwards. The left-hand door rebounded off the wall. A startled cry of "What the hell?" came from ahead and off to the left.

"*Shit*, Jack," Arianna hissed. "We're not even sure if he's in there! Now the whole damn hospital knows we're here."

"He's in there," Jack said, moving forward. A sound like static in his head had been increasing since they'd gotten off the elevator. In lieu of any other signs, he'd been using it like a mental compass. A sort of built-in mass murderer detector.

Arianna paced him until they reached the duty desk and came face to face with four astonished nurses who all began to talk at once.

"You can't come in here dressed like that! You need a gown and mask!"

"Did you just break the damn door?"

"Christ, is that a gun??"

"I'm calling security!"

"Special Agent Arianna Price. FBI." Arianna said. She pulled out her badge and the voices cut off. "Has anyone come on the ward in the past few minutes? A police officer? A doctor you're not familiar with?"

"I let an officer in no more than five minutes ago," a heavyset nurse, older than the others and obviously in charge, said. "He was down by the bathrooms last I saw of him."

She turned and looked down the empty hall.

"Dammit," she said, "I told him he didn't need to go into the rooms."

"Probably found Annie," the male nurse opined. "Decided to chat her up a bit."

Jack was already on the move. He checked the suites on the left side of the unit as Arianna turned and took the suites behind her, hurriedly looking into each, scanning for any sign of the man in yellow.

"Hey," the male nurse asked. "Isn't that the name the police gave us? Price?"

"The cops are looking for a couple," a nurse with close cropped purple hair, barely visible beneath the cap she wore, spoke over him. "A white guy and an African American woman posing as an FBI agent."

"Shit," said the other.

"Call security," the charge nurse said, before picking up the intercom and issuing a Code Silver in the Infectious Disease Unit.

THE NURSE IN ROOM 410 heard the door open behind her. The doors up here made a funny sucking sound when they opened, positive pressure forcing air into a negative space. A slight breeze pushed past her, and she turned to see who had come in.

Lonnie plunged the knife into her left eye before she could offer a welcoming smile. She jerked once, twice. Tremors ran up Lonnie's arm as her nervous system tried to sort out the erratic signals. Then her legs gave out. She made a sound in her throat that might have been *hoof*, or *woof*, but was likely surprised air exiting her lungs as her optic nerve and temporal lobe were destroyed. She crumpled to the floor. Lonnie let the knife fall with her. He wouldn't need it again.

He helped himself to the syringes, now whistling *doo-dah, doo-dah.* Jammed three into the pocket beneath the gown and stripped one from its package. He removed the Li-Ion battery *cum* heater from the other pants pocket, popped open the false port, and pushed the needle inside. He drew out a half milliliter of liquid death, then bent to the picc line in the boy's arm. Four lines from the infuser merged with a catheter just above the boy's elbow. Lonnie located the central port and began to insert the needle.

The ticking, which had become a steady *tickatickaticka* since he'd entered the ward doubled, trebled, then shrieked in his ears like feedback from a microphone in an empty auditorium. Or the shriek of a bird of prey.

He winced at the sound. *Cringed.* The syringe slipped from his fingers, dangled from the port momentarily, then fell off the bed, bouncing twice and spilling its contents on the floor.

Lonnie spat out an epithet and became aware of someone standing in the open doorway behind him.

JACK TOOK AIM FROM the hallway. One shot and this was over. He could flee the scene through the fire door thirty feet to his right, find his way out of the building, and disappear into the night. He didn't know whether Arianna would flee with him or not. To spare herself the arrest and trial that were sure to follow, the destruction of her reputation and career, the indignity of being punished for actions and events that were beyond her control. From what little he knew of her she'd likely stay to face the consequences. If only to be free of him.

Would she spin some delicate web of lies and deceit to explain away the events of the last two days? Or would she tell the truth as she knew it and damn the outrage and disbelief that truth yielded? Probably the latter. His sense was that she was too proud, too noble, for anything less.

Jack's finger tightened on the trigger, then he noticed the glass.

It was heavier than your average pane of glass, at least a half-inch thick and reinforced with wire. It made sense, he thought, as he realized the suites in this unit were probably designed to sustain negative air pressure, thus keeping any contagions present confined to that particular room.

A high caliber weapon like his .44 would be little affected by the 3/32nds of an inch thick glass in a standard pane, but this glass, no doubt made up of several standard sheets with polyvinyl butyral sandwiched in between for additional strength, could send even a large caliber round spinning off in any direction. It was far more likely to be deflected into a wall, a monitor, or into the body of the boy lying unconscious on the bed than to end up in his quarry's head.

Instead of firing, Jack pulled open the door.

There was a soft, sucking sound and air rushed past Jack and into the room.

The man inside winced. *Cringed.* The syringe slipped from his fingers, dangled from the tubing in the boys' arm momentarily, then fell off the bed. It bounced twice before its contents spilled out onto the floor.

A wave of static burst over Jack with the roar of a vile and venomous creature. His vision went white. He shook his head to clear it and saw the man turning, as if in slow motion. Another flash of white, a roar of sound, as if lightning had struck somewhere inside the room. The man was still there, highlighted on that field of pure white light, but behind his face and body—*beneath it? Superimposed over it?* —was the image of a lizard, a giant mechanical tail thrashing behind. Jack thought the image to be common objects in the room. The bed, the monitors, IV and EKG lines trailing between the boy and the machines. His brain was mashing them all together and turning them into a grand hallucination as it tried to interpret the dissonant signals roaring through his head.

His heart knew he had glimpsed the man's true form. His genuine nature. A monster. A beast. The demon from Arianna's vision.

As his own vision cleared, he noticed his quarry gaping at him. He looked as if he were about to scream. As if he'd something more terrifying than Jack had. *Another demon, perhaps?* Jack wondered. *An angel?* Both might be equally terrifying to this man.

Then the man bent at the waist and charged.

ARIANNA HEARD THE *Code Silver* go out over the intercom. A large number of states had mandated uniform coding systems for all hospitals within their borders. *Red* for Fire. *Blue* for medical emergencies or cardiac arrest. *Yellow* for disasters. While there was no national standard for the coding as of yet—*Pink* meant an infant abduction in Louisiana, while in Ohio it meant a child medical emergency—most systems were similar. *Code Black* universally stood for a bomb threat. *Code Silver* meant there was an active shooter or a hostage situation.

It also meant that the unit would soon be overrun by law enforcement.

She was hurrying past the rooms on her side of the teardrop, quickly scanning each while also tracking Jack's progress when she saw him stop outside one of the suites. He raised his weapon and took aim. She saw the man in the suite through the glass—it was the man from her vision, she had no doubt—and was mystified when Jack lowered his weapon, opened the door, and stepped into the room. He stopped inside. Paused.

He has the shot, she thought, confused. *Why doesn't he take the shot?*

Her confusion vanished when, behind her, two NOPD officers rushed through the doors and onto the unit. They were accompanied by a man in a dark suit and tie that had to be a federal agent. All three had their weapons out.

Reluctant to do so but without hesitation, Arianna spun on her heels, pointed her weapon at the trio and shouted: "Freeze!"

Take the damn shot, Jack!

The two uniformed officers faltered briefly, their eyes widening in response to the gun pointed at them, and half lowered their weapons before remembering they were supposed to be the ones in authority. The Fed, to his credit, didn't waver. "Don't move, Agent Price!" he called out, and continued to advance, his weapon high, body sideways to make as small a target of himself as possible.

Until the charge nurse danced out from behind the desk, waving her arms and shouting: "Don't shoot, *assholes*! There's kids in here!"

"Goddammit!" The agent muttered, trying to push the nurse aside, or at least away from his service pistol so that he could reacquire his target. The uniformed officer closest to the wall began bouncing his weapon back and forth between Arianna and the charge nurse, trying to decide which was the threat. The third had pointed his at the ceiling, a profound look of uncertainty on his face. He looked for all the world as if he wanted to be somewhere else.

You and me both, Arianna thought, then shifted her attention back to Jack just as he and the man in yellow sailed backwards through the door of suite 410 like a linebacker tackling a quarterback in the Super Bowl. They hit the floor three feet outside the open door, the air driven out of Jack's lungs with a *whoof!* The .44 flew out of his hand, bounced once, then spun across the floor before coming to rest at Arianna's feet.

The man in yellow scrambled up first, oblivious to the ongoing confusion, now added to by his own surprising appearance in the hallway. He screamed in Jack's face, a cry of outrage and hatred, then bounded to his feet and ran for the far end of the unit. An alarm blared as he straight-armed the fire door and fled into the corridor beyond.

Jack recovered quickly. He noted the momentary chaos taking place at the duty desk—two of the three remaining nurses had joined in the yelling, demanding the officers holster their weapons, *there are children here for chrissakes!,* while the fourth spoke rapidly into a phone. Jack rolled over twice, seized the fallen .44, and fired three rounds into the ceiling in rapid succession.

The noise, like cannons fired in a closet, was deafening.

The Fed ducked. The cops ducked. The nurses all hit the floor simultaneously, like puppets with their strings cut. It might have been funny if not for the seriousness of the situation.

Jack bounced into a crouch, his eyes on two more cops that were running onto the unit, nodded at Arianna—*Go!*—then turned and followed before any of the cops could regain their senses.

Arianna slammed through the fire door with Jack hot on her heels. She looked around for something to block it with. A gurney. A med cart. Anything. But found herself in an empty hallway save a deserted wheelchair in one corner. Jack crashed through the door behind her, slammed it behind them, and leaned against it. To the left was a short corridor fronting a junction that would take them back to the service elevator. To the right lay the broad, sweeping front of the building and the fourth-floor reception area. Heavy footfalls converged on their location from that direction.

Arianna cast Jack a desperate look: *What now?*

LONNIE'S RAGE WAS SO exquisite it felt like a white-hot dagger piercing his skull. He wanted to scream. He wanted to lash out at everything and everyone around him. He wanted to do the electric boogaloo on the graves of every last man, woman, and child in existence.

Instead, he ran, searching for a stairwell or elevator, anything that offered access to the lower floors where he would find an exit. He buried the raw emotion beneath a façade of calm, as he'd buried his true emotions, his true identity and ego, his entire life.

Forward motion was the key. Wallowing in regret and self-pity was as paralyzing as it was unproductive. It immobilized the intellect, leading to ennui and apathy. It murdered reason. No one who had ever achieved their grand destiny had done so under the mantle of irrationality.

He stripped off the cap and mask as he ran. The gloves, the gown, and booties. He almost tripped and fell face first to the floor as he struggled the left one from his loafer. And wouldn't that have been to his pursuers liking? You betcha!

And just who the fuck had that been, anyway?

The police weren't in the building because of him. Of that he was certain. Otherwise, he'd have never made it past the busy-body Captain in the lobby, let alone all the way to the fourth floor. So, who the hell was the Steve McQueen type in the Infectious Disease Unit? An assassin? Sent by those who governed the Mt. Nasak facility? That didn't track. Lone hit men were fine for people who'd seen too much. Knew too much. Hadn't paid a debt or had welshed on a deal. For someone they knew for certain had the ability to wipe out the human race, they'd have sent a squad if not an entire regiment.

So, who the hell had sent Steve-O? He and the black woman—he'd never forget her gaping mouth and wide eyes as he'd tackled Big Steve, then screamed in his face before fleeing—had been the focus of the cops' attention. If the fat quim running the ward hadn't interfered, they'd likely be in custody or dead right now, and not in his wake. *Their* focus, however, had been on *him*. It was ridiculous to think of it as a coincidence. That the pair had just happened to be on the fourth floor when he was, in the same suite he was in, up to whatever the hell they were up to.

They'd been there for him. To *stop* him. Which meant that someone out there knew of his plans and had sent them.

Who could know? he contemplated. *Who could possibly know?*

It was irrelevant, he decided. Confusion was as debilitating as anger. His focus now had to be on shaking his pursuers and escaping the building. He could mull over the perplexities and questions—and let his anger build to a sweltering boil—later. After he'd found refuge.

Because all was not yet lost.

Lonnie neared the end of the corridor and slowed as he spied what he'd been looking for: a door. It faced a stairwell, offset slightly from the corner of the building, with a service elevator, doors invitingly open, just a few feet beyond. At the same moment he heard voices coming from around the opposite corner. Hard footfalls, at least two pairs. He slowed further, to a casual walk, wiped sweat from his brow and willed his heartrate lower. He'd appear to them as nothing more than another police officer patrolling the halls, a little excited by all the commotion but otherwise harmless.

He eased his hand down over the butt of his Glock.

Inferno

Jack nearly lost his footing as the fire door was hit bodily from the other side. The thin green carpet underfoot saved him, offering him more traction than polished linoleum offered the police officers on the other side. Still, he wouldn't be able to hold the door for long. Multiple hands began knocking on the thick wood at his back while a voice yelled uselessly, "Open this damn door!" As if a fleeing suspect were likely to heed the order.

He spied a wheelchair in the corner.

He reached for it but came up several feet short. Arianna, either intuiting his intent or simply trusting him, quickly grabbed the frame of the chair and wheeled it closer. Jack bent as far as he could without losing leverage against the door, grabbed at the rigging supporting one footrest, pulled it free, then wedged it into the crack beneath the door.

"It'll hold," Jack said, "but not for long."

"Where to now?" Arianna asked. Rapid footfalls, louder, closer, came from their right.

"Away from that," Jack said, turning left towards the junction and breaking into a run.

"And our perp?" Arianna asked breathlessly.

As if in answer, gunfire erupted from the far end of the corridor.

Arianna, spurred on by the sound, took the lead.

Jack followed, easily outpaced by the younger woman. His heart pounded in his chest. His breathing was labored. *What's this?* he thought, realizing he was winded. He couldn't recall a time he'd ever felt this way. Fatigue, after being severely injured, sure. But this

251

feeling, like a depleted battery or a watch that has run down, never before.

He noted a discarded mask and a cast-off gown ahead, the sound of running footsteps behind. Their pursuers were slowing. Falling back. No doubt proceeding more cautiously than Jack and Arianna dared.

As he ran, Arianna easily overtaking and passing him, Jack contemplated what had happened when he encountered their target in room 410.

There had been a flash of bright white light, momentarily blinding in its intensity, a rocking crescendo like thunder. An afterimage of the man in yellow superimposed over—*something*—had bloomed before his eyes. Being in proximity to his quarry had felt like two bare, high-voltage lines of opposing polarity crossing. Overloading. Then it was gone. The noise. The light. The sound. Even the static, as if it had never been there in the first place. Like a power surge had destroyed a crucial circuit. He sensed an empty spot in his mind, as if someone had scooped out a vital component. A hole in his chest, as if part of his heart had withered and died. To his dismay he sensed the surge, the overload, whatever it had been, had also taken his connection with whatever force guided him with it.

Had taken *her* with it.

She's gone, he thought. *Completely, irrevocably, gone.*

He felt a sense of loss so great that his mind struggled for words to convey it.

Arianna entered the second junction and stopped. Jack caught up, surveying the carnage.

Two officers, SWAT emblazoned across their vests, lay dead on the floor. Each had a neat hole in his forehead, a second in their throats. Both bore a look of surprise, as if death had worn a friendly face when it came for them. The body nearest the elevator was in a seated position. Blood trailed down the wall behind him where he'd been standing when the pair had been ambushed. His MP5K was missing and several pouches on his vest and duty belt were open, as if they'd been rifled.

"He's bolstered his firepower," Jack pointed out.

The service elevator door was closed. Old gears ground and clanked in the shaft as the car moved downward. Footfalls, stealthy and quick, came from behind. Arianna turned to Jack, a mixture of grief and rage on her face.

"I've never wanted to kill anyone," she said. "I have. Twice. Both in the line of duty, and both in defense of others. I believe that every perpetrator, no matter their offense, deserves to be brought to justice. Judged by a jury of their peers. Sentenced by a duly elected official. Still, these deaths weigh on me.

"This man," she continued, "is the exception. I won't mourn this bastard. Won't even lose a night's sleep. He doesn't leave this place alive. Do you understand me?"

Jack nodded in agreement, but she'd already turned her attention back to the dead.

OUT! OUT! OUT! Lonnie's mind screamed as the elevator floor bucked and recoiled beneath his feet.

The heater that kept the GT-16 alive would soon fail, if it hadn't already. The toxin would die. He felt a brief stab of bitterness at the thought but pushed it aside as he attempted to pull the safety pin from a flashbang he'd liberated from the body of one of the cops upstairs. It was harder than it looked on TV and in the movies. The damn thing was bent over and ridged, and he had to apply considerable force to pull it free from the striker lever, or spoon, assembly. So much force, in fact, that he almost released the spoon along with the pin, and wouldn't that have been just the icing on the cake?

Securing the grenade against his chest, striker lever firmly against the primer assembly, he waited for the elevator car to settle on the basement sublevel.

Just as DNA remains in a cell after death, the building blocks for GT-16 would remain in the solution left in his improvised heater. Much as the toxin itself replicated and thrived in the dead cells of its host, it too could be replicated from the inert material. It would take time to find a suitable lab in which to do so. He'd shit the bed, so to speak, here in the states. Once the bigwigs running the Alaska operation found out what he'd done, if they hadn't already, he'd be the most wanted man in the country. Albeit quietly. He'd find no safe harbor within U.S. borders. But there was no end to the number of foreign governments who would be interested in the genotoxin. And would happily shelter him in secret, funding his project, while never suspecting his true motives.

Years of research and development would follow. Perhaps decades. But it could be done. He'd see to it personally. In retrospect, he knew, he'd view the current fuckarow as a small delay. A minor stone placed in his path on the road to destiny, easily sidestepped, effortlessly surmounted.

But before any of that could happen, he needed to find his way out of the building. Far away from pursuers.

The elevator ground to a halt.

"THIS WAY," JACK URGED, turning to the stairwell. He eased the door open. He cleared the doorway quickly before moving on to the landing. He then looked up, saw nothing but an empty set of stairs leading to the roof, the door closed tightly against the storm, then down. The stairwell was clear. He doublechecked their path out of habit, then descended, clearing the next landing, stairwell, and door as they proceeded.

Their footfalls echoed back at them from the steel risers. They froze and hugged the wall on three when a door opened and closed on the first floor. No one entered the stairwell.

A door crashed opened overhead as they traversed the first-floor landing. Voices and ringing steel risers clamored as law enforcement flooded the stairwell. Arianna paused at the door to that level, shot Jack a look:

Did he get off here? Or did he go all the way?

A loud thud shook the floor beneath their feet, accompanied by a flash of light muted by layers of concrete and steel. *Flashbang,* Arianna thought angrily. *Looted from the dead cop upstairs.* Automatic gunfire followed.

No longer hugging the walls out of caution, Jack took the remaining flight three stairs at a time and yanked the door to the loading dock open. Arianna followed as voices shouted from above:

"Hey, don't move!"

"Agent Price, Freeze!"

Jack nodded to her and eased to the left, between the doorframe and a cart of oxygen cylinders. Arianna let the door close softly behind her, keeping her back tight against the jamb. Another barrier for the agents descending from above, another obstacle to be cleared before they could safely proceed.

There was a scorch mark on the floor in front of them. Arianna thought it likely the safety door on the service elevator had been raised a few inches and the flashbang tossed out. The resulting explosion would have incapacitated anyone within twenty yards. Any sane and rational person would have then fled. Their perp, however, had then raised the door fully, stepped out of the elevator, and began firing. The bodies of three of New Orleans finest and one federal agent were ranged in a rough semi-circle on the concrete floor. The officers were all dead or unconscious. She could make out multiple gunshot wounds on their torsos, legs, and heads. The FBI agent moaned softly and appeared to stare into her eyes. It was unlikely he saw anything. As close to the flashbang as he'd been when it detonated, he was undoubtedly still blind. A bubble of blood formed, then popped on his lips. More ran down his chin. He'd been shot in the face, the bullet passing through his jaw and exiting somewhere near his spine.

Arianna's anger grew. The man had killed six LEO's—seven if the agents' wounds were as bad as she feared—in the course of one-half hour. God alone knew how many more he'd killed between here and wherever he'd come from.

Hazy smoke and the smell of cordite still hung in the air.

To their right was the empty elevator and an equally empty corridor. The corridor wouldn't remain empty for long, Arianna thought, not with the agents in the stairwell relaying their position to anyone with a radio. Which would be everyone with a gun. Straight ahead, across the loading dock, was another corridor. The one they'd traversed not fifteen minutes before. It was also empty. No sign of law enforcement officers. No sign of the fleeing murderer.

To her left stood Jack, a tall rack of oxygen cylinders, and the outer wall. Jack surveyed the dead officers, the basement, and the corridor beyond.

Arianna thought furiously. The corridor to the right would take their perp deeper into the hospital. Straight ahead led back to the basement stairs, the maintenance hallway, and out of the hospital, to freedom. The risk of encountering more law enforcement officers along either route was the same, however, she felt the stairwell and narrow maintenance hallway, where the cops investigating the body in the utility closet would have to line up more or less single file in order to pass, would offer a fleeing fugitive, dressed as a cop and blending in, a slightly better chance of surviving another confrontation. She started to move past the door and onto the dock, but Jack grabbed her arm and pulled her back.

His eyes shifted left, beyond the oxygen tanks. She followed suit. A sound came from beyond the tanks. Soft but rapid, like someone dialing a phone number on an old touchtone phone. Then a meaty thud, like a fist striking concrete.

"Goddammit!" a voice shouted. *"A code? It takes a fucking code?"*

Arianna realized it was the logical place for the controls to an electrically powered set of roll-up doors. It was also logical that a hospital would want to limit the number of people with access to the dock and would install a lock on the controls. The angry shout was followed by the sound of hands repeatedly hitting the closest rollup door angrily, as a trapped and panicked bird beats the bars of a cage with its wings.

Jack didn't hesitate. He drew his gun and threw his weight against the cart. It rolled and its unsecured payload began falling haphazardly, one tank clanging against the concrete floor as its center of gravity shifted too far for it to remain upright. The handle of the cart hit the perp in the waist, pinning him briefly against the concrete wall before he turned and, an expression of pure fury on his face, shoved it back violently. More cylinders fell.

The cart rolled into Jack's shin just as he fired.

The first round drove a hole in one of the cylinders. Arianna winced but didn't falter as she tried to take aim around Jack's body.

Oxygen cylinders don't explode when shot with a gun, the ending to Steven Spielberg's epic shark movie notwithstanding. The gas within the cylinder *does* exit violently through the hole, however, and the cylinder spun off the cart, taking more with it before hitting the floor where it spun in circles. The cylinder nearest Jack fell into his wrist as he fired his second shot, deflecting his aim and sending the round into one of the lines overhead. The line burst open, flooding the room with the stench of sulfur.

Jack's third shot came as he moved backwards and the man turned to the right, hopping over falling cylinders and trying to extricate himself from the jumble of the cart and its tumbling payload. The soft core .44 slug took off the tip of his nose before spanging off the concrete wall behind him. He screamed in pain, like an animal caught in a trap.

Jack pulled the trigger a fourth time. The killing shot.

The hammer clicked uselessly against a spent cylinder. There hadn't been time to reload after firing the first three rounds upstairs.

The man screamed again, his face a bloody, skeletal mask. He turned towards them, his eyes wide in surprise and recognition. He *shrieked*. The shriek became a howl that became an inhuman bellow of rage that could have come from no mortal vocal cords.

Arianna tried to line up a shot but couldn't. Not without firing through Jack. She was pinned between him and the closed door, could feel his body pushing her backwards as well as the impact of officers trying to force the thick steel barrier open from the other side, but was helpless to move otherwise. She watched the gunman raise the MP5K. Thought of the pure oxygen spewing from the damaged cylinder and the odor of rotten eggs filling the basement. She screamed:

"*No!*"

The man's finger tightened on the trigger and Arianna realized Jack had intentionally moved in front of her, directly into the line of fire, in an attempt to save her life.

She knew he needn't have bothered.

Her mind registered four rounds punching into him from bottom to top on a slight diagonal, puncturing his leg, liver, and heart. By the time the fourth round hit him in the cheek, spattering her face with his blood and bits of bone as it exited his spine, the previous rounds had already ignited the punctured gas line overhead.

Arianna gasped as a ball of white incandescence bloomed in front the perpetrator, moved upwards, then divided in two. The two points reddened oddly. Like two giant, glittering eyes staring at her with malice, before being consumed.

The loading dock became a white-hot inferno.

After

F rom the Times-Picayune, New Orleans
June 17th, 2023

MANHUNT ENDS IN EXPLOSION AT CHILDREN'S HOSPITAL – 11 DEAD

A nationwide manhunt conducted by the FBI in conjunction with local authorities ended in tragedy last evening as a rogue federal agent and an unknown accomplice set off an explosion inside the New Orleans Children's Hospital located on Hank Aaron Boulevard.

The former agent, a twenty-year veteran of the FBI's Behavioral Analysis Unit, identified as Arianna Mishelle Price, was wanted for questioning in connection to the slaying of five fellow agents in an abandoned parking garage in Boston, Massachusetts. The agents had been investigating the hijacking and abduction of twenty-seven children from an elementary school bus in connection to the attempted bombing of a local bank by the known terrorist organization *Freiheit Fur Immer* when they were gunned down by persons unknown. The suspected leader of the terrorist group, Timothy Coleman, was also killed. According to witnesses, Ms. Price then fled

261

the scene in the company of an unidentified male after the shooting.

The pair was then traced to the Children's Hospital in New Orleans where they murdered a nurse and three New Orleans police officers before being cornered by members of law enforcement.

Howard Sutherland, Director of the FBI, had this to say: "...[they] chose to detonate an incendiary device rather than surrender. The incendiary device caused damage to a gas line and several oxygen supply canisters that were temporarily being stored in the area, which resulted in an explosion that not only killed both perpetrators, but three more police officers, a federal agent, and an unknown hospital employee."

Witnesses said the explosion felt like a giant fist striking the building.

"We were incredibly lucky," Wayne Newsome, Chief Administrator at Children's Hospital said. "We recently installed a new emergency cutoff system for the gas lines that isolates certain areas when it senses a leak or dangerously high temperatures. Without that system in place, the entire hospital could have gone up and we'd be dealing with hundreds of casualties, most of them children."

Mr. Newsome also revealed that damages to the building are estimated to be in excess of four million dollars.

The investigation into what prompted the actions of Ms. Price and her accomplice, and what their connection to *Freiheit Fur Immer* may be, is still under investigation. Mike Conlon, Director of

- Continued on page 8 –

"BULLSHIT!" James Austin seethed. He pushed the newspaper away in disgust. It hit his coffee cup, sloshing hot liquid onto the tabletop. He absently wiped it away before it could spread further.

He sat in the dining room of the house he shared with his wife, Emily. Late afternoon sunlight shone through the windows, marching its way up the walls into evening. He was still wearing his pajamas and a robe. Unshaven, his hair unkempt, teeth unbrushed. After the events in Boston and New Orleans he'd been *advised* to take the six weeks of bereavement leave available to him. It hadn't been an order, but it had been made clear that it was to his benefit—and the furtherance of his career—to do so.

"What's bullshit?" his wife asked from across the dining room table. She was slowly munching on a piece of dry toast. Eight years they'd been married, and he still couldn't understand how she could eat toast without butter or jam.

"They're putting everything on Ari," he said. He ran his hands through his hair in frustration. "The deaths. The explosion. No way she killed a nurse or had a hand in the murders of those other cops."

"How can you be so certain?"

"Fifteen years, that's how," he said acidly. "Fifteen years of working together, investigating together. Hell, practically living together for weeks on end. Playing poker in our downtime or shooting pool. Weekend parties. Me, her, Decker, the entire unit.

You knew her. Spent time with her. Do you think she was capable of that? Conspiring with terrorists? Killing Matt and the others? Or Nurses and cops? *Blowing up a building full of kids, for chrissakes?*"

"I don't know, Jimmy," she said carefully. "She was quiet a lot. Withdrawn."

He said nothing. Just glared at her over the table and the copy of *Vanity Fair* she was reading.

"Can you ever really know anyone?" she asked.

He took a deep breath and slowly let it out, dispelling his misplaced anger. He had no cause to be exasperated with his wife. She had no knowledge of his conversation with Ari before her death. Knew nothing of her assertion that she was in the company of her long sought-after Unsub, or that they were pursuing a man possessing a biological weapon. He'd passed the information on to his superiors with the foreknowledge that the claim would likely be discounted out of hand. A smokescreen thrown up by fleeing criminals in the hopes of buying themselves more time. And Christ, who would believe it anyway? He wasn't sure he believed it himself.

But he'd believed in his coworker and friend.

There'd been no mention of a third perpetrator in the Times-Picayune article. Nor in any of the other articles about the incident that he'd read that morning. The deaths and the explosion were being laid solely at the feet of Arianna and her 'unknown accomplice.' If the FBI were taking the report seriously at all, they weren't going public with it. And that, he supposed, was par for the course for the FBI.

"The funerals are tomorrow?" Emily asked.

"Yes," he answered, thinking of his friends and what they would think of it. Five simultaneous funerals. Full honors. Entire lives reduced to stars on a wall.

"I'll get your suit ready. And that black dress I wore to my dad's wake. Do you think it's too short?"

"No."

There would be no memorial service for Arianna Price. No honor guard, nor heartfelt eulogy from Howard Sutherland. No pipe and drum corps or helicopter flyover. No one would present a flag to her loved ones.

And who would there be to take it, anyway? James wondered. To his knowledge she had no living relatives. *Her cat?*

She'd be buried in her family plot, if there was one. In lieu of that, a poorly marked grave. Forever branded a criminal. A *traitor.* Jimmy couldn't fathom such a thing.

He remembered a conversation he'd had with Dan Munoz, the FBI's on-scene forensic examiner, late last evening while wrapping up his gear in Boston. *Before* the conversation with FBI Assistant Deputy Director Laura Taylor. Before it was *suggested* he have no contact with anyone in the Bureau while on leave.

"Ballistics won't be back for a week," Dan had said, his cellphone crackling with distance and interference from the storm winding down over New Orleans. "But I've made my preliminary assessment. It looks like the gunfire started near the stairwell, where Agent Price and the unknown subject were found. One of the SWAT guys must have turned and got off a burst before the dock went up. The unsub was between your agent and the officer, shielding her. He took the rounds but heat and concussion from the blast killed her anyway. I'm sorry, Jimmy. But it looks like your agent was neck deep in it."

"Thanks, Dan," he'd said, disappointed with what the assessment meant.

"There is one funny thing, though," Dan continued. "Blast patterns indicate that the initial explosion originated in the middle of the room and radiated outward from there. If agent Price and her accomplice set off an explosive device that ruptured the gas line in turn, you'd expect to see a completely different blast pattern."

"What does that mean?" Jimmy asked.

"I don't know. Maybe nothing. And it's a tough scene, what with all the damage. The roof's completely gone and the rain's washed away a lot of the evidence. They're just lucky the loading dock is an external structure. If it wasn't, there wouldn't be much left of this side of the building."

He'd thanked Dan for his time and hung up. Continued packing up his gear for the long, and largely empty, return flight to Quantico. But Dan's words had stuck with him.

If agent Price and her accomplice set off an explosive device that ruptured the gas line in turn, you'd expect to see a completely different blast pattern.

"I'm gonna go shower and shave," Jimmy told his wife, getting up and rounding the table before planting a kiss on her lips. She smiled. "Then maybe I'll get dressed and take you out to dinner. Feed you something besides dry toast."

She stuck her tongue out at him.

"Good," she said. "Get your mind off everything. You have six weeks off. Maybe you can get to some of things that need to be done around here."

He playfully returned the tongue gesture.

"Real mature," she joked.

He smiled and walked away, out through the living room and towards the stairs.

"And brush your teeth while you're at it," she called after him. "Your breath could stop a wolf in its tracks!"

Tippy, Emily's occasionally derpy two-year-old Great Dane bounded from the couch, demanding a head scratch before he continued. The big animal had no objections about his breath as he absentmindedly stroked her head.

Who was the 'unknown' hospital employee? he wondered as he took the stairs. *What were they doing on the loading dock in the middle of a lockdown? In the middle of a* firefight? *Just some hapless joe caught unawares? Or the man Ari tried to warn us about?*

He shook off the questions and set his mind to the evening ahead.

He showered and shaved, then brushed his teeth. Took Emily to dinner. Made love to her afterwards. Attended the funeral for his colleagues and friends the next day. He finished up Emily's *to do* list over the following weeks.

He tried to put the questions he had regarding Arianna's death out of his mind, but, like a relentless machine, his mind kept circling back to them.

Who was the unknown person on the loading dock? Why didn't the blast patterns match up with the official account of what had happened? Then, after he'd returned to duty assigned to a new unit and finally seen the ballistics reports out of New Orleans: *How could Ari die with her service weapon in her hand, having killed all those people, yet not have fired a single shot?*

It was four months before he saw the story he'd missed on June 18th. The news article that changed everything.

He'd been reviewing the growing digital archive he'd begun to collect concerning the incidents in Boston and New Orleans. Notes he'd taken. Photos he'd saved. Links to news articles he'd read, and more he'd meant to. All the while telling himself to forget about it. Move on. It was what it was.

It was a small article. A footnote, really. It had been placed at the bottom of page 14, sandwiched between ads for a prominent restaurant, *Dooky Chase's – since 1941!* and Banner Chevrolet, *The Banner Way...a better way!* Nevertheless, he mentally kicked himself for missing it. Oh sure, he'd attended a six-hour funeral and a three-hour wake that day. And had had a generally shitty evening thereafter. Had to adapt to a new team, a new position, and a new office after returning to duty, and had been kept busy with chores by Emily in the interim.

Those were pretty good excuses, as excuses go.

But to overlook a *WTF* article like that? And to not follow up on Ari's funeral arrangements? What the hell had he been thinking?

BODY OF SUSPECTED TERRORIST STOLEN FROM MORGUE

The body of a former FBI agent accused of domestic terrorism was stolen from the office of the Orleans Parish Coroner this morning.

Thirty-five-year-old Arianna Mishelle Price was killed during an alleged bombing attack on the New Orleans Children Hospital yesterday. The body was then transported to the Coroner's Office for forensic examination.

At approximately 3:00 a.m., a disturbance was reported in the building by Jacob Deschamps, the assistant on duty during the time of the robbery.

"There was this loud hum, see," Mr. Deschamps recounted. "Then a really bright light coming from the coolers. That's where we keep the bodies, but we call it the holding room. I was in the bathroom next door and could see it coming in around the jamb like it was alive. Like it was looking for something."

Further investigation of the holding facility revealed no source for the aberrant light or sound, but did reveal that the body of Ms. Price, previously locked in a drawer and awaiting transport to Quantico, Virginia for burial, was missing.

Further investigation is underway, but at this time, no evidence of the perpetrator or a motive has been found.

AFTER READING THE ARTICLE, James Austin began an off the books (one might say rogue) investigation into the events surrounding the death and disappearance of Arianna Price.

Nobody

The little bell above the door of Yaya's didn't ring out when the door opened. Which was strange Jete Deveraux thought, because it had made plenty of racket when he and Ernie had come through it not five minutes earlier. That had been just before Ernie had blown the old woman looking over the table of herbs, spices, and candles out of her shoes with the big ass .357 Magnum he carried when they were out looking to pull down some green.

It *had* opened, though. Because the woman now standing there hadn't been in the shop when they had entered.

Yaya's was one of New Orleans less distinguished voodoo and occult shops, distinguished being a relative term in a city littered with such shops the way towns in the mid-west are littered with antique stores. The way tourist traps on the east coast are littered with clam shacks. It wasn't as famous as similar shops on Bourbon Street, being a full block away on Dauphine and tucked between a botanical apothecary and an antique bookstore as it was. Nor was it as impressive. It boasted no occult museum or psychic reading room, as did the famous Marie Laveau's. No souvenirs or ostentatious costumes like those available at Boutique du Vampyre.

Yaya's was a practical shop that sold genuine herbs, potions, oils, powders, and other paraphernalia associated with the practice of magick and witchcraft. Though it received its fair share of tourists, it didn't cater to them. Few stuffed alligators or shrunken heads could be found on the shelves. Most of those found in New Orleans were fakes anyway, designed to pique the interest—and open the wallets—of tourists who wanted to take them home and regale their friends with stories of their *authenticity*. If you wanted books on the occult, you could look next door. Diluted, in some cases completely phony but largely less expensive potions, powders, and the like could also be found, one door away in the opposite direction. Yaya herself, a fourth-generation Voodoo practitioner whose family roots lie in Haiti, would have it no other way.

She'd looked up from a box of month-old receipts she planned to enter into her QuickBooks spreadsheet later that afternoon—she thought computers and technology were a bit like sorcery in and of themselves but didn't hesitate to use either—as the bell over the door rang out. The receipts in her hand fluttered to the floor as two men brandishing weapons and wearing black leather great coats with matching ski masks barged in.

The first shot Glory Broussard in the ribs. Glory was an elderly and harmless practitioner of Wicca who'd frequented Yaya's shop for over twenty years. She'd been looking for a 'bit o' Henbane' this afternoon, she'd told Yaya, smiling conspiratorially before pushing her loose-fitting upper plate back into place on her gums as it tried to pop out onto the counter. Henbane seeds, Yaya knew, contain several psychoactive alkaloids including atropine and scopolamine and, when administered to the skin of the genitals, produce a flying sensation. The thought of the geriatric woman lying on her couch, high as a kite—literally, so far as Glory would be concerned—brought a smile of amusement to Yaya's lips.

The round punched through Glory's aged and paper-thin body, destroying her heart and lungs before knocking her into the table of herbs she'd been perusing. One shoe flew off. She was dead before she hit the floor. The man then stepped past her, to the back of the shop, and quickly looked around before turning to face the front door, his weapon ready for any sign of resistance.

The second man through the door stopped to flip the sign to CLOSED before leaning across the counter and holding the barrel of an impressive looking automatic about four inches from Yaya's nose. She saw her death reflected in his deep brown eyes.

"Howsyamammaanem?" he asked casually. All in one word. He was inquiring about the wellbeing of her family, in true New Orleanian style. As if they were old friends. As if he wasn't there to rob the place and wasn't right now holding a gun in her face. She stared at him incredulously.

When she didn't answer he impatiently tapped the counter with the barrel of his pistol.

"Da money, cher," he said. "Givit, or all da gris-gris in da worl' not 'elp you."

Out of the corner of her eye, Yaya saw motion near the front of the store. Fearing a third intruder, or, worse yet, another unsuspecting customer to be mercilessly shot down, she looked. Her jaw dropped. But not, she noticed, as far as the jaws of the two men holding her at gunpoint.

An African American woman had materialized just inside the entrance. Yaya thought *materialized* because the rough-cast brass bell hanging from a coil spring mounted to the door frame had not sounded. She could see the door swinging closed, the bell rocking back and forth, the spring recoiling. She'd entered the business just like anyone else, but no sound had signaled her arrival.

She was naked.

She didn't appear to be ashamed of the fact. Tight black braids descended down her back from her crown, her shoulders held back proudly, squared. Her breasts were high and proud, tipped with dark nipples. They moved gently up and down with the woman's breathing. Her feet were firmly planted on the floor. There was some mottling of the skin tone on her arms, hands, and face, as if she'd suffered a burn that was still healing, her skin was otherwise smooth and unblemished, like that of a child. Except for the scar on her abdomen. It began above her right breast, below the collarbone, and arced towards the sternum. The deep but healing incision was held closed with thick, waxed thread. A second incision above her left breast followed a similar course, forming a Y as it met the first and descended to the pubic bone.

Yaya had been born forty-seven years ago in the back bedroom above this very shop. At a very young age, Yaya's mother had told her that she'd been born with a caul over her face. It had been removed by her grandmother, stored in a jar of formaldehyde, and sat on the mantle in Yaya's bedroom to this day.

She'd been born with the sight. She had seen many a spirit, many an entity, and witnessed the acts of many Loa, or Voodoun gods. The woman in the doorway carried such a thing with her—or perhaps it carried her.

Ayezan, she thought in the mere seconds that had elapsed since the woman's arrival. In the short-lived stillness. In the hush of expectation. *Mother of many, protector of all. She who punishes those who have made mistakes. Not because she is sadistic, but to correct their behavior in future lives.*

The gun in Yayas face shifted to the new arrival.

"Dafuc 'oo, cher?" The man with the automatic demanded. *Who the fuck are you?*

The man in the back of the store may have just been itching for another victim, or he may have had a bit of the sight himself because what he saw—the nude woman, her steely gaze, the autopsy scar on a chest that still drew breath—was nothing like the avenging loa that Yaya saw. To him, the woman appeared as a visage of death.

"Ndzumbi!" he screamed the Haitian French word meaning a spirit that inhabits a corpse. A zombie. He started firing wildly.

The woman advanced on the nearest gunman as the shots rang out. He tried to get a shot off, but she ducked and got in underneath, knocking his arm skyward and his gun to the floor. She picked him up bodily and advanced towards the second gunman, using him as a human shield. He squawked in surprise at her strength and began pounding on her back, to no avail. His body bucked and shuddered as three slugs tore into his back: one in the shoulder, one in his lung, and one in the lower spine. As she closed within four feet of the second gunman, his weapon empty, now busy digging in his pocket for more rounds and screaming *'Djable!'*, or Devil, repeatedly, she threw the dead man. The body hit the remaining gunman square in the chest, driving him to the floor.

He began to flail, one arm trying to hold on to the Magnum and push his partner's weight off him at the same time. The other came up from his pocket, gleaming brass and lead clutched in his fingers as he tried to reload.

The woman seized his gun hand in one of hers and struck at his elbow with the other. The was a loud *snap* and the man screamed as his elbow turned inside out, his ulna punching through ligaments, skin, and the leather of his overcoat. Bone gleamed dully and a spray of blood jetted from the wound. The woman didn't relent. She twisted the arm further, separating his shoulder as she rotated the arm one-hundred and eighty degrees. Then she dropped to her knees, driving the exposed bone deep into the man's eye socket. His scream cut off and his leg kicked twice before his body realized it was dead.

The woman turned then and looked at Yaya. Shot her a warm and somehow comforting smile.

"You okay?" she asked.

"Uh. Yeah." Yaya answered, nearly speechless. The entire sequence of events had transpired in less than three minutes. She looked on in gratitude, amazement, and a little disgust as the woman turned back to the attackers, pulled the gunman's arm from his face—there was a brief wet sucking sound that Yaya would never forget as long as she lived—then extracted his legs out from under his associate. She began undressing him.

It took Yaya a moment to understand what she was doing, then realized the woman had come into the shop and had single handedly put down two armed gunmen who'd intended to rob it and kill her—rape certainly not being out of the question—while wearing not a single stitch of clothing.

The woman quickly pulled on the man's shirt and blue jeans, then slung his coat over her shoulders, snugging her arms down through the sleeves. The right sleeve was torn inside the elbow, but the dark colored leather hid the blood well. She pulled on his boots. Too big, but they would do until something better came along. The woman turned and stood, then headed for the door.

"You should call the police now," she said as she passed the counter, again offering that warm and easy smile.

"Wait," Yaya said. She stepped out from behind the counter and approached the woman. Picked the automatic up off the floor and placed it in the woman's hand. She had the feeling the woman have need for the weapon, more than either of the two men on the floor anyway.

"Are you Ayezan?" she asked respectfully as the woman accepted the pistol and tucked it into the waistline at the small of her back. "Spirit of Manbo, the first priestess?"

The woman paused for a moment and considered the question. She looked confused. As if she didn't know who she was. Or what.

She turned without a word, pushed the door open, and started out. The little bell above the door jingled. Before she turned right and disappeared from Yaya's view, she looked back and spoke two words.

"I'm Nobody."

Ad Infinitum

He heard *Ari scream: "No!" just before the rounds hit. Saw the killer turn, rage on his face like a living thing, his features stretched in an inhuman grin of cold malevolence.*

The madman brought up the MP5K. Fired.

In the milliseconds that followed, he was aware of the first round chewing through his knee. The second, his stomach. The third, his chest. He felt no pain as the slugs passed through, destroying the local nerve endings, the flesh, and his bones. There was insufficient time for the nerves that had survived to report the injuries to his brain. As bright light unfolded before the killer like a single white rose opening before the morning sun, expanding furiously outward and consuming everything in its path, the final round hit him in the face, just below the left eye. He felt that one as a brief sting. His hand began the journey upwards to meet it as he too was consumed by that terrible radiance.

She turned, giggling, and ran away. Black hair trailed out behind her, flashing iridescent hues of deep purple and blue in sunlight from above and reflected from snow that lay like a blanket upon the earth.

He frowned.

What's this?

He'd last been in a garage, or on a dock of some kind as rain and thunder lashed the sky outside and he and—someone else, what had her name been? —were fired on by a man with a nasty looking gun and a look of pure hatred on his face. Who had that been? Why was he firing at them? How had he ended up outside in the snow, on a fine winter's morning?

She stopped after a few yards and turned. Saw that he wasn't pursuing but was standing still, his hand to his cheek. A look of concern crossed her features, and she walked back to his side.

Closer, he could see that she had thick black hair and how the light played among the strands as if gently caressing them. He noted her fine features, her ivory skin smooth, fresh, and clean, so pristine that faint tracery veins could be seen just beneath the surface. Her eyes were so green that when they fixed upon his, his face flushed, and his heart fluttered in a way he didn't understand. She came closer and he found it hard to breathe.

"It's finished," she said. Her voice, a pleasant susurration in his ears, soothed him.

"I don't understand," he responded, surprised at the high register of his voice. He took his hand away from his face and studied the smooth, unlined skin there. He seemed to remember there being scars on his forearm, but why should there be? After all, he was just a kid.

"What's finished?"

She looked confused for a moment, then shrugged.

"The snowball fight, I guess," she said. She leaned in and brushed his cheek with her lips, the innocent butterfly kiss of a child.

Had any other girl save his mother done so he'd have pushed her away, angrily wiped the spot with the heel of his hand, perhaps retching as he did so. Instead, he blushed furiously as heat bloomed in his belly and rose to his face. He felt a dopey grin break out on his face but was powerless to stop it.

"C'mon," she said, her face as scarlet as his own, and took his hand. Though they both wore mittens against the cold, the skin of his palm tingled. The pain in his cheek was forgotten.

They ran. Together.

After a few steps the cold air cooled their faces and events neither of them was old enough to comprehend receded until they were just children again, laughing and playing, voices rising in an afternoon sunshine that smiled down upon them from a cloudless blue sky, bathing them in pure, clean energy as if it knew something of their future—and past—together.

As if it were somehow sentient.

And well pleased.

AFTERWORD and ACKNOWLEDGEMENTS

This novel began life in 2015 as I sat in a family restaurant much like the one described herein, munching on one of their tasty little burgers. As I finished the burger, picking lettuce and onion off the wrapper—it never all stays on the burger, have you noticed? —I looked around and thought: "What would happen if a gunman walked in here and started shooting the place up?" The layout of the place is pretty much as I described it in the book, leaving few places for anyone to run or hide in the event of such an atrocity. My mind told me it would be a bloodbath.

Still, the part of my mind that files such things away gobbled up the thought just as I had gobbled up that burger. And there it sat. Until the crazy clown sightings started in 2016. Then that part of my mind—I think it's clinically insane—put two and two together and in a fury of writing over three days, I punched out the first six chapters *sans* the flashbacks. Those came later. Then, as so often happens, that crazy little bastard in my head quit talking about this particular story and started babbling about others. I dutifully followed his lead, worked on other things, and by the time he did start talking about this story again, 2016 had progressed.

Sadly, in the real world, so had the mass casualty shootings, and the clown sightings, some of which had turned violent.

Uncomfortable with writing about something that horrible and ongoing—as if, as my vanity suggested, my thoughts could influence events occurring around me—I shelved the manuscript. Okay, what

I did was hit 'save' and closed the folder, but you get the idea. I didn't return to the story until 2019.

By that time the story was shaping up. I had a protagonist in Arianna Price. An anti-hero in Jack, whose back story had come to me via a song on the radio a few days earlier. And a wicked antagonist who wanted to wipe out humanity with a genotoxin that would initiate a pandemic of epic proportions.

Then the COVID-19 pandemic hit the news and I *really* started thinking my writing was, if not predicting, at least mirroring, reality. I again backed away from the story but didn't have the heart to delete it. I don't think I've ever deleted a story once I've begun it, no matter how bad it is. I'm not sure that I can.

Late in 2022, I resumed the story. For one, COVID had died down to its present dull roar. For another, the random shootings, during lockdown, had become nonexistent—they're back now, worse than ever I'm sorry to say, but I'm no longer deterred by events I'm not responsible for and cannot change. The biggest reason I took this tale back off the digital shelf, dusted it off, and began once again, is because that maddening voice simply would not. Shut. Up.

Since resuming the work, the world has changed yet again. The built in editor in my little machine tells me so, pointing out terms that may be considered derogatory, non-inclusive, homophobic, insensitive, and out and out racially biased. For these, I have no excuse other than they are what the story required. To explain motivations. To justify actions. To drive the fucker forward.

The editor just popped up to inform me that word may be offensive.

I certainly hope so. Because that's why I share what I write. That's what I believe fiction—rather, *art*, in any form—is for. Not just to engage, entertain, and educate, but to evoke an emotional response. Be it terror, disgust, or offense. So long as you feel *something*.

Since it would be criminal not to acknowledge the people that helped me write this novel, I'd like to thank Lynne Smith, who edited a large portion of the manuscript. James Tepper, Distinguished Professor, Center for Molecular and Behavioral Neuroscience, at Rutgers University in Newark, who gave me insight into genotoxins, how they can (and can't) behave without manipulation, and who Beta read the book. Twice. Michelle King, a long-time friend and fan, who also Beta read the novel for me. To Fallon Schwartz, who Beta read portions of the manuscript and allowed me to use her name and likeness so long as I spelled her name the way she always wanted it spelled, then became nervous and physically ill at the way I killed the character off and was unable to read more—now there's an emotional response! —and lastly, though there are many, many more I owe thanks to than will fit on these pages, my wife, Marie. Who holds my heart, and my soul, and quite frequently stops me from saying, doing, and writing stupid things. I love you, baby.

Now, if I've done my job well, you've enjoyed the novel and will come back for more. If not, I'm sorry I've wasted your time—and you your money—and promise to try harder on the next.

Cause that voice is talking again. Loudly. Something about the Multi-verse, Puckwudgies, and—really? *Werewolves?*

Shhh. I must listen.

T. Joseph Browder
Nobody
2015-2023

Don't miss out!

Visit the website below and you can sign up to receive emails whenever T. Joseph Browder publishes a new book. There's no charge and no obligation.

https://books2read.com/r/B-A-RXNY-NMAKC

BOOKS 2 READ

Connecting independent readers to independent writers.

Also by T. Joseph Browder

Dark Matters
Nobody

About the Author

T. Joseph Browder was born in Lima, Ohio in 1969 and is the author of 'Dark Matters,' 'Plague,' and 'Infernal,' the first in a series of novels about the Multiverse and the age-old battle between good and evil.

Of writing T. Joseph Browder says, "I'm an addict. Some people are addicted to alcohol, some to marijuana, coke, or heroin. I'm addicted to writing. It's my drug of choice and like the monkey on the back of the heroin user it compels me to sit down at my computer every day and check out of reality. If I don't 'use' often enough I suffer withdrawals. The pain is tangible. For me, writing is a high like no other. It's one helluva buzz."

A student of Psychology, T. Joseph Browder also holds Doctorates in Divinity, Metaphysics, and Religious Humanities. "I'm an ordained minister," Browder says, "but that's a prerequisite for the education I was pursuing. I've performed a wedding ceremony or two but have never felt the urge to preach before a congregation."

Like his education, Mr. Browder's writing is driven by an insatiable curiosity for what makes people behave the way they do, make the choices they make, and feel the way they feel. Drawing on an intimate knowledge of the evil alive in humanity his work centers on the darker aspects of life, the sudden changes and left turns life throws at all of us and how we react to those things that lurk around the next corner and go bump in the night.

Mr. Browder currently lives in Kansas with his wife, Marie, and is hard at work on a new novel.